in
Woolen
Bikinis

Catherine Dougherty

Catherine Dougherty

Raven's Wing Books

Concord, New Hampshire

in Woolen Bikinis
By
Catherine Dougherty

Library of Congress Control Number: 2013941564

Paperback ISBN 13: 978-1-61807-109-5
Mobi (Kindle) ISBN 13: 978-1-61807-110-1
ePub (Sony, Nook, iPad) ISBN 13: 978-1-61807-111-8

Book and Cover Design: Pam Marin-Kingsley,

Raven's Wing Books
an imprint of Grey Gate Media, LLC
Concord, New Hampshire
Email: info@greygatemedia.com
Web site: www.greygatemedia.com

*Dedicated to my "Cozy Cap" friends,
with gratitude.*

Acknowledgements

I'd especially like to acknowledge and thank my two sons, Mike & Billy, who surprised me with flowers and a very special message on the day my first novel *in Polyester Pajamas* was released in June 2012. Words cannot begin to express how much this meant to me.

Thanks is extended to Cynthia and Sue for their great marketing skills, Donna for traveling quite a distance to surprise me at my first author event, Pam and Cindy for the author photo, Scott for the cover and title suggestions, and Katie, an aspiring author, for being the first to interview and write about me when *in Polyester Pajamas* was released.

Also, a big thank you to the book clubs, bookstores, and other groups and media who promoted my first novel, as well as to the following two authors for their endorsements of *in Woolen Bikinis*:

Jim Novak, author of *Ora's Boy* (www.orasboy.com)

Chris Stralyn, author of *This Time You Lose* (www.thistimeyoulose.com)

(Both of their books are great reads—be sure to check them out!)

I couldn't have done this without my awesome publishing team at Grey Gate Media, LLC—Jason Reilly, Dana Blythe and Pam Marin-Kingsley. (Pam outdid herself with this fantastic book cover, don't you think?) And this novel wouldn't have become what it is without the hard work and help from my editor Lisa Christopher and line editor Kris Lang.

To the fellow writers I've met along this fantastic author journey, I greatly appreciate your support and continued encouragement.

Last, but not least, to my husband, my family, my co-workers, my friends, and all of my readers (this includes all of you!), I just want to say I am more than thankful for you and blessed because of you.

And now, with pleasure, I bring forth another Jean and Rosie adventure. I know you're going to love it!

Catherine Dougherty
June 2013

http://catherinedougherty.com
http://greygatemedia.com

Chapter 1

The time had almost come. It was really about to happen. Within days, the new yarn and book shop would be open for business. We're calling it *Simple Pleasures* and it's a dream come true.

As I placed another book on the shelf in front of me, I couldn't help but grin. There was so much to be thankful for—a husband I adored, two wonderful grown boys, this new venture, Jean as a best friend and now she was going to be my business partner, too.

There's only one thing left to do, I thought. The grin faded quickly as I squatted down, leaning my back against a nearby wall for sudden support. I had put this off for way too many years now. Maybe, maybe, it was also the time to....

"Rosie, where the hell are you?" shouted Jean as she walked downstairs from her new apartment above the shop.

I could already tell she was nervous. Her heels were clicking frantically across the wooden floor. She'd be even more nervous if she knew the surprise I had planned for her on our opening day. I've arranged the whole thing and haven't shared a word of it with anyone yet. It's going to knock her woolen socks off!

I began to grin again. So much to be thankful for, I reminded myself. As I stood upright, I wiped away a small tear that had trickled down my cheek. "I'm over here, Jean, just shelving some books. What's wrong?"

"One of the knitting suppliers called. Their last shipment was late getting out and there's a good chance it won't be here in time."

"Don't worry—look how much inventory you have already." I walked out from among the bookshelves and headed toward the yarn area to meet her. "Everything looks great. No one will even know."

Jean was standing in the middle of her vast assortment of yarn looking lost.

"What have I done, what have I done?" She placed her head in her hands. "I don't know the first thing about knitting. I'm only a beginner. I'm going to fall flat on my face."

That was Jean being Jean. She always sees the glass half-empty. This is where she needs me the most, for reassurance, since I tend to remain optimistic no matter what.

"Hey, calm down. I'll be here and I knit. And you even have that woman, Gertrude, from the nursing home who's going to volunteer. She's been knitting all her life. That's over 75 years of experience."

Jean looked a bit more relaxed. "You're right again, Rosie. I'm sorry. But it's still kind of scary. I've never done anything like this before."

She walked over and gave me a big hug. Little did she realize how much I needed one. Then, she pulled back and looked right at me.

"And how are you feeling? Are you ready for this?" she asked.

"I sure am," I said. "As ready as I'll ever be. There are only a few more books to price and put on the shelves. Then I'm finished with my area, it's all set to go."

"But wait a minute. I just remembered. There is still something you've got to do," I added.

Jean looked at me quizzically. "What could that be? I've worked my butt off here for the past few weeks and, except for a late shipment, everything should be in order."

"But you've forgotten one thing, Jean." I smiled at her and paused for a moment to get her worked up. I love seeing Jean get irritated every once in a while.

"Come on, Rosie. Cut the crap. Just tell me."

"Okay, okay, you've forgotten your promise, that's all. Remember what you promised Jacob? Remember the fish?"

"Aaagh! The betta fish! I said I would buy one and put it by the register." Jean started shaking her head frantically. "Oh, I don't know if I can do it, Rosie. I hate fish. I've hated them ever since I killed Robbie's when he was a kid. I didn't treat the water like I should've and the next thing I knew, his goldfish were floating dead on the top of the fish bowl. Robbie was traumatized and it was my fault. How can I go out and buy another fish again? I'll kill it for sure."

"Hey, take a breath, girl, and while you're at it, take one of your anxiety pills because you're way too stressed," I replied. "Now a promise is a promise, so let's go to the pet store right now before we forget again."

"Do I have to?" Jean whined and stood at a stance. She already knew what I was going to say next.

"YES!" I grabbed her firmly by the arm and dragged her out the door.

Chapter 2

Jean was still reluctant as we entered the pet store. "Hey, how about this betta?" I asked her as we walked towards the fish area, pointing to a pretty red and yellow one.

"No, it has to be blue. Remember? We need to call it Bluey, like in Jacob's books."

She was right. Bluey was the main character in all of Jacob's picture stories. Jean met Jacob this past summer while she was staying with her dying mother in Cleveland, and I've been a fan of his for years, but only met him recently. He's written dozens of children's stories and has won awards for several of them. I bought his books when Tommy was a tyke.

Now Tommy was on his way to college in a few short weeks, headed to the University of New Hampshire. I'm thrilled he'll only be a little over an hour away, but the thought of not seeing him on a daily basis scares me to death. When he leaves soon, it will only be Jack and I left in the house. And even though Jack is the love of my life, he isn't a conversationalist—not at all—and his attitude is more like Jean's, which is negative in nature and quite the opposite of mine. I'm worried how I'm going to handle it.

"Rosie, Rosie, ROSIE, are you listening?" Jean looked at me annoyed.

"Oh, I'm sorry, I spaced out for a moment." I gave her one of my smiles.

"Duhhh," she replied. "Now let's find the fish and the necessary supplies and get the hell out of here. I'm sick of having those goldfish over there eyeballing me. It's like they know I've killed their ancestors or something."

Her remark not only brought me back to the task at hand, but also made me crack up. Jean can be so dramatic and funny. But I knew she was asking me, in her own way, to take control, so that's what I did. After stifling my sudden laughter, I signaled one of the clerks to help us. A young girl came over—she looked like she was 12—and I explained what we wanted, expressing the fish had to be personable and it had to be blue. Glancing at the little display cups they kept them in, we agreed on one that didn't look sickly and who seemed to be begging to be picked. Then I asked for fish food, a net, some colorful rocks and a vase—the biggest vase they had. If the fish had to live alone, it at least needed plenty of room to swim in. I also requested a nice plant to go on the top of the vase, but they only sold artificial ones. The girl suggested we check out the florist nearby. Through all this, which took about ten minutes, Jean looked like she was going to pass out. She was still so stressed out about the whole thing.

When we left the pet store, after placing everything in the back seat of my Jeep (in a sheltered spot so the fish wouldn't fry), we strolled over to the florist shop a few steps away. Not knowing what type of plant to get, I mentioned what it was for. The woman, who appeared to be the owner, knew exactly what we needed. While there, I also decided to pick up a nice arrangement of fresh flowers.

As soon as we got back to our own soon-to-be shop, it was time to put the whole fish thing together. Jean attempted to make an excuse to leave, but I made her at least watch while setting everything up. That way, if everything went well, she could be over and done with her fish phobia.

After putting the colorful rocks in the bottom of the vase and filling it with bottled water, I opened the container and carefully dropped the fish into his new home. I could see Jean out of the corner of my eye squirming. The betta dropped right to the bottom, like it was in shock or something. Honestly, I thought it was done for—close to DEAD—even though I knew I'd done everything right. Jean came up closer to the glass. She stared at it, and then back at me, her eyes and mouth wide open in fear.

"See? That's what happens when fish are around me. I'm a fish killer," she gasped.

"First of all, it's not dead yet. The gills are moving. Look! Second, I'm the one who put the guy in there, not you. If it dies, it's my fault."

I stopped talking and held my breath. All eyes were now on the betta.

Slowly, it started to squirm, then move. Before long, it was swimming around the tank and looking back at us. I picked up the vase, found it a great location at the register counter, and placed the plant on the top of the vase in the special plastic cover made just for holding it. Voilà. Mission accomplished. We now had a new mascot, besides Max, of course.

Speaking of Max . . .

"Hey, Jean, where's Max today?"

"Bob has him. It's his dog custody time," she replied. "He's also bringing him in for a nice wash and cut because he wants him to look his best on opening day."

As I was arranging the flowers in another vase, I said, "It's hard to believe it's already the end of August and we're opening this shop up in only two days."

Only two days! I was beginning to feel butterflies in my own stomach.

"Yeah, could you ever have imagined earlier this year we'd be doing something like this? Never mind that we'd be best friends? Oh I can remember how much I didn't like you," Jean said as she shook her head. She then gave me a little nudge.

"Well, I grew on you, didn't I? And you did the same to me," I replied. "Now we're joined at the hip, so to speak. A business is a big step, but I'm excited about it. Thank you, Jean, for everything you've done to make it all come true."

"We'll just have to see how it goes. You might not be saying that in a few months. You know, we could fall flat on our faces together with this venture. After all, books and knitting supplies aren't always best sellers. More and more people are opting for those e-books lately, bookstores are closing left and right, and many people don't have the time these days to take up a new hobby like knitting. We're going to have to hook them somehow—have some knitting classes and book discussions, give them the extra something to keep them coming back."

"We shouldn't even wait to plan those things," I said. "Let's put our thoughts together and come up with some ideas. Then, we can place some flyers in the windows."

"Well, since I now know how to make hats and scarves and even socks ..." Jean lifted her right pant leg to display her newly-made colorful knit socks. "I can set up a class one evening a week for a few weeks. I have plenty of colorful yarn already for people to buy. But the class itself, let's make it a freebie—no charge—so it'll entice others to join in."

"Ohhh, that sounds wonderful. Great idea. I can choose another evening for a book discussion, so I'll have to pick the book to read and display. Right now, I haven't a clue which one to choose."

"How about *The Cheerleader*?" Jean suggested. "You said it was written by a New Hampshire author, right? So it would be a great one to start with. You already have several copies, too."

"Perfect," I replied. "Now that we've decided, let's go upstairs and relax a bit. We've worked pretty hard today and besides, it's almost three—time for tea."

Myra, the previous owner, was a big tea fan, so it had become a ritual for us to drink tea most weekday afternoons since Jean had moved in here. It's also something we've decided to integrate into the shop—tea at three for all customers who want to join us. We've discovered it's a great way to celebrate each and every day. And, as Jean has said, it's also a great way to take a breather and keep our heads on straight when life, and love, can get so confusing.

"How's Bob?" I asked while she was filling the tea kettle with water. "You are still dating, right?"

Jean stopped what she was doing, turned to face me and replied "He's fine and yes, we are dating, but I just don't know, Rosie." She shook her head in confusion.

When it comes to love and confusion, Jean's the expert. Bob, her husband, left her last year for a younger woman and, at one time, wanted a divorce. Now he's back on the scene and doesn't see the need for one.

I was good at reading Jean's mind. "You're also thinking about Jacob. I can tell you miss him. Don't worry. I'm sure you'll see him again."

"Yeah, yeah," Jean said as she placed the kettle on the stove. "I doubt it. But, at least we talk everyday on Skype. Guess that's better than nothing." She turned the burner on before coming to sit beside me at the table.

"I can't live without him, but he doesn't turn me on so I don't want to sleep with him. What's wrong with me, Rosie?"

"Nothing, so don't beat yourself up over all this." I reached over and gently patted her shoulder for reassurance.

"I'm doomed at love, Rosie. I really am. Look at all the men in my life lately and not one of them is right for me."

I couldn't argue with that. There had been a lot of men in her life recently. For a while, she was hot for a long-time friend who stuttered. Then, there was the night when she almost gave in to Justin's charm. He's an ex-fiancé of mine who is now serving time.

I laughed. "Face it, Jean; you're crazy about men, all sorts. I can't even compare my romantic life to yours, nor do I care to."

Jean started to laugh. "Maybe you can't, but I can."

I pulled my hand away from her.

"Hey, wait a minute," I protested. "Jack's the only man in my life besides my two boys. Now, how can we compare?"

"Well, he's not the boys' father, is he?" she chortled.

Okay, you're right, but he's been a good dad to them. My first husband, Charlie, is their biological father, but he's a two-timing jerk. Besides, he doesn't stay in touch often enough and he has a drinking problem."

"Calm down, Rosie. I'm just getting on you, don't take offense. We both have had our man problems. And it wasn't so long ago, was it, when another man in your life caused quite a stir?"

I rolled my eyes. "Don't remind me!"

Jean was referring to Justin. I was only 20 when I met him. He was my very first love and we were going to be married. At least until he went and slept with my best friend before the wedding date, and until I found out he embezzled money from the bank he was working at. Justin disappeared right before we tied the knot, and it wasn't until I saw him again this past spring that I found out he had spent two years in jail after he left me at the altar. It would be great if I could forget all about him, but I was already two months pregnant when he deserted me way back then. I put the child up for adoption, haven't heard from or seen the child since, and I've never told Justin he was the father.

Thoughts of Justin brought me immediately back to this unfinished business I'd been mulling over all day in my mind. Now I'm hoping to finally find out who my biological child is, I want to meet them. It's been 25 years and I'm curious. My stepmom, Eloise, knows the adoptive parents, one is a distant relative, and has gathered photos and information from them over the years. The photos are now in a sealed envelope in my safety deposit box—I haven't looked at them yet—and I've been wondering if I should. The boys are old enough to know what happened so many years ago, and it's not fair not to tell them they have a half-brother or sister somewhere. Jack is on the mend from a heart attack, but I think he's well enough to deal with it, too. He knows some of the story already, but not all of it. As for me, it's still conflicting. I want to know, but should I know? I just don't know.

The kettle started whistling, which brought my attention back again to the present moment. As Jean was preparing the tea, I figured I might as well bring the subject up.

"Remember when I shared my secret about giving up a child for adoption?" I asked her.

She glanced over at me. "How can I forget it, Rosie? I can't believe that you haven't looked at those photos yet. Don't you want to know if it was a girl or a boy? Don't you want to finally meet them?" She appeared anxious to hear my reply.

"That's why I'm mentioning it. I'm thinking that once this shop opens, well, then, maybe it's time to."

"Woo Whooo!" Jean exclaimed, almost dropping the filled tea cups as she brought them over to the table for us.

As she sat down again, she leaned forward and said, "Ever since you told me at our first pajama party, I've been waiting for this. So, no more delays, let's crack that envelope open, girl!"

"Hold on a second. Not yet." I said as I took a sip of tea. "After the shop opens; I don't want to rush things. We've got enough to handle right now. Besides, there's something else I have to do first, something really important."

Chapter 3

The following morning, I decided to take the opportunity to go to the nursing home where Eloise lived. It was located about 50 miles away and there was another planned stop I could tie it in with. I didn't ask Jean to come with me, I didn't even tell her I was going. Instead, I told her Jack had a doctor's appointment, which he did, but, unbeknownst to Jean, I wasn't going with him.

Eloise no longer has much of a long-term memory, but with any luck, she would still remember a little bit about the adoption. It happened so long ago, I couldn't be sure. I also wanted to share the exciting news about the book and yarn shop with her so I came equipped with some pictures since she wouldn't be able to attend the grand opening.

Two years ago, Eloise suffered a stroke. Besides robbing her of some of her memory, it left her partially paralyzed. Luckily, she's still able to speak. Her face droops a bit on her left side and she hasn't much use of her left hand, but she does okay. I think she may be one of the youngest nursing home residents—only 72—and one would think this would get her down, but it doesn't. According to Eloise, she is where she's meant to be because that's where the Good Lord decided she's needed most.

And she does make a difference. She enjoys playing card games and cribbage with other residents. Bingo, too. Then, there are trips they take to the mall every other week. The men fight over who will scoot her around in her wheelchair. Despite the paralysis, she's still great looking and you couldn't find anyone with a better personality and disposition. She just warms your heart.

I love Eloise and enjoy visiting with her, which I try to

do at least once a month. I've thought of taking her in to live with the family and even mentioned it once after her stroke when she was in the hospital. She told me she wouldn't go. Not that she didn't enjoy being around me, but she felt she belonged where she is now, not stuck in a home without any company her own age. I didn't understand at first, but now I do, and I can tell she's happy.

It was mid-morning when I arrived. She was already in the front lobby waiting for me and reached out her right arm to give me a hug. It was so good to see her again.

We spent the first hour on the nursing home's large screened-in patio breathing in the fresh late summer air and talking about the new shop. I showed her the pictures of what it looked like and also gave her a book to read. I knew she couldn't knit anymore, so I brought along a few samples of yarn, too. She enjoyed weaving the strands repeatedly through her fingers.

"Oh, how I used to love to knit. Just feeling the yarn moving through these old fingers of mine is bliss," she said. Her eyes closed briefly, like she was cherishing a memory.

"I used to watch you," I replied. "You taught me how to knit, remember?"

"Yes, I do. The first thing you made was a bright orange scarf for your dad. It almost glowed in the dark." She chuckled. "It was absolutely horrid."

Her memory was very good today.

"It wasn't that bad," I replied. Sure, it was filled with mistakes and uneven knitting, but everyone's first project is bad anyway. Still, my Dad wore it proudly.

"Knitting is a gift and so is reading," I continued. "I know neither are big money makers, but I'm hoping we can be successful enough to keep Simple Pleasures going. As you know, I've wanted a bookstore for a long time."

"Yes, you have, Rosie. And you've also wanted to write for a newspaper. Are you still hoping to do that?"

"Not just hoping, I'm planning on it. I've already approached our weekly paper and they've agreed I can do a write-up about the shop every week. They'll even pay me for it. It won't be only for self-promotion, but also to share what's new in the world of knitting or reading or whatever else I care to focus on."

This was something I hadn't even told Jean about yet. I wanted it to be another surprise and was going to wait until my first column was in print to announce it.

Eloise and I enjoyed a nice lunch in the cafeteria before we headed back to her room. Plans were to ask her about the adoption once we could be in private. I was hoping she could give me more information about the adoptive parents and how they would feel if I contacted them.

As we settled into chairs in her small, but well-arranged sitting corner, I started in with my questions.

"I need to ask you about the people who adopted my first child. I haven't looked at the photos or any information you've given me yet, but I want to know if you are still in contact with them and if you think they'd be put out if I ever decided to introduce myself. Be honest, because if it would bother them, I don't want to pursue this."

Eloise reached towards me and held my hands with her own aged-softened ones. "Oh, Rosie, I do know more. I'm so glad you brought this up because it has weighed heavy on my own mind. I've recently heard from the mother, my distant cousin. There have been some health concerns with the child. It may be nothing, but their doctor mentioned the possibility of contacting blood relatives to find out if there might be any solutions found."

"When did you hear this?" I was startled. What could be wrong?

"Calm down, only yesterday, dear. And then you called and said you were coming today. I didn't want to alarm you, so I was hoping you'd bring this discussion up first. I prayed for it to happen, and thank God, it did. I really have tried not to interfere with any of your decisions about this, and I don't want to pressure you to open that envelope if you're not ready to."

She was right, she had never pressured me and it had

been seven years since she had given me the photos. The envelope they were kept in had remained sealed, but it was time to find out, it was time to know.

"What is wrong? Is it serious?" I didn't know how I was going to deal with this right away since the grand opening was tomorrow. And then there was Jean's surprise that would take away being able to do anything for at least the next few days. Also, I didn't know how I was going to tell Jack or the kids yet.

"Oh, I can see you're still concerned. Don't be because it isn't urgent. There's some depression, and overuse of pain pills and alcohol, but treatment is ongoing and another week or two won't make a difference. The child was even in a facility for help earlier this summer; she's being well taken care of." Still holding onto me, Eloise patted my hands to reassure me.

"Are they planning to call again soon?" I asked.

"Yes, yes. They will call again—maybe in a few days, maybe next week."

"Then give them my number please. I'll be busy with the shop, that's for sure, but soon, real soon, I plan on opening that envelope. And if I can be of any help to them, and especially to the child I gave up, I'd be more than happy to do whatever I can."

"I know you would, Rosie. I do."

I couldn't help it, tears started to flow from my eyes. Eloise pulled me towards her and we embraced.

She felt my pain. She always could.

Chapter 4

Iarrived at my next stop right on time, and the ride back home was interesting. After doing a few more errands and checking in with Jack, I went straight to Jean's. We still needed to prepare flyers to put up in the shop before opening tomorrow. There was also an informal celebration dinner planned. Jack and Tommy were picking up pizzas and joining us in about an hour. Bob was also going to come.

Jean was in a tirade when I got there. I didn't know what had gotten into her. It was something about what Jacob did, or maybe didn't do. She just kept rambling on and was clearly upset. I could tell the stress was really getting to her and was glad the others hadn't arrived here yet. I had to calm her down before she ruined the evening.

"HEY!" I said loud enough to get her attention. She stopped complaining and looked straight at me like she was scared of something. You'd think she'd seen a ghost.

"Hey," I said again, this time not as loud. "Calm down. Nothing can be that bad. I'm thinking maybe you're just burnt out from all of the preparation."

She took in a deep breath. It was working—she was beginning to calm down.

"Oh, thank God you're finally here. Where the hell have you been all day? I thought I'd hear from you before now."

This time it was my turn to take a deep breath. Sometimes that woman can really get on my nerves.

"I went to visit Eloise. I wanted to share some pictures of the shop since she's not able to be here tomorrow. Plus, I wanted to find out more about the envelope."

Jean turned red. I could see she was getting mad again.

"You didn't open it without me, did you? How could you? You promised I could be there when you did."

"Calm down, woman. Of course I didn't. I just needed to make sure she thought I was doing the right thing. She does. We'll open it in a few days, okay? After our grand opening, and after I figure out how to tell Jack and the boys."

Looking like she was about to cry, Jean reached out her hands to me but then put them again by her side.

"I'm sorry, Rosie. I'm just scared to death about tomorrow. I don't think I can go through with it." She began wringing her hands and pacing back and forth.

"Of course you can." I tried to reassure her by stopping her in her tracks. I then wrapped my arms around her and patted her softly on the back. I could feel the tension starting to leave her as she sunk into me.

"And then there's Jacob," she went on, her voice muffled into my shoulder. "He hasn't been in touch with me all day. I even tried to call Aunt Helen and Walter, but there was no answer. Where could they be? Do you think something is wrong?"

"No news is good news," I replied and gave her a squeeze. "Everything will be fine and I'm sure you'll be hearing from Jacob soon. He's probably been busy."

She pulled away and started pacing again and getting herself all worked up.

"Yeah, right, Rosie. Doing what? Pulling weeds without me? Working on a new story? He knows the shop is opening tomorrow and he's nowhere to be found. It's not like he ventures far with that agoraphobia of his. If he did, he'd be here."

"Forget it. He'll be in touch soon. Right now, we need to get those flyers done and then enjoy an evening together— all of us—so put the smiley face back on and let's get going. We can start celebrating while we work. I'll pour us some wine. It might calm you down."

"Wine, did you say wine? Damn! I knew there was something I'd forgotten to get. What is wrong with me these days?" Jean was in a panic. She continued to move back and forth, now having something new to worry about.

It was going to be a long evening. Somehow I had to find a way to calm this harried woman down.

"Just give Bob a call. He knows what you like and I'm sure he'll bring it with him. Besides, maybe we shouldn't drink while we're working after all—wrong idea. You know how that can be. In less than an hour, we'll all be celebrating anyway."

Jean put in a distress call to Bob. No problem—the wine was on its way. A little more relaxed again, she finally sat down at her computer and we soon became involved in creating the flyers. She seemed to forget all about how nervous she was and how upset she'd been about not hearing from Jacob. Phew, what a relief.

Using some nice colorful graphics of yarn and a pair of knitting needles we found by searching online, Jean created a flyer for the upcoming knitting class she was offering. She also put in a graphic of a hat—a "cozy cap" she called it.

"I've thought about it some more and hats will be a better first project. That colorful yarn will be perfect for them. Socks are just, well, too hard for a first project and might discourage the newbies. Besides, we can even donate them to chemo patients if we want to, like Jacob does."

Silence all of a sudden. I thought she was going to start up again about not hearing from him, but she didn't.

"I hope we can get enough people involved," she commented.

It was decided the knitting class would be on Thursday evenings for four weeks beginning in September. As for my book discussion, I opted for Tuesday nights, beginning the same week. Tuesday was a night Jack had plenty to watch on TV so he wouldn't miss me as much and I could prepare his dinner beforehand. Still, he wouldn't be too thrilled about it. But, hey, maybe he could join in? I was going to see if I could convince him. Jack was an avid reader, but, unfortunately, not a social person. If he would only give it a chance, I think he'd enjoy it, especially seeing he doesn't know what to do with his time since the heart operation. Recently, he's been busy helping to get the shop ready by making bins and bookcases for us. The work has uplifted him; he hasn't been so depressed. It has given him some purpose, but all the preparation is about finished. So, honestly, I'm a bit worried about him. His depressed mood is coming back. He doesn't even have a desire to have any intimate relations with me, either, not since the heart attack, and that was several months ago. He's scared it will cause another one. We've discussed it with his doctor and the doctor says it is fine—go ahead, do it—but Jack is still nervous. I wish there was some way I could convince him otherwise. Maybe I should get a few tips from Jean. Nah...she hasn't had sex in a long time either.

We proceeded downstairs to the shop after creating the flyers to post them. We made three of each—one for the entrance door, one for near the cash register where I took a moment to say hello to Bluey, and one randomly placed in our separate sections of the store. Now all we needed were for people to sign up. Hopefully that would happen in the next few days.

Jean and I were finished just in time to see Jack and Tommy walk through the door with several pizza boxes. Then, in walked Bob behind them. He was toting a case of wine with a grin plastered on his face.

"Turn around and close your eyes, Jean. We have a surprise for you," Bob announced.

This was the moment I had been waiting for. I was about to return a favor to her for letting me be a co-owner of this shop and making my dreams come true. Now I wanted to make her dreams a reality.

Jean did as Bob said and then we all called out "SURPRISE". I told her to turn back towards us and open her eyes. When she did, you should've seen her! Her face was white as a sheet—she was in shock. I thought she might even have a panic attack right in front of us, but she didn't. Instead, she fainted.

Chapter 5

"**H**ow the hell did they get you here?" Jean asked once she came around. Jacob was holding her head up a few inches from the floor staring down at her. He appeared as pale as she was, having had to overcome his agoraphobia to fly all the way from Cleveland.

"It didn't take too much convincing," he replied as he grinned at her. "I've been going to meetings, you know. I wanted to be here for the grand opening, but I never said anything so you wouldn't get your hopes up." He pushed aside the graying hair from his face to reveal his gentle blue eyes.

That's when I joined in the conversation. "Jacob called me last week and we planned it all out. I picked him up at the Manchester airport today after visiting with Eloise." I shot a glance over at Jacob and smiled. "He even contemplated bringing Aunt Helen and Walter, too, but decided that they're both too fragile to come all this way."

"They went on a week-long retreat with other people from their church. At least I won't have to worry about them," Jacob said.

By this point, she was sitting up and gaining some color back in her cheeks.

"I can't believe it. It's so awesome you're here. She then grabbed hold of Jacob's face with both of her hands and planted a big kiss right on his lips. He looked a bit surprised. When she pulled back, she said, "Well, where are your bags? You're staying with me, you know."

At that comment, I glanced over at Bob who didn't seem to be smiling anymore. No doubt about it, he was jealous.

I needed to get everyone redirected. After all, the pizza was getting cold.

"Get yourself off the floor, Jean. I'm hungry, so let's go upstairs and eat," I commanded.

"And don't forget I brought wine," added Bob, trying to be noticed. I could tell he was still bothered, but knew there was nothing he could do about it. Jean had already informed him months ago how important Jacob was to her. She also told him she didn't feel any romantic sparks with Jacob, like she still did with Bob. Is he forgetting that? Maybe later I can remind him, if for no other reason than to keep the peace between them.

We all slid a few slices onto our plates and poured some wine into our glasses. Then we sat around Jean's small living room chatting about opening day. Jean did most of the talking, but it was exciting news and, of course, she had someone to impress. She held up her glass of wine and proposed a toast.

"To the beginning of a prosperous and fun adventure," she said. We clinked glasses, all agreeing it would be fun. As for prosperous, well, time would only tell. As Jean mentioned earlier, books and yarn aren't always top sellers. We'll have to be innovative enough to keep them coming through the doors. Having Jacob, a popular author, around for the first few days of business will help, that's for sure. I must remember to check with him later to see if he can read a few stories to kids while he's here.

My personal collection of all Jacob's picture books were already displayed in different areas of the shop for customers to enjoy. None of them were for sale, though, because they meant too much to me. Also, I'm hoping someday to hand them down to a grandchild. I don't have one yet, but my oldest boy, Jonathan, has just found, in his exact words, "the woman of his dreams." He lives in Maine, is an outdoorsy type, and teaches at an elementary school. The girl he met is another teacher who was hired for this upcoming school year. Jonathan is still young, only 23, but usually knows what he wants when he sees it. He always knew he would be a teacher, he loves kids, and he's only had a couple of girlfriends before. I can't wait to meet this girl—Laura, that's her name—because I already know I'm going to like her.

After eating, Jean took Jacob's hand and led him back downstairs to the shop for a personal tour. Jack and Tommy were anxious to get home to watch TV—they were bored—so they bowed out early. I promised to come soon after. Jack was not at all thrilled about me hanging out so late with the big day tomorrow, but I wanted a few extra minutes to talk with Bob alone. He continued to be concerned by Jean's ogling over Jacob tonight.

Once we were alone, I poured another glass of wine for both of us and then started the conversation.

"Are you all right with Jacob being here?" Before he had a chance to answer, I added, "I appreciate your help in bringing him tonight. As you know, it means a lot to Jean."

"Oh, Rosie, what am I going to do? She may not think she's romantically attracted to the guy, but just look at her. She's had her hands all over him tonight and … and that kiss she gave him."

I put my glass down and leaned forward. "Well, if she is, then she hasn't told me. I know he means a lot to her, and so do you. I really think what she feels for Jacob is quite similar to your feelings about her."

"What do you mean by that? Romantically, Jean and I have, or should I say had, it really good. I'm sure she's told you we have plenty of great memories together in that way."

It was a bit embarrassing talking about this subject, but I knew it was important to get around to what I had to say next.

"I don't mean that exactly. Yes, she's told me about the two of you, just a bit. She's also told me how much she loves you, but she doesn't feel it's mutual. Not in the way that makes a real marriage work between two people."

He didn't respond. I had said something he knew was true, so I went on to finish explaining how this tied in with Jacob.

"As for Jacob, well, I think he truly loves Jean, or at least thinks he does, and she loves him, too, but not completely, not romantically, so that's not going to work either. It wouldn't be fair for either one of them. You still mean a lot to her, so don't forget it. If she could bottle you both up into one ideal man, you know she would."

"But she can't," replied Bob as he frowned and looked defeated.

"No, she can't," I agreed. "That's something Jean is going to have to realize for herself. Until then, you'll just have to accept things as they are."

Bob looked more relaxed, but still concerned. "Hey, you know I wish I could love her completely. I really do."

"I know you do, but trying doesn't make it so. To be blunt, it would be a good idea if you both faced that fact and got on with the divorce. It doesn't mean you can't still be friends, or keep on dating even, but it's not good for either one of you to continue to deceive yourselves into thinking this time around it could be different."

Bob added, "If it didn't happen in 32 years, it won't happen now. That's what the kids keep telling me. I don't want to hear it, but maybe they're right."

After that comment, he stood up. Leaning over, he kissed me on the forehead and said, "Thanks, Rosie. Such a hard discussion, but I'm glad we've had it. I'll say goodbye to Jean and Jacob as I leave."

I also rose from my chair. "Hey, let me get my purse and walk down with you," I said. "I've got to get home myself. It's a big day tomorrow—I still can't believe it's happening."

"Yeah, we've all done plenty to prepare for this. I'm happy for you two. Wish I didn't have to miss it, but things have been tough at work lately. If I don't get into the office, they'll probably fire me. Max will be here, though."

"Well, I'm sorry you won't be here, but think of us and be sure to call Jean tomorrow night when you get back home. I know she'll want to share all of the details with you."

"Sure, sure. Like she'll even notice I'm not around." He dropped his head and groaned.

"Ahh, come on, Bob. You know she will."

Chapter 6

Even though I was in bed early enough, I didn't sleep well. I kept thinking about the grand opening the next day and also kept reviewing my conversation with Bob. Sure, I spoke my mind regarding his relationship with Jean, and sure, he thanked me for it, but maybe it wasn't my place to butt in. After all, did I really know if they could work it out or not? And if Jean knew about our talk, how would she feel? She'd probably tell me to mind my own business. I managed to get my two cents in where it didn't belong, but I hoped she'd realize it was in the best interest of both of them. At least their kids agreed with me so I couldn't be that much off base.

When I arrived at Simple Pleasures early the next morning, Jean and Jacob were already downstairs. They both greeted me with a smile. This was it! Soon enough, we'd have customers coming in the door.

By 9 am, when we opened the shop, a small group of women, some with young children, and even a few men, were gathered outside waiting. Word had gotten out, even though we opted not to advertise in any papers yet. Besides the nice window display of yarn and books we had put together, along with the flyers for the upcoming book discussion and knitting group, the only advertising done was by word of mouth. Of course, both of us have pretty big mouths when it comes to bragging about our new venture, so the results were impressive.

In no time, there were at least a dozen people roaming around both areas of Simple Pleasures, reading books, feeling yarn, and ooohing and aaahing at the knitted shawls, scarves, socks and hats the women at the senior center knitted up for Jean to display. They were also gathering around Jacob, who was already reading a Bluey book to a few wide-eyed children. I didn't even have to ask him to read to them, either, and I thought he'd have a hard time being around so many strangers with his agoraphobia, but it seemed like he had come a long way in only a few months. Instead, he was in his glory.

And then there was Max, all prettied up and in his glory as well. Bob must have brought him back earlier this morning. He was lying down with his head nestled in a little girl's lap. Jean was right, he was the perfect mascot. Many bookstores have mascots, and they're usually cats. But, we're different. Instead, we have Max and Bluey.

Bluey was fluttering about and getting his own attention, determined not to go unnoticed. I have heard that some betta fish stay at the bottom of the vase and don't move much, but not so with this one because he's entertaining and lively. We made a good choice with him.

Jean was calmer than I expected. She roamed throughout the shop smiling and discussing yarns with many of the customers. She may not have that much knitting experience, but she has been studying up on all of the items she purchased and she's also good at striking up a conversation. She glanced over my way and winked. All was going well.

As for the bookstore section, it was busy, too. Most of the men opted to go in that direction and, before I knew it, I was at the register ringing up sales. Every time I tried to get away from the register, someone else came along.

"Hey there, kiddo, you've been here long enough," Jean said as she came up beside me. "Gertrude has just arrived to help, so why don't you go and take a lunch break? Bring Jacob with you if you can tear him away from the kids. I'm sure he's hungry, too."

It didn't seem right eating without Jean, especially with Jacob who was here to see her, not me.

"How about you? Aren't you hungry?" I asked.

"I couldn't eat if my friggin life depended on it. I'm too excited and don't want to miss anything. No, you go ahead.

I'll take a quick break afterwards. Besides, I had Jacob all night." Jean gave me a sheepish smile and winked again before she started ringing up a large purchase of yarn.

What the heck did she mean by that? I was too afraid to ask and it wasn't an appropriate time, but I'd be sure to find out later—as soon as I could catch her alone.

Jacob had just finished a story, so when I asked him to join me for lunch upstairs, he put his book down and announced to his small group of new friends, "It's time for lunch, guys and gals. I've enjoyed our time together, but I'm getting hungry."

"AWWW" the six preschool children said in unison. They were all disappointed. I felt like a criminal taking him away from them.

"Will you be here tomorrow afternoon?" one little girl asked. She was the cutest thing, about 4 years old, with shoulder-length curly blonde hair and big blue eyes. She grinned up at him in anticipation.

"I'll not only be here tomorrow afternoon, but I'll be here all week." Jacob grinned back at her. He patted her on the head as we walked towards the stairs. "I hope you'll come back and visit me."

The little girl nodded while they all cheered and clapped. It made me think it was too bad Jacob never had any children of his own because he would've made a great dad.

"What's for lunch?" I asked him as he began to reach into the refrigerator.

"Something Jean and I made last night—a tomato pie. There are also some spiced peach slices. How does that sound?"

"It sounds great. I'm starving." I sunk into the nearest kitchen chair. He handed me a plate of food and I didn't even wait for him to sit beside me before I started eating.

"Yummm. Jacob, the pie is delicious."

"The tomatoes come from my garden. I brought them with me. Pretty good, huh?"

"They're beyond pretty good, they're awesome. I should've known—I've heard you're quite the gardener."

"Yes, and so is Jean. I've missed her."

"I know she's missed you, too. You mean a lot to her."

"I'm aware of that, but I did have some reservations about coming here. I didn't know how she'd react to what I had to say to her." Jacob stopped for a moment as if he was unsure if he should go on.

I had a sense he was about to tell me something I maybe didn't want to know.

"Rosie, you're Jean's closest friend, and I'm so glad we have this time alone to talk. Maybe you can help me out. You see, I'm trying to convince Jean to move forward with the divorce. When it's finalized, if things keep progressing the way they seem to be, I'm thinking of asking her to marry me."

WHAT? This took me totally by surprise. I was sure she had already told him how she felt about him. She must have shared that she didn't have those romantic feelings for him—the one's needed for a marriage. I couldn't believe what he was saying. What was he thinking?

"Jacob," I said quietly after regaining my composure. "Has something changed between you two? I mean, I know you're good friends, even soul mates maybe, but...."

"But you didn't think Jean wanted to be romantically involved with me, right? Never mind, consider a marriage proposal?"

"Well?"

"Well, I didn't either, but that all started changing last night. We didn't actually sleep together, but we did do some serious necking. You know, I haven't done that in so long."

I blushed. I really didn't want to hear this, but I should've known. That was why Jean was smiling. And I'll bet she also knew beforehand that Jacob would bring this up over lunch. I wasn't sure if her feelings had changed toward Jacob. If not, how dare she? He was too nice of a guy to hurt, and if Jean didn't plan for this to become a romance, she was setting it up to break his heart.

And what about Bob?

"I hope you know what you're doing with him," I blurted out to Jean the moment she stepped into the apartment. Jacob had gone back down to help Gertrude cover the shop so Jean could also eat some lunch. I promised I would be right behind him as soon as I had a quick conversation with her. I'm sure he knew what about.

"What?" she looked surprised.

"Necking with Jacob?" I replied. "He told me, Jean. He told me what happened last night. No details, mind you, but it just blew me away. I thought you didn't feel that way about him." I put my hands on my hips and frowned at her. "How could you?"

Jean turned away and began to prepare her lunch. She didn't turn back when she started talking.

"First of all, what I do is my business, remember?" she said as she cut herself a big slice of tomato pie. "And I'm 51 years old, old enough to make my own decisions," she continued, as she scooped up a few slices of peaches. "Besides it's nice to get a little special attention."

"Sure, as long as it doesn't hurt anyone," I scoffed.

She put her plate of food on the table, along with a fork, napkin and a glass of milk. Then she stomped down the hall and into the bathroom a few feet away, shut the door on me, and gave me the answer I knew I would hear.

"I really don't know how I feel yet," she said through the closed door. "It's not like being with Bob, but, well, Jacob came all this way and, and, and, well, I thought I should at least give him a chance."

"And did you FEEL any differently? Does he turn you on now?"

She didn't respond. Silence. So I walked away planning to just leave her there and go back downstairs. I couldn't even stand being near her right now.

I had only taken a few steps, though, when the bathroom door opened.

"Rosie?" she said softly, as she emerged back into the hallway.

I turned to look at her. Tears were falling from her eyes. "I really do want to feel that way about him, but no, it didn't happen. What can I do to make it different?"

"Nothing, Jean, but you have to promise me you'll be upfront and honest with him. Don't lead him on."

"I don't want to hurt him. I really don't," Jean said as she started walking toward me.

"I know, I know. But sometimes you only think about yourself." I reached out my arms to her. Jean is always dramatic, but I couldn't help but care. After all, she is my best friend.

"Have something to eat and get yourself together. Remember, it's our grand opening so we have a lot to be thankful for. I'll see you downstairs in a little bit, but take your time." I gave her a hug, then pulled back to look at her. "Cheer up," I added.

"What would I do without you, Rosie? Thank you. Thank you so much." She lifted the corners of her mouth slightly.

Everything was going to be all right between the two of them, I thought, as I walked back down to the shop. For some reason, I started believing that. Or maybe I just hoped it to be true, for both of their sakes.

Simple Pleasures stayed busy throughout the day. Sales were overwhelming and when teatime came around at 3 pm, there were still several customers in the store and most decided to join us.

"What a lovely place," one elderly woman named Emma commented as she sat in a comfortable chair clicking away with her knitting needles. "We've needed a place like this for a long time. I'll have to tell George about it."

"Is George your husband?" I asked, leaning closer to her to see what she was knitting.

She noticed and said, "This is a baby sweater for my soon-to-be first great grandchild. My granddaughter is seven months pregnant." Her smile was broad.

"Oh, how I wish I had a grandchild," I mentioned. Of course, my oldest son, Jonathan, has just met someone and

Tommy's just entering college. It's too soon for both of them.

"And George isn't my husband, he's my youngest son," Emma continued. "He's a wonderful man, but so, so lonely. He lives with me and doesn't leave the house, not even to get the mail. You see, he lost his wife three years ago."

I looked quickly over at Jacob who had bowed his head. Jean also glanced over at him.

"How did his wife die?" Jacob questioned.

"She had breast cancer. Poor thing, they didn't discover it in time. And when she passed away, George closed himself up in his house, didn't even work. Oh, and he had a nice job, too—he was a stockbroker—but they fired him and then he lost his home. That's when he moved in with me."

"Sounds like he may have agoraphobia," Jacob commented.

"Agora what?" Emma looked perplexed.

"Agoraphobia. It's a fear of open spaces. People who have it tend to suffer from anxiety attacks and shut themselves up in their house or wherever else their safe place tends to be." Jacob kept his head down, but continued talking. "They're afraid of dying sometimes. The fear is paralyzing and very real to them."

"Really?" Emma replied. "Well, I don't think that's what he has."

"Has he ever been checked by a doctor for it?" He glanced over at her finally.

"No, he's just depressed. He'll come out of it, I know he will." Emma set her needles down to reach for her teacup.

Jacob frowned, "Not necessarily. I know because I've had agoraphobia for years. I needed to go to therapy to finally start overcoming it. If I didn't, I wouldn't be here today."

"Oh, so you know what he's going through then? Well, maybe you can help him?" Emma picked up her knitting again, but her eyes were on Jacob.

"Maybe," Jacob replied, "Would you mind if I stopped by your place tomorrow morning to talk to him? At least he'll know he's not the only one going through this and that there are ways to get some help."

Chapter 7

It was almost six-thirty by the time I arrived home that night. Jack was sitting in his chair staring at a *Law & Order* rerun. He didn't even turn around to say hello, although he's probably watched the same episode a dozen times already. I knew right away he wasn't happy with me.

"Aren't you going to ask me how the day went?" I said. I came up close to him to get a glance at his demeanor.

"No comment," he replied and frowned at me. *Uh Oh.* I was glad I picked up his favorite pizza on the way home. Maybe that would change his apparent bad attitude.

"I got your favorite meal—a Margarita extra thin with garlic and slightly overdone." I opened the box and put it up next to his face hoping the aroma would cheer him up.

He didn't even look at it . . . or at me again.

"We just had pizza last night. Remember? Besides, it's probably cold by now," he said in his usual gruff tone. Okay, he wanted to remain ugly.

"No, it's not," I said as I closed the cover, walked into the kitchen only a few steps away, and placed the box down on the counter. Then I went back over to him again and sat in his lap facing him. He wasn't going to get me down—especially not on the day of our successful launch.

"Ah, don't be that way, honey. You love pizza, especially this kind. And it was a great day and we made some good money. You had to realize that I might be a bit late tonight. I would've called, but I wanted to get home as soon as possible."

"How much money?" he mumbled, still not looking at me.

"We made about $700 in the yarn section and another $500 worth of books. That's pretty good for a first day, don't you think?" When I saw him finally glancing my way, I gave him one of my cute smiles to try to charm him.

It worked. I saw him relax a bit.

"Hey, where's Tommy?" It occurred to me that besides the noise from the TV, the house was quiet.

"He's taken some girl out—it's only you and me."

"That's all right. Maybe we can work up a bigger appetite and fool around while we're alone. Especially since dinner may already be cold. I could heat it up later. Whattaya think?" I wiggled my eyebrows up and down, hoping he'd take the suggestion.

But he didn't. I should've known.

I should've eased off while I was gaining ground. His softened mood turned sour again, so I quietly got off his lap and went to get the pizza, zapping it for a few quick seconds in the microwave to make sure it was, in fact, hot enough. Hopefully, a little food would change his mindset. Otherwise, it was going to be a long, long night.

After eating and washing our two plates, Jack was still distant, glued to the TV set. I decided to go downstairs to our family room area. That's where my desk and computer are and that's where Tommy spends most of his free time when he's home. He has a TV, his own computer, a great sound system, everything set up. At least, until a couple of days ago. Now, most of his stuff is packed away. I couldn't stand thinking about him leaving in less than two weeks. It was going to be so lonely without him here to talk to in the evenings. He's gone more and more these days anyway— maybe it won't be too bad. *Hey, who am I kidding?*

I wanted to check my emails, as I did every evening, then my Facebook quickly and maybe there'd be some time to search the Internet for suggestions on getting a man interested in sex after a heart attack. I needed some help on this.

There were four messages in my Inbox. Three of them were Spam—advertisements for real estate. The remaining e-mail was from the editor of the local weekly paper.

```
TO: Rosie
FROM: Chad
_____

Rosie-
Congrats re: opening day. Looking fwd to 1st
write-up. How soon will u b ready?
Chad
```

I had told Chad, who was a high school friend from way back when, that I would have my first column ready within a week after we opened the shop. Now, I was getting second thoughts. Can I even write well enough? Will anyone want to read it? I guess there was only one way to find out. While the thoughts of our business launch were fresh in my mind, I opened up Word on my computer and stared at a blank page. Searching the Internet and checking Facebook could wait. I placed my fingers on the keyboard. This was scary. It took several minutes before I started to actually write something, but in no time I was on a roll. I didn't stop until I heard Tommy come in through the basement door, the usual entryway for him. Glancing up at the clock, I was in shock. Two hours had passed since dinner and it felt like only a few minutes. I quickly shot off a couple of lines back to Chad saying I was working on it and then shut down the computer.

"Hey, Tommy, did you have a good night?"

He yawned. "It was all right. Girls around here act so immature. I can't wait to get to college and meet someone new."

"Well, I can wait because I'm going to miss you." I gave him a quick hug. "Are you hungry?"

"I'm always hungry."

"Good, I'll heat up the leftover pizza for you, but only on one condition."

"And what's that?" he asked.

"Get your stepdad in a good mood. He's been a crank all

evening."

Tommy then shrugged his shoulders. "That's nothing new, but sure, okay. I'll try."

Jack must have been sleeping in his chair since I had left him and gone downstairs. He was just waking up. He gave out a big yawn, rubbed both of his eyes and didn't appear so unfriendly anymore. I'm sure having Tommy home helped. He started right in talking about sports.

"Tommy, there's a game starting in, aahh…" He looked at his watch. "I must have dozed off for quite a while." He then looked up at me and said, "Sorry, Rosie."

Little did he know I had been engrossed in writing the whole time and he hadn't even noticed. "Thank you, Lord," I said under my breath. If he had been awake and I had ignored him for that long, he wouldn't have been in a better mood—Tommy here or not.

Jack pressed the remote to get the right channel for the game. "It started around eight, but we can pick it up from here."

I went and heated up the pizza again. There was still enough for both of them. I also poured them both a glass of iced tea.

"Thanks, Mom," Tommy said as I delivered it. Jack was already talking to the TV set.

No need for me to stay around. Besides, I was beat. I gave Jack a kiss on the cheek. "Goodnight, hon. I'm going to bed."

He looked up again and smiled. "Thanks for putting up with me, and sorry about being so crabby. You know how I get. Despite my ugly mood, I'm glad you had a great day."

"Yeah, Mom. Congrats," Tommy added.

Hey, I got their attention for a couple of seconds. Amazing!

I couldn't sleep again. It must have been because I was overtired. I kept thinking about the shop, about Jean and

Jacob and even Jack. Then my mind started thinking about my firstborn child. I still hadn't told Jack about visiting Eloise, discussing the child I gave up, and also finding out that the adoptive parents really needed my help. I had to tell him I planned on opening that envelope. I also had to tell him who the biological father was. Oh, that was going to be hard, but it had to be done soon. It was important to be ready to help in any way I could when the call came in from the parents. That could be any day now. As far as the boys were concerned, I would let them know as soon as I found out more myself. I wanted to be able to tell them whether they had a half-sister or a half-brother. And how were they going to react? It wasn't going to be easy and I dreaded it. My mind kept reeling and reeling thinking about it.

Then I recalled how I felt when I had to give the baby up for adoption. I was not much more than a child myself. Justin had left me right before we were to be married and I was pregnant, but didn't know it. Then I found out about his embezzling from the bank he worked at. No wonder he skipped town. Still, part of me had wanted him back. I thought I was in love with him and we could make it all right. Thank God he didn't return.

I can still remember the afternoon when I went into the bathroom with the pregnancy test and it turned blue. Or was it pink? What was I going to do? I was so scared and didn't know where to turn. At first, I thought an abortion was the only solution. Luckily, I asked Eloise for help.

When I went into labor, they knocked me out. I didn't get to see the child afterwards, they wouldn't let me. Then, later when I woke up, I just felt empty and alone. The baby had been inside of me rolling and kicking. I had already bonded with it and loved it. I didn't want to give it up, even though I knew it was the best thing to do. Then, it was suddenly gone, somewhere in the hospital, and I couldn't see it. I would never know, at least not for many years, at least not yet. It's awful, it's awful—the pain I felt. I cried and cried and wanted to change my mind. The paperwork had already been done, though. The baby wasn't mine. I was only the surrogate mom, so to speak. How could anyone do this? Give up their child? What a bad person I was. There was an empty hole in my heart that wouldn't heal.

Eloise knew, though. She knew how I would feel, so she made an arrangement with the new parents—they would keep her informed of the child. They would send her pictures every year and when the child turned 18, she would give them to me. Then I would finally be able to find out. It was years ago when she handed me the envelope, but I've been afraid to know. Now it's time to and I'm still afraid.

Chapter 8

When I walked into the shop the next morning, I was expecting to see Jacob, but he wasn't there, only Jean and Max. At first, I thought they might've talked last night, and Jean had told him the romantic feelings still weren't there for her. I imagined Jacob possibly leaving early knowing there was no hope for them, but soon found out that wasn't the case.

Jean seemed as cheerful as ever. "Welcome to day two, Rosie. Let's hope it's as good as yesterday. I can't wait to open up." She was already busy arranging some yarn in various areas of the shop.

I smiled at her. "Hey, where's Jacob?" I asked as I placed my pocketbook out of view behind the counter. "Is he still sleeping?" Max came up to me wagging his tail, waiting for a pat.

"Not a chance. He was up at five this morning, and was already starting in with his gardening routine."

She didn't have any yard with this commercial property, so what did she mean by gardening? By the confused look on my face, Jean knew an explanation was in order. She began to chuckle.

"Jacob is setting up flower boxes with all sorts of beautiful fall flowers in them. They're on the deck. Also, he made a terrarium to bring some of the outdoors inside. He even started a small herb garden for the kitchen. Oh how I wish I could keep him. He's already given me ideas for container gardens on the deck next spring."

"Where is he now?" I asked as I started to unload a box of new books that had arrived.

"He left with Emma who stopped by a few minutes ago. They went to visit her son. Remember? The guy with agoraphobia? But he promised to be back soon in case any kids were looking for a story."

"He sure is something," I commented.

"Yeah, he sure is. If only he turned me on."

"I know, Jean, I know. Don't keep beating yourself up over it." I finally reached down to Max who was now whining for attention and ruffled up the top of his head.

By the time we opened for business, there was again a group of people gathered at the door. Word must've gotten out. One young woman looked quite disheveled and found her way quickly to the books. Soon after, she emerged from an aisle with a trade paperback, chose a comfortable chair to sit in and started reading. She looked like a street person the way she was dressed—ragged t-shirt, worn and tattered jeans—and I immediately wondered who she was and if she'd eaten recently. I grabbed a couple of munchkins I had picked up on my way in to work and, putting them onto a paper plate, I carried them over to her.

"Hey, would you like some?" I asked.

She put the book down in her lap, looked up at me and lunged for them. Forget the plate—she grabbed the munchkins in both of her hands and proceeded to stuff one into her mouth.

"Ahhh, how about some coffee to go with that? Or maybe a bottle of water?"

"Water," she mumbled. I went and got a bottle and smiled when I brought it to her. It looked like this young woman not only needed food, but also needed a friend. I took a glance at what she was reading—*The Accidental Tourist* by Anne Tyler, my favorite author. "Good choice," I commented, but she didn't respond. Guessing she wasn't very sociable, I then left her alone.

As the morning hours went by, I noticed the young woman hadn't risen from the spot where she'd been sitting. She was still engrossed in the book. I imagined she couldn't even afford the few dollars to purchase it. It didn't matter. It was nice to see someone enjoying it as much as I did.

Customers came and went most of the morning, lots of purchases were made, and then there was a lull right before lunch. It was only at that point when Jean and I both realized the girl had finally disappeared and also that Jacob hadn't returned yet.

"Where do you think he is?" Jean said. "I'm starting to get worried. He promised he wouldn't be gone long."

"Well, maybe he's really enjoying his visit with this guy," I commented. "Besides, I didn't see any children in here yet, so at least he didn't miss story time. The kids would've been so disappointed."

As if he knew we were talking about him, Jacob arrived a minute or two later carrying a big brown paper bag. He held it up and grinned at Jean. "Lunch," he said as he proceeded up the stairs.

"Go ahead," I said to Jean. "Go join him, I'll cover."

"Are you sure, Rosie?"

"Yes, I am. I'll come join you as soon as Gertrude gets here. She's coming around twelve-thirty today, right?"

"Oh, that's right. She'll be here soon. Come up when you can." Jean was gone in a flash. I knew why, too—the aroma from the food Jacob brought in was heavenly. It must be Chinese food, I thought. My stomach started to grumble. Hunger pains.

There was no one in the shop so I decided to do a bit of rearranging while waiting for Gertrude. Several of the more current bestsellers displayed earlier on a round table in the center of the room had been purchased, so I rummaged through another box to find their replacements.

It's important to always have some fresh stock available—something I knew, firsthand, from visiting so many bookstores myself. Jack and I had visited about every bookstore on the east coast. It was one of our favorite pastimes.

Thinking of Jack made me realize it might be a good idea to give him a call so he knew I was missing him. It may also be nice to suggest dinner out tonight—just the two of us—so we can spend some quality time together. And maybe, possibly, if Tommy is out again tonight, we could even do a bit of snuggling and necking ourselves later on, maybe more. I sure did miss the active sex life we once had before Jack's heart attack. Somehow I had to get him over that fear and back to his old frisky self again.

I reached for the phone and dialed home. The phone rang only once.

"Hi Jack. Whatcha up to?"

"Nothing much," he grumbled. I could tell he had been lonely without me for so long.

"Hey, come on honey, cheer up. If you don't have anything to do, why don't you come over to the shop and help me out." Part of me wanted him to, but part of me didn't if he was going to stay in this rotten mood.

"No thank you—you don't need me," he said.

"Of course I do," I replied, trying to be cheerful for the both of us. "Hey, why don't we go out to eat tonight, maybe to L'Italiano's? I think it might be nice to get out for a change."

"Whatever. What time are you coming home?" I could tell he already wanted to get off the phone.

"I'll be there by six and will just need to freshen up a bit. Then we'll enjoy our evening together and have a chance to talk for a while. Maybe even . . ." I stopped talking, already sensing what his response would be. Too late.

"HEY," he said rather loudly. "I'm not going to say this again. There isn't going to be any hanky panky for a while, got that straight, Rosie? I'm not in the mood tonight or maybe any night. And I'm definitely not in the mood as long as you're pushing me on this." He took a deep breath.

"I'm sorry," I said. And I was. I didn't mean to get him so upset.

After a moment of silence, he said softly, "Me, too. I was a bit gruff. As for dinner, sounds like a good idea."

47

Well, that's a start, I thought. "Thanks, Jack. I'm looking forward to it."

Okay, so maybe no hanky panky tonight, but there were other important things to do. I needed to tell him about wanting to find out who my birth child is. Maybe, if all went well, tonight might be a good night to discuss it after we both have had a nice meal together. Eloise had said the parents planned on calling again, so it had to be done. I wasn't too anxious about also telling him that Justin was the father. Maybe I'd wait a little while longer on that one.

L'Italianos was crowded. I expected Jack to turn around and suggest we grab some takeout instead and go back home, but he didn't. The wait was over thirty minutes, and he sat there holding onto the pager that lights up when the table is ready and seemed relaxed for a change. He was also in a great mood. Amazing!

"Hey, why such a good mood? What's gotten into you?" I asked.

He turned my way. "I know I've been a real jerk lately. It's a great thing, this new shop of yours, and I really liked helping you get it ready to open."

"I know you did," I replied.

"And after it opened," Jack went on, "I didn't think you could use my help anymore. But then Jean called me today."

"She did?" That woman! She didn't tell me. "What did she want?"

"She told me how busy it's been and how much you could use my assistance there. So, I've decided maybe you need me after all and I'll come in a few mornings a week to help you stock the shelves. How does that sound?"

"Oh that would be wonderful, Jack." I reached over and hugged him. Then I planted a big wet kiss on his lips. "I can't believe it. Jean sure is amazing sometimes. I guess she knew how much I needed you."

Jack returned the kiss. It was passionate, too. This wasn't something he usually would display in public.

Now we're getting somewhere, I thought. Maybe there could be some fooling around between us before the night ended after all. However, I wasn't about to say anything again to suggest it. It would have to be Jack's idea.

The table was situated in a quiet corner—nice and romantic. The scenery at L'Italiano's was always lovely with soft candlelight and music in the background. Knowing what we wanted, we ordered some wine and our meals--lasagna for him and fettuccini alfredo for me. Everything seemed set for a good evening, except . . .

Was that Luanne a few tables down? Sitting with Charlene, the sales manager at Home Sweet Home Realty? OH NO! I can't say that they are two of my favorite people. Hoping neither one would spot me, I turned away from them and tried to concentrate on the menu. Fat chance. Before I knew it, there was a tap on my shoulder. Jack looked up first. I turned around to see who it was and wasn't surprised to see Luanne's smiley face looking right at me.

"Rosie, oh Rosie, it's so good to see you!" Luanne looked a bit out of it and I could smell whiskey on her breath. No surprise. Luanne's a lush. She's also a former client—the owner of the multi-million dollar property on Lake Winnipesaukee I had sold earlier this summer for her. The property where Justin took us all hostage and did indecent things to me, things I'd rather not remember.

"Hi there, Luanne." I smiled back at her, appearing surprised. "How's it going?"

She put her hands on her hips. "Oh well, it's going great now that my rotten ex-husband Lars is out of the picture. Hey, did you know I just got hired to work at your old real estate office? I've been bored out of my mind, and even though I don't need the money, I took the job at the front desk greeting customers."

That explained it. That's why she was here with Charlene. They were two of a kind. I couldn't wait to share this news with Jean.

"What about you? How's it going with the new venture?" She seemed genuinely interested, but I wanted to be with my husband alone tonight. Somehow I had to convey that to her before Charlene decided to come over here also.

"It's going great, we just opened for business, and I'd love to tell you about it, but, ahh, this is kind of a special night for me and my husband."

"Oh, your anniversary? I'm so sorry. I'll let you be then. It was great to see you and to meet your handsome husband."

"Jack, my name is Jack."

"Yeah, great to meet you, Jack." She extended her professionally manicured hand to him. There were diamonds on most of her fingers.

"Likewise," he mumbled as he reached out and shook it.

When she left, he looked over at me and chuckled. "Anniversary, huh?"

"I know, I know, it isn't for a few months. Besides, I didn't say it, she did. If that's what she wants to think, then fine." I smiled back. "And we need to be alone tonight. I want to talk to you about something important—something other than the shop."

Our meals came right at that moment, so he didn't ask me what about. It was on the ride home I brought it up again.

"Jack, I've decided I'm finally ready to meet the child I gave up for adoption."

"Oh?" he said glancing quickly over at me. "Why now after all these years?"

I didn't sense any agitation in his voice—definitely a good sign.

"Because it's been on my mind lately and Eloise told me the parents called her recently—there are some emotional issues involving drinking and/or drug use. They want to contact me."

"And how does that involve you? Are you sure you want to do this?" Jack continued to concentrate on driving, but took a moment to glance my way again. He still seemed calm.

"I have to do this, Jack. Otherwise, I'll always wonder. Maybe I can help out in some way. Maybe it's time to."

Jack took it quite well and never once asked who the father was. He told me to do what I had to do and when I'd found everything out, then we'd tell the boys. Why tell them now without knowing anything? He was right and I thanked him for it. Secretly, I was also thankful for not having to announce Justin was the father. It would have ruined his good mood.

But his mood wasn't good enough to prompt him to want to consider making love to me when we got home, and, like I said, I wasn't going to suggest it again. Instead, we sat close together on the couch and enjoyed some popcorn and a nice movie. It turned out to be the best of evenings, well, minus the sex we missed out on, and it was also a relief to be one step closer to meeting the child I didn't know, the child who now was a young adult and maybe needed my help.

Chapter 9

The disheveled girl returned the next morning. She went directly to the book section and picked the same Anne Tyler novel she was interested in yesterday. Finding a quiet corner, she sat down and immediately started reading.

Bets are she was also hungry again, I thought. I grabbed a bottle of water for her and one of Jacob's freshly baked carrot muffins and walked over to her. She smiled up at me this time—a nice smile.

"Hey, it's nice to see you again." I smiled back at her, showing her she was welcomed.

She gently placed the book face down on a nearby table, keeping it open to the page she was reading. I put the water down next to it and handed her the muffin. She devoured it in two bites. Then, she wiped her mouth with the napkin, stuffed it into her front jeans pocket and reached for the water.

"Uh, thanks," she mumbled. She looked over at the book, like she wanted to pick it up.

"I see you're reading the same book as yesterday. Tyler's a great writer," I said quickly, not wanting to lose her attention yet.

She seemed bothered now. "I wish I had enough money to buy it, it's at a bargain price, but, ah, I don't."

I stopped her before she went on. "Hey, don't worry. Come in any time. You enjoy reading and, and . . ." I stopped briefly. My eyes lit up. "Wait a minute, I've got an idea. What if you could help out here in exchange for the book, for any of the books? Volunteer kind of. Would you consider it?"

The girl seemed puzzled. She took a sip of water before answering. "Whattaya mean? Earn the book?"

"That's right. I need some help here. My husband's going to come in a few mornings a week, but what if you could come on the other mornings—maybe Tuesdays and Thursdays for a couple of hours? I'm not in a position to pay wages yet, but I could at least offer you breakfast and books. How does that sound?"

She brightened up again. "Really? That would be great. When do you want me to start?"

"How about starting today? That way, you can bring the book with you when you leave and enjoy the rest of it at your leisure." I then hesitated. "But, there's just one catch."

"There always is," she replied. The smile quickly went from her face.

"Oh, no, I'm sorry. It's just I need to know your name, your first name at least."

The smile returned. "Mary, my name is Mary."

"Great. Now, let's get to work, Mary. I'll show you how to stock the shelves."

"That was real nice of you, Rosie," Jean said later on during lunch upstairs. "You know, what you did for that girl."

"Her name is Mary," I replied. "It thrills me to watch her read. She reminds me of myself when I was younger. Once I discovered books, I couldn't get my nose out of them."

"Do you know anything about her, though?" Jean's demeanor turned to concern. "Like, aren't you worried she might steal something? Or that she's a drug addict or alcoholic or something? She looks like she lives on the streets. Maybe you should've found out more about her before you asked her to help out."

"And what would that do to make it any different? Geez, Jean, what's with you? What if she is a drug addict or alcoholic? That's all the more reason to offer her an alternative."

I put down my fork and pushed away my leftover meal from L'Italianos that I had just finished heating up in her microwave. All of a sudden, I'd lost my appetite. I didn't want to admit it, but maybe Jean was right. Maybe I should've found out more about her first. But, no, why second guess myself? I knew in my gut this girl was special in some sort of way. She needed me, I could tell, and it was the only way I could help her right now.

"It's the right thing to do and it will all work out fine. You wait and see," I replied. I reached for my plate, picked up my fork again, and started eating.

The shop had just closed when Jean announced "We're $10 short in the register." Jean looked at me suspiciously as she counted it again. "Wonder why," she said. Right away, I knew she suspected Mary and I became defensive.

"One of us must have given someone too much change back. It can happen," I commented.

"I guess so," Jean replied. "But let's keep a watch so it doesn't happen again. If it does . . ."

"I know what you're going to say. You're going to blame Mary. Don't. Give her a chance. Besides, I don't even think she went near the register."

But I didn't have a clue as to how we could be short. Did Mary go near it while she was here? Could she have opened it without one of us noticing? No, it couldn't have happened. I felt guilty even considering it. My mind was lost in thought when Jean started waving a $10 bill in the air.

"Whoops, here it is. Sorry about that. It was caught in the back of the drawer somehow."

"Good," I replied half-heartedly and still deep in thought. The few seconds of suspicion started me wondering why we tend to judge people like Mary simply because they're less fortunate. People that live in shelters, or even on the streets. I didn't know if that was her case, but because of how disheveled she appeared, and her wrinkly clothing, her unkempt hair, I suspected it.

"Street people," I must have said out loud.

"What about them?" Jean asked.

"Well, I'm wondering if there might be a way to help them out." I looked over at Jean. She was still listening. "I mean, our shop is in the downtown district. The emergency shelter is nearby and the food pantry is only a few stores down. Maybe we can help in some way?"

"There you go again, Rosie. Who do you think you are, Mother Teresa or something? Look, you're already helping Mary by offering her some work in exchange for free food and books."

"I know, I know, but . . ."

She cut in. "But nothing. There's already too much on your plate. First of all, there's Jack who's a handful himself. Then the shop. And Tommy is heading to college soon and, remember, you still need to open that envelope."

"You're right, Jean. Sorry I mentioned it." I flashed a grin. "Hey, speaking of that, I told Jack last night I was finally ready to meet my birth child. Gosh, that sounds strange to say."

"And?" This caught Jean's full attention. She had finished the deposit and had put the day's sales into a blue zippered bag for me to drop in the night deposit at the bank.

As she handed the bag to me, I replied, "And he's okay with it, at least at this point, but he wants me to wait until later to tell the boys."

"Are you ready to open the envelope? Can I still be there when you do?" Jean asked in anticipation.

"Yes, Jean, I didn't forget. We'll open the envelope this weekend if that's all right with you. As long as it doesn't interfere with your plans with Jacob before he leaves on Sunday."

Jean frowned. "Don't remind me. I'm going to hate to see him go. It's hard to believe the week is half over already and do you think he cares? He's going back to see that guy tomorrow morning, the one with agoraphobia. And he's got 'other plans' tomorrow night and those plans don't include me. What's going on, Rosie? Just a day ago, he was hot on me and now it seems like it's fizzling out."

"Hey, cheer up," I replied. "He's found someone who needs his help. I can understand and so should you. Besides, why wait until this weekend? Why don't we open the envelope tomorrow after work? You're free then, right?"

"Who says I'm free? Damn, Rosie, you think I was going to sit around all evening? No, no, I've already made my own plans."

"Oh, let me guess."

"Yep, you've got it. I've got a date with Bob. And I'm going to tell Jacob all about it when I get back from it."

Chapter 10

It was already Friday, and the first week of business was almost over. Having picked up a copy of the weekly local newspaper on the way into work, I couldn't wait to skim through it to find out if my first column had been published. I came charging into the shop, not even saying hello to Jean and Jacob who were sitting there drinking coffee.

"Not even a hello?" Jean barked out. "What the hell's the matter with you today, Rosie?"

I didn't respond.

Max came over to greet me while I spread out the newspaper on the counter next to the cash register. He nudged his nose against my leg, insisting he wasn't going to go unnoticed. While I was frantically searching the paper, I reached down to give him a pat.

Then I spotted it. "It's here! They put it in, just like they promised," I screeched.

"What's here? What're you talking about?" Jean asked. She quickly came over to join me. Jacob glanced our way, but continued to sit still.

"My first column about Simple Pleasures. They've printed it." I pointed to it several times. "It's my first column, Jean." I peered up at her. "Can you believe it?"

That's when I noticed her eyes, they were red, and her face was blotchy.

"Hey, I'm sorry," I said. "Did I interrupt anything? You've been crying."

"Yeah, yeah, just ignore it. Everything's okay." She sniffled and then blew her nose in the tissue she had been holding onto.

I glanced over at Jacob and then back at Jean again.

"Ignore it?" I placed my hands on her shoulders forcing her to look straight at me. "I won't ignore it, now what's going on?"

"Jacob broke up with me," she managed to say. Then she started crying again.

It took all I had inside of me not to break out laughing at what she said. Broke up with her? I didn't even think they were going together! Sure, Jean had done a little necking with him, and she considered him her soul mate, but she made it quite obvious, to me anyway, that she didn't have those romantic feelings about him. It made me wonder if she'd ever told Jacob after getting his hopes up, like she said she would.

"Look, I want to know all about it, but we're opening the shop in fifteen minutes. Why don't you two take it upstairs and come down when you're ready, okay?"

"No need," Jacob interjected as he stood up and placed his empty coffee mug on the counter. "I need to go. I'm on my way over to George's this morning. Jean, are you going to be okay?"

Jacob appeared concerned. He still cared about Jean— he cared a lot. I was sure he didn't like seeing her so upset.

Jean went over to him and gave him a kiss on the cheek. "I'll be okay. Thanks for doing what you needed to do."

"I plan on coming back early enough to tell stories for the kids this afternoon. I promised them I'd be here. Do you want me to bring lunch again today?" he asked both of us as he headed towards the front entrance.

"That would be great," Jean replied. Her mood had already improved at the mention of something to eat. "Food always helps when I'm depressed."

Somehow I didn't think she'd be depressed for long.

"How about pizza again?" she added. "There's a great place around the corner that serves an awesome pie—thin crust, lots of cheese, so much grease that it drips down your arm when you eat it. It's even better than the pizza we ate the other night."

I rolled my eyes, but, luckily Jean didn't see me. Oh no, pizza again?

Once Jacob left, I looked at her again and frowned. "You didn't tell him, did you? You said you would days ago, but you kept leading him on and he was smart enough to know it."

"That's not fair, I did so, well, kind of," she replied not looking directly at me. "I told him we needed to go slow, that I wasn't sure what I wanted and that's the truth, you know. THAT'S THE TRUTH!" Jean walked away from me and then stomped all the way up the stairs and out of sight.

There she goes again, I thought. Being so dramatic. Sometimes I wonder how we ever became friends because we are opposites in almost every way. But despite her outbursts and daily drama with the men in her life, Jean has a heart of gold, I know she does, and that's why I love her.

There was no time to discuss this anymore. The shop was due to open in a few minutes. It was a rainy day and several people were already waiting at the door. Plus, the cash drawer hadn't even been set up yet. I glanced at my watch—five till—just enough time to get it all done. I quickly peered down at my column in the newspaper one last time, and then folded it up and put it under the counter. Jean and I would have to read it later. Gosh, I hope there aren't any typos in it.

Later that morning, Jack came up to me, looking kind of lost.

"What else can I do to help?" he said.

"You've already put all of the new books on the shelves?" I asked.

"Yeah, already done." He seemed a little edgy. "Hey, Rosie, do you think I can take a quick break? Maybe run to the coffee shop and sit at the counter with a couple of friends for a while? Joe called yesterday afternoon and invited me, but I had already promised to help you here."

I was thrilled to hear it. Jack was actually starting to get a life again. He used to always get together with his buddies in the mornings, at least a couple of days a week. It was part of his regular schedule and he enjoyed it. Ever since his heart attack and heart surgery, though, he'd been afraid to do anything.

"Of course you can. I'll be fine. Tell the guys I said hello." I gave him a quick kiss and grinned.

As he was leaving, I added, "Don't eat too many of those homemade donuts there. Remember, they're not good for you."

"Nothing is good for me," he grumbled as he walked away.

But sex was good for him, the doctor even encouraged it the last time we went to see him. And it's not even fattening, either. Why can't Jack realize that?

Emma came in for tea again, as well as a few young mothers. Two young girls and a boy pleaded with Jacob to tell them a story. He obliged, and they found a spot in the far corner of the book area so as not to intrude on our social time. We could hear them in the distance, but it wasn't too loud.

We were all sitting, enjoying our tea, and chatting. Emma was clicking away again on her knitting needles, her baby outfit almost finished.

"Oh that Jacob, he's such a wonder," she said. "He's helped my son tremendously in just a few days. We'll miss him when he goes this weekend."

"Don't remind me," replied Jean. "I'll miss him the most."

I glanced over at Jean and knew she meant it. She would miss him. It was going to be hard for her to bring him to the airport and say goodbye to him. Well, at least they had that Skype thing going on the computer. They could still keep in touch regularly. And it might be safer, too. That way, Jean won't lead him on anymore. It was time for both of them to move forward with their lives. It didn't mean they still couldn't be good friends, or even soul mates for that matter.

"Hey, Emma, are you planning on coming to the knitting group once it starts next month?" I asked, hoping to change the subject. I had to keep Jean's mind off of Jacob's leaving soon or she would be in a bitter mood for the rest of the day.

"Of course, dear, I wouldn't miss it," she replied. "I've already signed up and so have two of my friends."

One of the young mothers, Morgan, who'd been sitting there sipping her tea, glanced up and finally spoke. "Knitting group? I don't know anything about it. I don't even knit well yet, I just started."

"All the more reason to join," piped in Jean. She put her cup down, went over to the counter and came back with the flyer and the sign-up sheet. "We have four people right now and two of them are brand new at knitting. Why don't you give it a try?" she said. "After all, it's free, except for the supplies. All you'll have to do is find a project and some yarn and I can help you with that."

She handed both items to Morgan and after looking over the flyer quickly, Morgan said, "Well, I guess that I can try it out. It might do me some good to get out one night a week." She pushed her long blonde hair back, and wrote down her name and contact information with the pen Jean also handed to her.

"How about it, Heather?" Morgan asked the other young mother sitting next to her. "We could come together. It might be nice."

"Well, I don't know. I'd like to learn how to knit, but I also like to read books. I can't go to both."

Emma looked over at both Jean and I. "Hey, I've got an idea. How about if you make the knitting and reading group meet at the same time on the same evening each week? Most knitters like to read also and those who don't knit might want to give knitting a try once they see how enjoyable it is. Besides, it would be fun."

Jean watched to see my reaction. I wasn't sure if Jack would join in, but I thought it was a great idea. That way, we could do it together and Emma was right, I enjoyed both knitting and reading, but couldn't be out two nights a week either.

"You know, I think that's a great idea. Why don't you say we try it, Jean? If it doesn't work out, we could always change things," I said.

"Sounds good to me," she replied. "I don't think the others that have already signed up would mind. How many do you have on your list, Rosie?"

"There are only three names so far and I was hoping Jack would join in also. Every Tuesday night he's glued to the TV set, so Thursday, the night you planned for the knitting classes, may work out better."

Jean started counting on her fingers. "Let me see. There are six names on the knitting list right now, and three on your list. Add Jack, you and me and that makes 12. That's a good class size. How about calling it the limit?"

Emma piped in. "Hey, wait. I was hoping George would join in. He's still afraid to go outside, but Jacob has been a big help to him. Maybe he'll come."

"Okay, okay, 13 is the absolute limit. Now let's take down the flyers, Rosie. Unless someone objects, I'm happy to announce we have a full class and we'll begin the second Thursday of September!"

SIMPLE PLEASURES

A weekly column by Rosie Blume

I've wanted to open a book store for many years now. There's nothing like the feel of a good book in my hands, and many times I've even found myself holding one up to my heart and hugging it tightly because it has become such a treasure.

The first treasure I can remember reading was *My Side of the Mountain*, a young-adult fiction novel written by Jean Craighead George. It's a story about a young boy who ventures out into the Catskill Mountains to live on his own. He hollows out a tree for a home, finds a falcon for a pet, makes clothes out of deerskin, and grinds acorns into flour. I first read it in sixth grade, many, many years ago, and became so immersed in the story that I felt I was also out there in the wilderness, living off the land, and having the greatest adventures of all!

Now I'm selling copies of this book, along with many others, at Simple Pleasures, the new yarn and book shop on Main Street. I'm co-owner of the shop, along with my best friend Jean, and it's a dream come true for both of us.

At Simple Pleasures, we offer all sorts of books, old and new, at very reasonable prices. You can spend an entire day browsing through the thousands of titles we have.

Plus, the yarn area has all types of yarn imaginable for the beginner up to the expert knitter. We also offer accessories of every kind—needles, spindles, winders, etc.

And if you happen to be in our shop around 3 pm, we brew a nice pot of English tea daily to share with all of our customers. It's a great way to take a break in the day and engage in some good conversations.

Simple pleasures are things that don't cost much, but are totally satisfying. To read a good book is satisfying to me, as well as to feel warm fuzzy yarn through my fingers as I knit. I also like a good cup of hot tea or coffee, chatting with girlfriends, an energizing walk, spending time with my family, taking a scenic drive, dancing and singing to a favorite song. Oh, I could go on and on.

In this day and age, it is easy to hear about all that's going wrong in the world. The news is saturated with horror stories and bad news. To engage in a simple pleasure allows one to realize there is still so much good around—so much to make us smile, relax, and be thankful for.

So, this is what my weekly column is going to be about. I'll share stories about our shop from time to time, but it will mostly be about the simple things in life that don't cost much, if anything, and make us truly happy. It'll be some good news for a change.

Until next week, be sure to find the time to engage in some of these simple joys. Take a nice walk, pick up those knitting needles, read a book, dance and sing to your heart's content, and don't forgot to also stop by and find some treasures at Simple Pleasures. We're open from 9-5 weekdays and from 10-3 on Saturdays.

Chapter 11

By the start of the weekend, I was exhausted. We were only open a half-day on Saturdays and didn't open until ten, but it was hard to get out of bed. I hit the snooze after the alarm went off.

Jack was already up—I could hear him in the shower. Wanting to get a few more minutes of rest, I kept my eyes closed, but it wasn't long before my mind started racing. I had planned on opening the envelope this weekend, but I was still nervous about it. Is this really the right time? "Oh God, give me a clue," I prayed. It didn't take long to get an answer because the phone rang. I reached over to pick it up.

"Hello?" I said in a sleepy tone.

"Rosie? Oh, I'm so sorry to wake you."

I recognized the voice right away. It was Eloise. Immediately, I was concerned.

"No, I wasn't sleeping. What's wrong?" I blurted out.

"Oh nothing, dear. It's just, well, the parents of the child called me this morning, rather the mother did. She wanted me to tell you they've put everything on hold right now. You won't be hearing from them, at least not for another few weeks."

This was the answer to my prayers—I knew it. It wasn't time to open the envelope yet, although I had been prepared to. Tommy was moving out and going to college next weekend. The shop continued to be busy. There was too much going on right now and I was already stressed beyond my limit. Still, I remained concerned about why the sudden change in plans.

"Oh?" I said. "I thought they needed me."

65

"I'm sure they do, but they assured me it's only on hold, something has come up and they don't want you to worry."

The alarm clock went off again. Eloise could hear it through the phone.

"I knew you were still sleeping. I'm sorry, Rosie. I should've waited until later to call you."

"That's all right. I'm awake. And I'm glad you called. The timing was perfect."

Now, how am I going to break this to Jean, I thought, after hanging up the phone? She's been hoping to see those pictures, too, and she's going to think I chickened out all of a sudden.

Since I can look at those photos anytime, and have had the opportunity for years now, maybe she's right. Maybe I am chickening out again.

"Hey, who was that?" Jack asked emerging from the bathroom with only a towel around his waist.

I gazed at his hairy chest—mostly gray now, except for a bald spot where his scar from heart surgery was still visible. His spare tire was still there, too, but smaller since he had been eating better. Seeing him in front of me made me yearn for him. I wanted to reach out and yank the towel off, leaving him totally naked and vulnerable. And then I wanted to entice him to join me back in bed to resume the lovemaking I've missed so much. If we could do it just once, nice and slow even, he wouldn't be afraid anymore. He'd see how good it is for both of us. But . . .

"Don't get any ideas. I know that look," he remarked. Then he grabbed his clothes and went back into the bathroom to change.

Jean was already downstairs and alone in the sitting area knitting something, possibly another scarf, when I arrived. She seemed content. Soft music played in the background. She glanced up as I approached her.

"What a beautiful day," she remarked. "I'm glad you're early. I wanted to chat with you."

I put my purse down and sat beside her.

"What about?" I asked.

"Well, as you know, I went out with Bob on Thursday night and . . . " She hesitated and put the knitting down on the table.

"And?"

"And he asked me to go with him to California to visit the kids for a week. He'd like to leave next Thursday."

"Gosh, Jean, we're moving Tommy out next Saturday. I can't possibly cover the shop next weekend, never mind for a whole week."

Jean's face brightened. "You don't have to, Rosie. I've got it all taken care of. Gertrude is going to put some extra time in and Emma has volunteered to take my place while I'm gone. Also, I'll book Max into that posh pet motel near the airport. It won't be a burden to you at all. You can have the time off as planned."

"Why so early?" I asked. "Why such a sudden decision?"

"Because Bob is thinking of moving out there. He mentioned it to me earlier, but he also wants to see if we can work things out. If we can, then he'll stay. It's kind of like a test to see if we're able to live together and stand each other for a whole week."

My eyebrows went up. "Does that mean you'll be sharing a bed? Gee, I didn't realize it had progressed to this?"

"Well, it hasn't yet," Jean replied. "But I'm willing to give it a try. Besides, we're still married, you know."

"And what does Jacob think about all this? You did tell him, didn't you?"

"Yessss, I did, but Jacob is so mellow, too mellow. He still thinks we're meant to be together, meaning Jacob and I, but he understands. Besides, he's too damn busy for me these days and broke it off with me yesterday, remember?"

"And he's leaving tomorrow," I added.

"Don't remind me!" Jean snapped back.

Chapter 12

Who could've imagined what would happen that same afternoon. I had gotten home around four after talking more with Jean after the shop closed, and I was about to start preparing dinner when there was a knock on the door. Jack was in the basement working on a project and Tommy was out, so I went to answer it. Standing there, on our doorstep, was a tall, lanky guy, about 20 maybe, blonde hair, blue eyes, wearing jeans and a t-shirt with a backpack slung over his right shoulder. I'd never seen him before, but at first, I thought he might be a friend of Tommy's.

"Hi," he said quietly. He appeared nervous which made me nervous. Who was this stranger?

"Uhh, are you looking for my son? He's not home right now," I said.

"No, I'm looking for Jack Blume. Does he live here?"

"Aahh, yes. Does he know you?" I was real curious now as to why he wanted Jack. Jack never mentioned anyone fitting his description before.

"No, he doesn't, but it's important I speak with him. Real important. Is he home?"

Okay, I didn't know him and maybe it was being rude, but I wasn't going to let him in until I did. After all, he could be a thief or something. I've heard of terrible things happening to decent people right here in New Hampshire when they let strangers into their homes. No, he'd have to wait outside.

"Wait right here and I'll get him," I shut and locked the door. Rushing downstairs, I yelled out, "Jack, there's someone at the door. JACK?"

He was there. I could see him engaged in making a set of bookshelves. I wondered if they were for the shop. I could also hear him sputtering and grumbling.

"Damn, where are those tools I need? I'm always looking for them. Rosie, did you . . ."

There was no way I was going to let him finish his sentence. He was always passing the blame on me when he'd lose something. Besides, I had to get his attention before this stranger tried to climb in a window.

"Jack, stop what you're doing. Hey, LISTEN TO ME!

That definitely got his attention. He finally looked up knowing I meant business.

"WHAT?" he yelled back.

I frowned and my tone softened, "Jack, there's a guy at the door asking for you. A young guy. I've never seen him before so he makes me nervous. Anyway, I told him to wait outside until I got you."

"Who the hell is it?" he replied. I could tell he was still annoyed about being interrupted. He resumed searching for his tools.

"I told you, I don't know," I said.

Jack sighed in defeat, stood up and walked upstairs with me. I watched from the window as he went outside to talk to the guy. They were deep in discussion for close to an hour. As I watched them, my initial thoughts began to change about the kid—he didn't appear harmful anymore. Now, I was just curious as to who he was. And I couldn't wait until Jack came back inside so I could ask him.

When Jack did come back in, he seemed unusually quiet. He didn't even look at me. He passed right by me without saying a word and went downstairs again. When I followed him minutes later (not wanting him to think I was pressing him for information), I saw him sitting on his workbench, head down and leaning forward, with his hands rubbing his head. I knew by looking at him that the guy had said something bothersome.

"Are you all right?" I asked as I walked slowly up to him. I stood next to him and put my hand on his arm.

"Yeah, Rosie, sorry. I just need some time to think for a while. When is supper going to be ready?"

Supper? Uh Oh! I'd totally forgotten to prepare it after the knock on the door. "Oh, Jack, I'm sorry. I was about to make it when he came by."

"Ahh, that's okay. Maybe we should go out to dinner anyway. Leave a note for Tommy. I've got something I need to talk to you about. Alone."

Now I was scared again. What could this guy, this stranger, have said to Jack?

What did he need to tell me that he couldn't also share with Tommy?

It wasn't my idea of going "out to dinner", but at least I didn't have to cook. We picked up a couple of subs and Jack drove to a nearby park that looked out over Lake Winnipesaukee. We sat across from each other at a picnic table.

With the setting sun and light breeze off of the water, it was a bit chilly. I wished I'd brought my sweater and my napkin kept blowing off of my lap. Frustrated, I tried to hold it down by squeezing it between my knees. It wasn't very comfortable, but, that aside, at least Jack was going to talk to me about this unknown guy finally. At least that's what I thought he wanted to talk about and I was more than curious by now.

We had also forgotten to order drinks to go along with the sandwiches. It's awful hard to eat a whole Italian sub without anything to wash it down with. Still, there was no one around, and Jack still seemed bothered. I didn't even dare complain.

He didn't talk until he finished eating. Then, once I'd thrown all of the paper wrappings into a nearby trash bin and came back and sat down again, he looked over at me for the first time since we'd gotten here.

"Rosie, I'm having a hard time with this and I don't even know if I believe it yet, but I have to talk to you about the kid who came by today.

"Who is he?" I asked.

"I know you've had a lot on your mind lately, wanting to find your birth child and all, and then there's the shop. I just hate to hit you with this news."

I started trembling inside. I knew what he wanted to tell me was something big, but I didn't have a clue. What could it be about?

He went on. "Well, Rosie, I guess I have say it anyway. Before I met you, there was this other woman in my life. It was kind of serious and we lived together for several years."

"You're not telling me anything new, Jack. You've told me this already, all except the serious part. You must have loved her."

"Yeah, I did. At least I thought so until I met you and found out what real love is." He reached over and held onto my hands. Looking straight at me now, he continued, "She left me and I haven't seen her since. I just found out she passed away."

"I'm sorry to hear that, Jack."

"Well, it's not really what's so important. I don't want to upset you, but the boy . . . the boy who came to our house today . . . ," Jack hesitated.

"Yes?" I asked.

"Rosie, he's claiming to be my son."

Chapter 13

"**H**ey, Rosie, are you awake?"

I glanced over at my alarm clock. It was 7 am. It was Sunday. What was Jean calling me about so early?

"Uhhh no, I wasn't, but now I am," I said while letting out a yawn.

"Good. I'm about to take Jacob to the airport, but I'm wondering if you're heading to that prayer group thing this morning. If you are, could you pray for me? I'm starting to have second thoughts about going with Bob to California later this week."

"We discussed this yesterday. You were all gung-ho about it. What happened?"

"Nothing, I'm just thinking, you know how that goes." Jean snickered. For some reason she thought this was amusing. At 7 am on a Sunday, I didn't think so.

"I'm not going today, but I'll pray for you. I'll also stop by later this evening because I need your advice about something."

"My advice?"

"Yes," I continued, "Believe it or not, I do. I'll call you before I come over, but right now I'm going back to sleep."

"Okay, okay. I'll have dinner ready. Pizza?"

"No, not pizza! I've had it three times already this week and I've probably gained five pounds."

"Chinese?"

"Not that either, it's time to start eating right. How about salad? I'll bring the ingredients."

"Won't Jack mind you not being home for dinner?" Jean asked.

Usually he would, but not tonight. He knew I needed to talk to my best friend.

"No, he's okay with it. I'll explain later."

"Great, but don't bring tomatoes. I still have some here from Jacob. Oh no, Jacob! I need to go or he'll miss his flight. See you tonight." Jean hung up and I was wide-awake. No use trying to go back to sleep now. I sat up on the side of the bed, put on the Crocs I always wore for slippers, and shuffled into the kitchen. When I got there, Jack was on his cell phone speaking softly. He must be thinking Tommy might still be asleep.

When he was done with his call, he poured us some fresh brewed coffee and told me he had been talking to the boy—his name is Kevin—and Kevin would be stopping by around noon. I didn't know how I felt about this new news, but at least he shared it with me.

"Okay," I said, "Should I make some lunch for you?"

"No, I don't know how Tommy would react to this. I told Kevin we'd go out to lunch so we could talk some more. Is that okay with you? I know it's your only day off, but this is kind of important."

"I know, Jack, I can understand. Go ahead. Maybe Tommy will go out with me to eat somewhere else, kind of a special mother and son lunch before he leaves. That would be nice. And then I have to see Jean this evening, for a little while, and I said we'd have salads, but I'll make you a dinner beforehand. I'm sorry, Jack."

"I understand, Rosie. You need to talk to someone also and Jean's your best friend. I'm glad you're going. No need to make dinner either, I'll find something to eat. There's a game on tonight, too, and Tommy's staying in. That'll give us a little time together as well."

"I'm glad, Jack. I'm going to miss him." The thought of Tommy leaving for college soon made me sad all of a sudden. I placed my coffee down on the counter and hung my head low.

"Me, too. He's a great boy." Jack said. Then, after placing his own coffee down on the counter, he reached out to me, drew me close to him, and let me cry in his arms.

Tommy was available for lunch and seemed kind of excited about the two of us going out. He chose the restaurant—a little coffee shop around the corner that served great organic soups and sandwiches. We both ordered the tomato bisque soup, along with chicken salad mixed with yogurt on fresh baked wheat bread.

We sat in a booth in the corner and it wasn't busy, so it was a good place for us to talk. I wanted to somehow let him know how much he meant to me, and how much I would miss him, without seeming overly mushy. He knew how I could get and would get irritated if I began to treat him as younger than he was. No, he was now a young man and didn't need a mother to baby him anymore. Still, he'll always be my baby, and it's not easy to just let go. Most mothers would understand this, but sometimes it's hard for kids to realize how difficult it is for the parents, especially mothers. Having gone through it with his older brother already and sometimes feeling like Jonathan was a stranger now, I knew it all would be different once Tommy left. No longer would I know who all of his friends were, what he did in the evenings, if he was eating all right. I'd have to trust him when he said he would never drink and drive—I realized college life encouraged parties—and I believed God would protect him, even if Tommy didn't know if he believed in God yet.

"So, are you excited about leaving next weekend?" I asked him as a starter to the conversation.

"I am, but I'm a bit nervous, too. All of my friends are here—I've grown up with most of them—and now we're all headed in different directions. Did you know Sean's going to Florida State? I think I mentioned it earlier."

Sean was Tommy's best friend. They'd been almost inseparable since sixth grade when Sean moved into the area. Tommy would spend many weekends over at Sean's house since his parents were easier going than Jack. Jack always had set rules—curfew at 11 pm, even on weekends, and no Internet after nine. It would drive Tommy crazy. Still, they enjoyed sports together and Jack really loved Tommy like he was his own. It's just sometimes when Jack was being his usual "bear" self (and I don't mean the cuddly kind), Tommy would forget that. In some ways, I think he was happy about soon getting away and having his own say about what he did and didn't do.

"Florida is pretty far. It'll be tough on you with him away, but there must be some friends that are staying near-by. How about Keith?" I asked.

"Keith's going to UNH, too, which is great. It'll be good to have someone I know around. There are also some others from school that'll be there. Plus some will visit. Still, it's a bit scary. I'm sure I'll get used to it."

"I'm sure you will, and I will too, but I'm going to miss you. It won't be the same without you to talk to in the evenings. And I won't hear your car drive in the driveway every night. I do that, you know, when you're out or at work, or especially when you go somewhere farther than town. I wait for you, worry about you, and don't feel relaxed until I know you're home safe again. That's the way mothers are, but soon you won't be here. I'm going to have to stop worrying. Otherwise, I'll drive myself crazy."

"And you'll drive me crazy calling and emailing me all the time. You can't do that, Mom. Promise me. Once a week—that's it—unless you have something you need to tell me that can't wait."

He was setting the ground rules early. I guess it was necessary to do, but it made me even sadder about him leaving. I didn't want him to see me cry, though, so although I wanted to, I held back and kept on trying to be cheerful. Still, how will I be able to make it an entire week without talking to him when I'm used to saying goodnight to him almost every evening? Even when he would be staying over at Sean's or some other friend's house, I'd call him on his cell phone. Oh gosh, I must have driven him crazy. In fact,

I know I did. How many times did he tell me before to let go a bit, to not call him all the time and I brushed it off and never listened? This time, I had no choice, I'd have to.

"Tommy, I get the message. I understand. I won't call you more than once a week unless I absolutely have to," I said.

"Promise?"

"I promise." It was hard to do this, but necessary—for Tommy's sake. I wanted him to become independent, to do what he wanted to do, not what his mother or stepfather wanted or even what his own father wished for. We didn't talk about his father much, but he was still around. He lived in the next town over and would see the kids every once in a while. When they were young, he used to take them every other weekend, but now that they were older and Jonathan was living in Maine, they didn't see each other as often and only talked on the phone occasionally.

"Have you spoken with your dad lately? Is he planning on visiting on Parent Weekend?" I knew I was prodding, but I wanted to ask.

"I spoke to him a couple of months ago, but not recently. I really don't want to talk about him, okay?"

I looked over at Tommy and could see the topic of his father was disturbing to him.

"What's wrong? Has he been drinking again?" Uh oh, I might be crossing the line here.

Tommy glared at me with the look that I wasn't listening again, but I guess because he was also doing his best to have a nice lunch with me, knowing he would be leaving next weekend, he kept any usual remarks about my prying and asking the wrong questions to himself. Instead, his glare softened.

"What do you think?" he replied a bit sarcastically.

That's it. No more questions were needed. I knew how Tommy's father could be when he drank. It was one of the reasons why I left him. That was so long ago, when Tommy was really young. Now he's heading off to college. Time sure does fly by.

Chapter 14

Since Jack had returned back home, after having lunch with Kevin, he hadn't said more than a couple of words to me. Instead, he spent most of the afternoon working down in the basement on the bookshelf he was making. Whenever Jack's disturbed about something, he engages himself in a project like that to keep his mind off of things. Still thinking about Tommy leaving and the situation with Jack, as well as wanting to know my birth child, I took the opportunity while he was busy to also engage in my own project. I started searching and sorting through my collection of knitting magazines hoping to find a knitting pattern to begin. Maybe I'd even share it with Jean later on. If I found something interesting, I could pick out the yarn when I went over to visit with her tonight.

It was about 6 pm when I gave Jean a call. She didn't sound too upbeat and seemed a bit tired, but that was to be expected after having said goodbye to Jacob. I'm sure it had been an emotional day.

As I was driving over to see her, I swung in to the Park and Shop grocery store near the downtown district to purchase the necessary items for our dinner salads. Usually, I don't shop at Park and Shop because the prices tend to be higher, but they have a good selection of organic vegetables and it was the most convenient store on the way. I chose three different types of lettuce, some apples, a cucumber, a couple of carrots and some bean sprouts. I also picked up some locally made balsamic dressing I already knew was not only healthy, but delicious. As I was on my way to the cheese section, I passed by the pre-packaged nuts and berries section and grabbed some dried cranberries. I was also fortunate to find a rare treat—maple glazed walnuts. Yummm. After also grabbing some cheddar cubes and crumpled feta, I proceeded to the check out.

All of this stuff was going to be costly, but my mouth was already watering for the delicious salad it would make. Jean would be thrilled. It was so much better than the usual pizza she suggested that I was sick of having. "Three times in one week is enough," I muttered under my breath. Now, don't get me wrong, I love pizza, especially the thin New York style kind, just not that often.

When I arrived at the shop, I let myself in and proceeded up the stairs. I stopped when I heard Jean talking on the telephone.

"Hey, if you'd rather take her, than me, to California, then be my guest," She commented sarcastically. She was pacing back and forth between the kitchen and the living room. She didn't sound so tired anymore. Instead, she appeared a bit worked up.

Oh, no, it must be Bob she's talking to. I wondered what had happened now. I had just talked to her less than an hour ago. Honestly, too much has been going on these past few days—most of it good—but I don't know, I think I could stand for a little boring stretch. There's only so much one can take at one time. I'm sure Jean felt the same way right about now.

I proceeded into her apartment and she gave me a fretful look while she remained on the phone.

"Hey, I've gotta go, Bob. Make up your mind and let me know. And tell Ginny to make up her mind also!" She slammed the phone down and came and grabbed one of the two bags of groceries I still held in my hands.

"What's that all about?" I asked.

"Oh, well, you know how it goes. You make plans and then a kink comes into them. Something you wouldn't think would ever happen." Jean walked into the kitchen area again and placed the bag on the counter. I followed her and did the same. Then she gave me a quick hug.

"I'm glad you came. Don't worry about Bob—he's all right. Ginny happened to call him today so he had to mention it to me. It was probably his way for getting me back for turning him down for a date yesterday and going out with Jacob instead. It was his last night here, what did he expect me to do?"

I was more curious about Ginny, and wondering if she was having second thoughts about breaking up with Bob. "Does she want to come back to him?" I asked. Although, I knew Bob and Jean should get their divorce and get on with their lives, I didn't think Ginny was the one for him, although I'd never met her. I also thought that Jean and Bob going together to California for a week, and even "playing house" together while they were over there, might be a good idea. That way, they could see for themselves, and remember, what it was like to live with each other. I think they've both forgotten. Reality should set in within a few days if living together was anything close to what Jean has mentioned to me.

"Oh, God no! She made it quite clear she's happy now in Florida. No, I just wanted to give him a hard time like he seemed to be giving me. Before he mentioned Ginny, he was talking about Jacob and I could sense the jealousy in his voice. I'm convinced that's the reason we haven't seen him hanging around the shop while Jacob was here. Next week might be a different story."

"Well, that's good. I've missed Bob." I smiled. "Speaking of Bob, does he have Max again? I miss him also when he's not around."

"Yes, it's his dog custody time, but Max will be back in tomorrow morning. You'll see him soon enough."

We prepared the salads together and enjoyed every bite. They were better than any salad I've ever eaten in a restaurant. And they were healthy, too, even though I'm sure there were more than enough calories consumed with all the delicious stuff we put on them.

After we ate, we sat down in Jean's living room and that's when I reached into my pocketbook and pulled out a large envelope.

"I can't wait to open it, Rosie. Go ahead, let's find out." Jean sat forward in her chair, eager to see what was inside.

It suddenly occurred to me I hadn't told Jean I wanted to wait a bit longer. The last conversation was a couple of days earlier when I asked her if we could get together to find out. Since that time, I hadn't even gone back to the bank to get the envelope out of the safety deposit box again. I had been stalling.

"Oh, Jean, I didn't mean to get your hopes up. I know I said I wanted to find out this weekend, but since I mentioned it to you, I've talked to Eloise and she's heard from the mother. They want to wait a few more weeks before contacting me, so under the present circumstances, I've decided to wait a couple of weeks also, at least until you come back from California."

Jean looked angry. "Oh, come on Rosie. You're just putting it off some more. Maybe you'll never want to open that envelope." She sat back hard, almost sinking into the cushions, and folded her arms.

"I will so! I just think now is not the right time. When I tell you why I need your advice, you'll understand."

She wasn't buying it. "Yeah, yeah, sure. So what's in THIS envelope?"

I opened it up, unfolded the sheet inside and showed her the pattern I had found earlier in the day. It was from an old knitting magazine, circa 1974. "Look at this!" I was excited to start the project and thought Jean would be excited about it also. "A bikini pattern. Isn't it cute? And how cute would it be to make a woolen bikini? Think of it. I plan on making one and then modeling it in front of Jack. My body isn't like this model's is, but maybe it might just turn Jack on, being so different and all."

"This is definitely different." Jean seemed interested and leaned forward again. She wasn't mad at me anymore. "Maybe I can make copies of this to hand out with purchases.

It could create a craze. Can you imagine us all knitting woolen bikinis? Sounds like fun."

It sure did and I could already imagine having mannequins modeling them in our shop windows. It would cause quite a stir and also some great publicity.

I was about to bring up the subject of Jack's newfound possible son arriving on our doorstep, but in a flash, Jean jumped up and headed for the stairs. I knew why, too—she was eager to choose some yarn and get started right away on her bikini.

Discussing Jack's situation would have to wait. "Not a bad idea," I said as I rose from the living room chair. "I need to get some yarn too." I headed toward the kitchen before following her.

"I'll grab some wine and glasses and we can knit down there while I tell you what's been happening at my house the past few days."

She looked back at me like she was going to ask me something, but then looked straight ahead, waved her free hand in the air motioning me to follow, and continued down the stairs. With the pattern still in her hands, she was on a mission.

It was nice to have the time to browse around looking at the yarn and admiring the knitted items the senior citizens, friends of Gertrude's, had made. I started to see the shop from a customer's point of view for the first time and liked what I saw. No wonder several of them kept returning even though we'd been open for only a week. The atmosphere was cozy, friendly and inviting. We had done well setting it up. I had to give most of the decorating credit to Jean, though. She has a knack for it and it showed.

In my browsing and admiring, I was able to find the perfect yarn for my bikini in no time—wool and self-striping. Three shades of blue—Jack's favorite color. I could picture what it would look like when it was done and it pleased me. The yarn was a sporting weight and seemed rugged enough to hold up. It wasn't scratchy either, which was VERY important, and I also didn't think it would shrink or stretch—also very important for swimming attire—although I couldn't envision myself ever being seen in public in the thing. No, I just wanted to wear it for Jack. And if he wanted to take it right off of me when I did model it, then all the better.

While I was waiting for Jean to choose her yarn, I strolled over to the book area and again, did my best to view it through customer eyes. The shelves were beautiful, stained a deep dark color. Jack had done a great job making them, and the books were all neatly lined up. The bestsellers and other new titles displayed on the two round oak tables were well arranged and the various types of chairs situated in several locations were inviting. I could see why someone would want to come into the shop and spend hours browsing and reading. Besides Mary, I'd spotted several others doing just that this past week and they also bought books to take home. Our clientele was already growing and news of the book and yarn shop was spreading. I'm sure the column I wrote for the newspaper the other day also helped to get the word out.

"Okay, I found my yarn," Jean called out. She lifted it up to show me. Unlike mine, hers was a solid color—a beautiful turquoise. It would look great on her with her green eyes and auburn hair. While I was looking her way, I also noticed what great shape she was in. Somewhere, somehow, she must have found the time to maintain her daily run in the mornings. I admired her for the many positive changes she had made since meeting her earlier in the year when we both were realtors at Home Sweet Home Realty. It seemed like eons ago, but it was only months. So much has changed since then, including our careers.

I went to join her in the larger sitting area where we gathered in the afternoons at three every business day to share tea with the customers and to get to know them better. Some customers, like Emma, knit during these daily chats. That's what we envisioned before the shop even opened and that's what Jean and I planned to do right now.

We both sat down on the large velvet sofa Bob purchased from an antique store. It was his gift to our venture and it was lovely. I ran my fingers along it before picking up my needles.

Jean placed the pattern on the table between us so we both could view it.

After casting on, I reached for the wine to open it, but noticed I'd forgotten to also bring down a corkscrew.

Jean could tell what I was thinking. "Don't bother. We'll have a glass in a while. Why don't we just knit first?"

"Okay." I went back to my knitting, now starting on the first row.

Wine was always relaxing, but so much so it made me tired. It had been a long week and it probably was a good idea to at least begin the project before having any.

I opened my mouth ready to share the events of the weekend with Jean, but before I could begin, she started up her own conversation.

"It was sad seeing Jacob go. We parted as friends, not lovers, and I think he realizes his first intentions when he came here, after we did a little fooling around, were a bit farfetched. He told me he had mentioned to you he wanted to marry me, Rosie. How crazy is that?"

I chuckled. "Yeah, it took me by surprise and I was a bit worried about both of you getting hurt, but I'm glad to hear the week turned out okay. And I'll bet he was glad he came to visit. It seems like you both had a good time together, well except for the break up as you so called it. He also enjoyed reading to the kids and helping Emma's son. I'm sure he'll visit again."

Jean recounted the stitches she had cast on her size 3 needles. "Damn, this is the worst part. I always get distracted and lose count. Wait a minute," she grumbled.

I knew what she meant. It was easy to lose count and it was important to have the right number of stitches to begin with. Sometimes, even after knitting for so many years, I would still cast on the wrong amount. Or I would drop a stitch or do the pattern wrong and have to rip back or begin again. And sometimes the pattern itself would be wrong and then it became a disaster. Knitting is relaxing for the most part, but not always. It definitely has its challenges—plenty of them.

"Shit," Jean sputtered. "I mean, am I stupid or something? This is the third time I've counted and I've lost track again."

"Hey, maybe we do need the wine after all, as long as we don't drink too much. It'll put me to sleep if I have more than a glass, but it'll help you relax. Let me go get the corkscrew upstairs. I'll be right back."

At this point, I could do without the wine, but I wanted to get her attention to talk to her about what happened the other night. It was already getting late and we both were working tomorrow. If I was going to tell her, I'd better tell her soon.

As I was proceeding to the stairs, I had a thought and turned to Jean. "Better yet, let's take the wine and glasses back upstairs. We can both knit on our own later tonight and continue to knit tomorrow during tea. Right now, I need to share something with you. Remember, I need your advice, and it's almost eight already. I told Jack I'd be home by nine."

"Awwww, Rosie. I was looking forward to knitting together, but okay. I know you came here especially to talk, but let's do it here. We don't have to go upstairs. I don't need to drink to relax."

Jean placed her yarn and needles down on the table next to where I had already put mine. I came back to sit beside her. Then, after adjusting comfortably on the sofa again and leaning back a little into the cushions, I turned sideways to look directly at her, making sure she was giving me her undivided attention.

"Well, I know you enjoy my stories, even if you never admit it, so I have a new one to share with you," I knew that would get her riveted from the get go. It did, so I went on.

"Last night, before dinner, there was a knock on the door. It was a stranger—a young man not much older than Tommy."

"Was it Tommy's friend?" Jean asked right away.

"That's what I thought, but no. The guy, who I later

discovered is named Kevin, asked to speak with Jack."

"Jack? Why'd he want to talk to Jack?"

"Again, that's what I thought. But, after shutting and locking the door on him in case he was trying to get in to rob the place or something, I ran downstairs to get Jack. Jack was as confused as I was at first, until they spent some time talking to each other."

"Did you find out who he was? I mean, what's this got to do with having to talk to me?" Jean looked perplexed.

"It has everything to do with it. Let's just say another kink came into the plans as you mentioned earlier. This time it was my plan. I was so excited about finding out who my first-born child was, and it never occurred to me that . . . well . . ."

"Well what, well what, Rosie? You drive me crazy, you know!"

"Well, the guy alleges he is Jack's son from a previous relationship. Jack said he never knew about him. The woman passed away recently and told her son about Jack on her deathbed. So, he came to find his father. I know everything works out the way it is meant to. I believe God has his plan for me, for all of us, but that was nowhere near the plan I had in my own head. I find myself asking myself why another situation? Haven't we had enough happening this past year already? Let's see, holdup at the lake, Jack's heart attack, the new shop and let's not forget still wanting to find my own child?"

"Okay, no need for lists," Jean commented. "I could add at least a half of a dozen more to yours."

"And what if Jack loves this boy more than his stepsons? Anyway, I just needed to share my frustrations with my best friend." I sighed and already felt more relaxed now I had spoken it out loud.

"Rosie, I'm surprised at you. I would think you'd be ecstatic about Jack having a child. After all, it's not like the woman is still in the picture. She's dead. She won't come knocking at the door hoping to steal your husband back."

She was right. There was no reason to feel bad about this. Jack loved Jonathan and Tommy. He would love my other child, too, in time. And I would welcome Kevin as part of the family if, in fact, it turns out he really is Jack's son. For some reason, however, I still had my doubts about it. Why? I didn't know.

Chapter 15

When I arrived back home, it was a few minutes after nine, and Jack didn't even notice. He was watching a ballgame on TV with Tommy and someone else. One of Tommy's friends? I looked closer. No, I couldn't believe it—it was Kevin.

"Hey," I said, shooting him a look of concern.

Jack glanced up at me before quickly turning his eyes back to the set. "Hey, welcome home. We're kind of hungry now. Is there anything you could fix up real quick for us to snack on?" It was like he didn't even notice me or seem to care how I felt about this. But Tommy was glancing my way also and was better at reading my mind.

"Hi, Mom," Tommy added. "Have you met Kevin yet? Jack asked if it was all right if he watched the game with us. He explained the whole thing and I'm okay with it, I really am." He managed a smile of assurance.

I smiled back at him. "Oh, okay. I'll see what I can find in the kitchen." I started to walk away when Kevin added, "Thank you, Mrs. Blume."

Hmmm. What a nice gesture of appreciation, I thought, but I still remained skeptical. And I was also still a little peeved at Jack for confiding in Tommy and inviting Kevin into our living room without even asking me first.

As I prepared some cheese and crackers on a plate for the three of them, and poured them each a glass of iced tea, I thought some more and began to calm down. If it were my daughter or son I had just met, I would probably do the same. Jack is doing what he thinks is best, so I won't mention anything. I'll accept Kevin until we find out for sure if he's really Jack's son.

Since they were engaged in the ballgame and it was only half over, I retreated to the bedroom for a little peace and quiet. After getting into some pajamas, I leaned back in bed, pulled out the yarn and needles from my handbag and started knitting again. I could probably get several rows done while waiting for the game to end. Although I wasn't interested in joining them, I wasn't one for going to sleep before Jack came to bed either.

At 10:30, I was still knitting and had a good portion of the bottom half of the bikini finished. The talking became louder in the living room, then the TV went off and I heard Jack get up from his chair, walk over and open the front door and say goodnight to Kevin. I also heard him say he would see Kevin again tomorrow. I wondered what they had planned, and hoped Jack remembered he was helping in the shop tomorrow morning.

After putting the knitting away in my bag, not wanting him to get a glimpse of it, I got out of bed and strolled into the kitchen. Jack and Tommy were cleaning up the plates and glasses left behind. As I entered, Jack was thanking Tommy for letting Kevin join in.

"No problem. Hey, I'm happy for you. For both of you. I can't imagine growing up and not knowing who my real dad is."

"I know, Tommy," I said, wanting them to realize I was there.

Tommy had his hands in the sink scrubbing a plate, but turned and looked back at me.

"Mom, I didn't know you were still awake."

"It's late, but I couldn't go to sleep without saying goodnight."

"Okay, goodnight," He replied. "It is kind of late, isn't it? You have to go to the shop tomorrow, right?"

"Yeah, I do. And so do you, Jack. Are you coming to bed?" I asked, looking over at him.

"I'll be there in a minute, hon. We need to finish up in here, then I'll make sure everything's locked up. I'm sorry the game ran so long."

"It's okay, I've been knitting."

"That's nice. Whatcha making?"

I smiled at the thought of the bikini and how he was going to react to it—or at least how I hoped he would react.

"Can't tell you, it's a secret." I winked at him and then went back to the bedroom.

The next morning, I was dragging. Even though we were all in bed by eleven the night before, Jack and I had spent some time talking about Kevin, and Tommy, and all sorts of things before going to sleep. It was a good conversation and it was nice he confided in me about all of his feelings. Jack wasn't one to share his feeling often enough and he'd definitely been quiet since Kevin came on the scene.

He's thrilled about having a son, but he's also scared. He doesn't want to get attached to Kevin until he's sure. But, Kevin is visiting for a few days with his grandmother. The funeral took place about a week ago and he's grieving for his mom. Making a connection with who he believes is his dad is important and Jack doesn't want to let him down. Once he travels back to Pennsylvania where he lives, Jack will do a little more research. He's going to talk to Kevin about how important it is to have some tests done to make sure he's really the father.

Max had returned to greet me when I arrived at Simple Pleasures. His tail was wagging furiously and he was moaning and groaning. I reached down to pat the top of his head. "Hey, Max, I missed you, too. Welcome back."

"Hey, kiddo," Jean exclaimed from across the shop. "Get any knitting done last night?"

"I sure did and I brought my unfinished sexy bikini to prove it," I said.

Jean appeared to be in a good mood. I was sure she'd be a little down now that Jacob wasn't around, but she seemed more relaxed than last night. Maybe it was because she'd been knitting also. Knitting is great for the body and mind. When one knits, they have time to contemplate and work out all of their issues and problems. It had helped me and I'm sure it helped Jean as well with her own situations.

"I can tell you've done some knitting yourself. You seem relaxed, Jean—and happy—even though Jacob's gone back home."

"I am, I am. I talked with Bob again and we planned our upcoming trip. Also, I Skyped Jacob this morning. He got home safe and sound and Aunt Helen and Walter also returned home from their retreat. He says they looked well rested and they also seemed a little cozy to each other. He's wondering if a romance is starting to emerge between the two of them."

"How do you feel about that?" I asked as I pulled my partially finished bikini out to show her my progress. "Walter was married to your mother. It hasn't been that long since she passed away, either."

"Wow, you did get a lot done! Me, not as much, but I still did quite a bit. I'm happy with it, too." Jean flashed me a quick smile. "As for Walter and Aunt Helen, I think it's great. They're both old, ANCIENT, so all the more reason not to wait if they both want an intimate relationship, whatever that is at their age. As I mentioned to Jacob, this may mean he can visit more, knowing the two of them can take care of each other whenever he's away. There was a time when we didn't know if Walter was going to remain living with Aunt Helen or if he was hoping to move back in with Jacob. Now it looks like Walter plans to stay there with her."

"That's great, Jean. Everything works out for the best."

"Hah, you remember that, Rosie. Take your own advice and don't worry about Jack and Kevin, okay?"

"Yes, yes, you're right. Okay, then, let's get the cash register set up and let's open the shop. Hopefully, it'll be another busy day at Simple Pleasures."

And it was. Several people came in during the first hour. Then, around ten, Jack showed up, not forgetting he was scheduled to help out for a few hours. He went right to work putting new books on the shelves and dusting all of the furnishings, not only in the book area, but in Jean's knitting area also. He spoke with a few of the customers as they passed by, discussing the new titles he'd recently read. It was nice to see him cheerful again.

"Are you up for a little lunch together today?" I asked him at noon.

"No. Sorry, Rosie. I'm taking Kevin out for lunch. I was thinking of bringing him to the coffee shop where the guys hang out, to introduce him to them all."

Huh? He's already planning on letting everyone know about Kevin? Sure we're both mature about this, and if others found out about Kevin sooner rather than later, that didn't really bother me. Again, I thought about if it were my own son or daughter who had shown up on my doorstep. I'd want to shout it to the whole world, but I'd also want to make sure they were my own flesh and blood first. Jack may be setting himself up for heartbreak if Kevin turns out to not be his son like he claims he is. There's no indication at this point it isn't the truth, but I'm still concerned. There's something in me that keeps saying to be cautious with this.

I wanted to express my concern to him, but Kevin walked into the shop at that very moment. He came over to me, gave me a big hug, and kissed me on the forehead. "Hey, there, Mrs. Blume, it's nice to see you again so soon."

Jean was quietly checking things out from the sidelines. She walked over, extended her hand and introduced herself to him.

"You must be the co-owner of the shop. Nice to meet you." He reached for her hand and shook it.

As soon as they left, Gertrude arrived, so Jean and I let her take charge and went upstairs to have some more salad, made with leftovers from the night before.

Before I even had a chance to pull the lettuce and other ingredients out of the refrigerator to put them on the counter, Jean started up.

"Rosie, we have to do something and quick. That guy, Kevin, I don't trust him. There's something about him that seems familiar. Don't you think so? In fact, he reminds me of that loser Justin, your ex-fiancé, who held us up at the lake."

Justin, as I've mentioned, is also the father of the child I still haven't met, although he doesn't know that yet. After Jack and Kevin were reunited, I began to wonder if I'd done the wrong thing by not telling him earlier. Justin left me before I knew I was pregnant, over 25 years ago. I hadn't seen him again until he appeared as Jean's potential buyer for a lakeside property I listed earlier this year. Believe me, it was quite a surprise to see him. He held us up at the property, took me into the lake house and felt me over, telling me he wanted me to remember how good it was between us way back when, but Jean interrupted and then, with some quick thinking on my part, the police arrived. That was right after both Jean and I made him drop his gun and I pulled it on him. Gosh, it's hard to believe all of that actually happened earlier this year. We were going to have to go to trial over this whole thing, but Justin got into another jam—he was caught trafficking drugs into the country. They've put him away in Federal jail in California and he received a stiff sentence of 15-20 years. Hopefully, they won't grant him an early release.

"Rosie, ROSIE, why aren't you listening to me?" Jean screeched.

The refrigerator was still open and I still had all of the vegetables in my hands. I put them down on the counter closing the door with my hip.

"Oh, sorry, I'm just thinking back to the lake house and about Justin. What were you saying about Kevin again? I thought you told me not to worry about it."

"I was saying he may claim to be Jack's son, but he reminds me of Justin for some reason. In fact, he looks like him. He doesn't even resemble Jack, not one bit. Forget what I said about not worrying earlier. I've changed my mind."

"Now that you mention it, I agree with you. You're right

again, but how can he resemble Justin? That doesn't make any sense."

"Doesn't it?" Jean started tapping her left foot. She put her hands on her hips. "What if this Kevin guy is actually related to Justin? What if Justin put him up to this to get closer to you? Or to do some harm to Jack?"

"Nonsense. You have too much of an imagination. There's no way something that far-fetched could be happening here."

I started to make the salads, but began shaking a bit. What Jean said may have sounded far-fetched, but what if she was right or even partially right? What if Jack's life could be in danger?

The salad looked as delicious as it was last night, but after two small bites, I couldn't eat anymore. My mind was whirling at the thought of what Jean suggested.

"Hey, what if we could find out more about Jack's ex-lover? Like if she really did die and who Kevin's grandmother is? Jack hasn't mentioned any names, but I could find out tonight. We could do a little of our own investigating before you leave on Thursday."

"You got it, Rosie. Gather the information and get it to me as fast as you can. I'll give Scott Walker a call. Maybe he can help out a bit. After all, even if he is back with his wife, it doesn't mean he won't be able to be charmed into doing it. You know how I can be with men."

Scott Walker was the cop who helped us when Justin took us hostage. He also was a high school friend of Jean's. He had a crush on her and they almost slept together, but he went back to his wife and now lives in Dracut, Massachusetts.

"Yeah, I know, Jean. Just be easy on Scott. And don't get carried away. This is a crazy notion, you know. Chances are it's also totally bogus."

"You never know, Rosie. Truth can be stranger than fiction. Don't you forget it."

The way my life had been going this past year, I had to agree with her.

Chapter 16

"How'd your lunch go with Kevin?" I asked Jack as soon as I arrived home that evening. It had been a great afternoon at the shop chatting and knitting with several customers, and we had also sold plenty of knitting supplies and books. Being so busy helped me take my mind off of my conversation at lunch with Jean, but now it was forefront on my mind again. Somehow I had to get the necessary information from Jack and get it all to Jean as soon as I could.

"Lunch went great. The guys all liked Kevin. I wish he was staying for a few more weeks so I could continue to get to know him better, but he mentioned today that he'd be leaving by Thursday. That's only a few days from now, so I asked him to spend the afternoon with me tomorrow. I thought I'd take him for a drive up north to the mountains—show him a little bit of New Hampshire's beauty."

"Oh, okay," I said. What else could I say? I couldn't tell him he couldn't go. I couldn't mention, without warrant, that his life could be in danger.

"Speaking of Kevin," I said. "You never mentioned who his mother was, other than saying she was a former live-in girlfriend."

"What does that matter, Rosie? What difference does it make now? She's no threat to you—she's dead." He came over and wrapped his arms around me. The warmth of his body felt good against mine.

"I love you, only you," he whispered into my ear. It gave me instant goose bumps.

My mind was distracted for a moment and I was hoping this might be the beginning of a little hanky panky, but, no, the cuddling only lasted a few seconds. Jack pulled back and proceeded to walk over to his chair in front of the television set. He picked up the remote.

"The news is on in a minute. Are you going to make us some dinner?" he asked.

I went and stood in the doorway between the kitchen and living room. My arms were crossed and I was a bit bothered, but didn't want to show it. I still needed answers from him.

"Yes, but first I want you to tell me what her name was. You may not think it's important, but it is to me. I want to know." I was almost pleading.

"Oh, all right. Her name was Karen . . . Karen Knight."

"Was she from around here? I mean, did she grow up in this area? Maybe I knew her."

"No, I don't think so. She was from Pennsylvania where Kevin lives now. When she graduated from high school, she moved up here with her mother and went to nursing school. Then, she got a job as a nurse at the hospital. That's when I met her. I was in my early 30's, just out of the Air Force, and had gotten in a car accident. The car was totaled and I had smashed my head on the windshield, so I ended up in the emergency room with a concussion. Anyway, she was working that night."

I could feel a little jealousy coming on, even with her being dead and all, but that was stupid. It all had happened years ago before Jack and I had even met. I wanted to ask him if it was love at first sight, but decided it would be best if I didn't. Better not to know.

"I assume that you met her mother at some point. Where does she live?"

"Mrs. Rodgers? She lives somewhere off of Main Street in Meredith. I can't remember the name of the street. At least, that's where I think she still lives. Why are you asking so many questions?" I could tell he was beginning to get annoyed.

"I'm just curious, Jack. That's all," I replied sweetly. "Besides, Kevin has suddenly walked into your life and I want to know more about where he comes from."

There was one more question I had to get out of Jack to be able to research this all correctly and find out more information, but I also had to give it a little time so as not to seem like I was prying a little further than I needed to. So, instead of continuing to bug him, I left him alone to watch his news while I prepared our dinner. I cooked up some hamburgers on the grill outside, and steamed some fresh butter and sugar corn I purchased at the local farm stand on the way home.

We enjoyed a good home cooked meal for a change. Too bad Tommy was out again—this time working his next to last shift at L'Italiano's—so he couldn't join us.

Jack cleaned up the plates from dinner and started to wash them in the sink. That's the way it works at our house, I usually cook and he usually cleans up.

When he finished with the dishes and had returned to his chair in the living room, I gave him the Jumble puzzle section of the daily newspaper and started in on the crossword puzzle. This is another nightly ritual. We worked on the puzzles in front of the TV set airing another *Law and Order* rerun.

After asking Jack for help with one of the words, I decided to also ask him one last question—the one I needed to gather the information with.

"You said her name is Karen Knight, but her mother's last name is Rodgers. Was Karen married or something?"

"Yep, after we broke up. That's when she moved back to Pennsylvania. I think the guy's still alive, but they got divorced."

"How do you know all of this?"

"Kevin told me. He thought the guy was his father until his mother told him otherwise. I kind of feel sorry for the kid. He's a bit messed up."

"I'll bet he is," I commented. I finished the puzzle, threw it in the garbage and announced I was going downstairs on the computer. I had some serious work to do.

Before emailing Jean with the info, I did a little research on my own. First, I Googled the name Karen Rodgers. Five of them found. I clicked all the links, but they led nowhere. Darn. Then, I Googled Karen Knight. Again, plenty of Karen Knights, but none of them her, not even an obituary listed. Maybe it's too soon for that, but I can't give up now. That's when it hit me. Hmmm, I wonder if... I logged into Facebook and did a search for Karen Knight. There were plenty of them, but I got lucky. One of them was from Pennsylvania and she looked about my age. I clicked on her page and was relieved to see her information wasn't confidential. It could definitely be her. Then, I clicked on "about" and saw she once lived in Meredith. Bingo! I'd found her!

Now I wanted to know more, so I began to read her posts. *That's funny, there's an entry here from only a day ago. Isn't she supposed to be dead?* Next, I clicked on her photos and started looking through them. There were some nice ones of her—she was pretty. Another pang of jealousy hit me, but I quickly pushed it away. No time for that—Jack may be in danger. Besides, stupid.

Back to looking. Some photos showed her with men, many of them recent pictures, but she had an album titled older photos. I clicked there. To my surprise, I saw three old photos in there of her with Jack. Yes, he was in his early 30's then, so they were taken definitely way before Jack and I met. Still, I didn't know if I liked them being posted and accessible to everyone. I clicked out of there and scrolled through the new photos again. No pictures of Kevin. Hmmm, strange. But wait, what is this photo? I enlarged it to view it better. Could it be? I couldn't believe it! It was Karen in a sequined gold evening gown looking quite elegant. Standing right beside her was a man. Not any man. That man was .. . Justin! I was sure of it!

Forget the email now. Instead, I needed to call Jean right away. Her notions about Kevin could be right. I didn't know if he was Justin's son, but he sure looked like him. And the photo was proof Karen knew Justin. I couldn't believe it. Here was Justin, in a jail thousands of miles away, and he's still haunting me and now may even be going after Jack. Why's this happening? How am I going to explain this all to my husband? One thing I do know is sooner, rather than later, Mrs. Rodgers of Meredith will have to be paid a little visit.

Chapter 17

"**J**ean, you're not going to believe this," I whispered into my cell phone. "Jack's old flame's name is Karen Knight, formerly Karen Rodgers. I found her on Facebook and she posted on her wall yesterday, so I don't think she's deceased. Plus, and this is a big PLUS, there are photos. I saw some of Jack and . . ." I paused before I went on.

"Stop doing that to me, stop stalling right before you tell me the most important part," Jean huffed.

"I just wanted to make sure you were listening and I knew I'd get that reaction from you if you were," I continued whispering. "I still can't believe it. There's a photo of Karen with Justin on there. It looks pretty recent."

"This is awful, Rosie. I knew it when I saw that kid, Kevin. I think he's Justin's son and why he's saying Jack is his father now, I don't know for sure, but I've got a suspicion somehow Justin put him up to this and maybe so did that woman Karen."

Jean was worked up. I could tell because she was rambling.

"Maybe Karen's trying to get close to Jack again and I'm thinking maybe Justin's trying to get close to you in the only way he's able to. This is awful, Rosie, we're going to have to do something. I'm going to call Scott right away."

"No, hold off a bit. I'm thinking Karen's mother needs a visit tomorrow. Maybe I can slip out for an hour or two in the afternoon if it's all right. Her name is Mrs. Rodgers and she lives in Meredith."

"If you think I'm letting you go there by yourself, you're crazy, kiddo. No, I'll find coverage for part of the afternoon and we'll both go. In the meantime, try to find a way to deter Jack from hanging out with Kevin tomorrow."

"I don't know how to do that. He's planning on taking him up to the mountains in the afternoon to show him the sights. How am I going to keep him from going?" I started thinking things through in my head. There must be a way.

"I know," I continued. "I'll get Tommy to say he needs Jack for the afternoon—to help him pack or something. I don't want to upset Tommy, but I'll have to confide in him so he can help us. I'll just tell Jack to delay his trip by a day. Kevin isn't planning on going back to Pennsylvania until Thursday so that ought to work. Then, maybe by tomorrow evening, we'll have more info and can finally let Jack in on what's going on. He's going to be upset, but at least he'll be safe."

"Thatta girl, Rosie. You're good—you're real good. We should open a detective agency on the side," Jean chuckled. "Just kidding, of course. I'll see you in the morning."

Tommy called later to say he was staying at his best friend Sean's house. They were throwing a little going away party for him and then he was going with Sean's parents to bring Sean to the airport tomorrow. I couldn't tell him he couldn't go because I needed him. Change of plans. My original idea to get Tommy to engage Jack for the afternoon wasn't going to work. It was too late to call Jean on it, but we'd have to think of another way.

The next morning, before heading into work, I invited Jack to bring Kevin into the shop around noon. We'd eat lunch together at a diner next door before they were supposed to take their sightseeing tour. Luckily, Jack agreed to that. I could see him beaming—he was thinking I was starting to want to spend some time with Kevin myself. Little did he know I only wanted to gather more information to incriminate Kevin. I also wanted to come up with a way to postpone Jack's afternoon plans with him.

When I entered the shop, Max was there as usual, tail wagging. I pulled a dog biscuit out of my coat pocket.

"Here you go, Max. Here's a little surprise for you." I reached down to give it to him.

Jean came walking downstairs. "Where'd you get the treats? You're going to win his heart over. He'll adopt you as his second mother."

"That's fine by me. I got it when I went through the drive-thru window at the bank this morning. I had to cash a check for Tommy. They give them out to customers' dogs. Since I knew I'd be seeing Max this morning, I asked if they could give me one to bring to him."

Max had devoured the biscuit and was licking his mouth looking up at me.

"That's it, Max. Only one. Maybe I'll get you another one later." I briefly scratched his ears and he closed his eyes. He enjoyed it as much as the biscuit.

As we were preparing to open, I mentioned to Jean we'd have to come up with a different plan to keep Jack from spending the afternoon with Kevin. I did say I had invited them to join me for lunch first—that they'd be coming in around noon and we'd go across the street to the diner.

"I don't like the idea of you spending any more time with that creep," Jean said. "You may be concerned about Jack's safety, but I'm concerned about yours."

"I know. That's why I won't go any farther than next door with them. Everyone knows us over there. Kevin wouldn't dare try anything. Besides, he's still playing the act."

"Okay, okay," Jean replied. "There's another kink, though. I couldn't get full coverage for this afternoon. Gertrude has a doctor's appointment today—she can't come in. None of her senior citizen friends are able to either. So, I figure I'll find a way to visit Mrs. Rodgers myself. I'll have to announce I have to leave unexpectedly and that means you're going to be left in the shop alone for the rest of the afternoon. I'll tell Jack he needs to stay with you for safety purposes.

"I was planning to go myself, but okay. Hey, what if Mary offers to stay? She's coming in this morning and she'll still

be here at noon when he shows up. Also, you shouldn't be
going there alone."

"Don't worry. I'll do it when you get back from lunch.
Mary should be gone by then, and even if she isn't, and
she offers to stay, I'll take Jack aside and tell him I'm not
comfortable with that arrangement. Don't worry—I'll find
a way. Hey, Bob's around, so I'll have him come with me if
you're worried."

"What a good idea. I hope it works. You'd better call Bob
and explain before we get busy."

There were a few women standing outside waiting to
come in at the start of business. I went over to the door and
unlocked it.

"Hi there, welcome to Simple Pleasures," I said cheerfully.

Jean was already upstairs making the important phone
call. She came back fifteen minutes later and winked at me.
"All set," she said as she passed by me and went over to one
of the ladies.

"Is there anything I can help you with today? Don't you
just love the feel of that yarn? It's alpaca, comes from a local
farm, and is heaven to knit with."

"Is that so," the unknown woman exclaimed. "Why, how
many skeins do you think it would take to knit a nice scarf
for my daughter?"

I grinned. Jean was so good at enticing people to buy yarn
and other items. I'd have to take some tips from her. I love to
read and have read several books now on the display tables,
but to just walk up to someone and start a conversation
wasn't going to be easy for me. There was a young gentle-
men browsing at a table of books. Okay, there's no time like
the present. I slowly walked over to him and started talking. It worked—he bought the book because I suggested it
would be a great gift for one of his female friends.

Mary came in around ten and went right to the social
area. She grabbed the bagel with cream cheese I had placed
on the counter for her, along with a bottle of water. On the

days she comes here, I want to make sure she has something to eat. It's part of our deal in exchange for her helping us. I wasn't sure she was eating much anyway. So, since Jacob's no longer with us providing us with sustenance in the morning hours, I brought the bagel from home. I was hoping she liked cream cheese, some people don't, but I took a chance and I could tell she liked it. She gobbled it up in no time.

"Hey," she said. She didn't seem to be one for many words.

"Hey, yourself. I hope you had a good weekend."

"It was okay, but I'm ready to work again. Whattaya want me to do first?" she asked.

"Why don't you clean up the counter area? It could use a good cleaning and arranging. Also, maybe make the social area more inviting. Feel free to arrange the cushions, as well as the knitting magazines and books on the table."

"Okay, I'll have that done in no time and then I'll tidy up the shelves."

I looked around. Everything seemed pretty much in order. With Jack also helping during the week, there wasn't much cleaning and shelving left to do. Still, I felt it was important to keep Mary coming in. Besides, I liked seeing her.

"Do you think you'd mind changing Bluey's water?" I added hesitantly. Having never done it before, it was something I wasn't looking forward to.

"No problem," she replied. "I'll get to it right away."

Chapter 18

When Jack walked in around noontime and Kevin arrived soon after, I tried not to look apprehensive about our lunch together. I really wasn't looking forward to spending an hour with that guy posing to be Jack's son, especially since I knew his mother, or so-called mother, was still alive and knew Justin.

I noticed Mary shot a glance at Kevin as she was putting her coat on and getting ready to leave. I wondered if she wanted to join us for lunch. It wouldn't matter if she came back to the shop afterwards and was here when Jean made her getaway. Jean had already told me she had it all covered to make sure Jack would stay on with me.

"Hey, Mary, how'd you like to come with us to the diner for lunch? My treat."

"No, thank you. I have someplace to go." She left quickly, giving Kevin another look as she passed by him.

When we returned from lunch, I had no idea how Jean was going to pull off getting Jack to change his plans and stay with me, but earlier she had assured me not to worry. No matter what happened, she would take care of it. Bob was in on it, too, and would go with her to visit Mrs. Rodgers.

There were no customers in the shop at this time—a simple blessing. Jack had just announced he and Kevin were heading out on their afternoon excursion when Jean yelled out,

"I CAN'T BREATH. I CAN'T BREATH. HURRY, GET ME A BAG."

She started reeling around in the middle of her yarn section like she was dizzy or something. She looked in distress. Her breathing became loud and labored. For a moment, I wondered if this was her plan or if this was the real deal.

Jack rushed over to grab a hold of her. Kevin just stood there doing nothing. I wasn't surprised. Max scurried over also, whining, tail between his legs. He was concerned. I raced to the check-out area, grabbed a medium plastic bag from behind the counter and brought it to Jean.

At that moment, Bob walked into the shop.

"Hey, what's going on?" he said. Max took a few steps toward him, whined some more, then turned back to Jean not wanting to get far from her. Bob came right over and grabbed the other side of her, the side Jack wasn't already holding onto.

"Jean, are you okay?" he asked.

She clutched the bag in her hands now and brought it up to her mouth. Bob and Jack moved her gently to a nearby chair. Then, she started breathing slowly into the bag.

Jean's doing a great job of pretending, I thought. Her face was ashen, the color all drained from it. Her eyes were watery. No one would believe this was just an act.

After several slow breaths, Jean took the bag away and dropped it on the floor. She looked up at Bob.

"I need to go to the hospital. This is not like the other attacks. I can't feel my arms and legs."

"It's only a panic attack," I said. "You need to stay here with me. You'll feel better in a minute." I tried to sound reassuring, but I knew this was part of the skit I was joining in on.

That's when Bob said to Jack, "I think Jean's right. She's been having these too often and this is the worst one I've witnessed. I want her to get checked out."

"But Rosie is going to be alone for the afternoon. She needs someone with her in case it gets busy," Jean said.

Then, she started to breathe heavy again. "OH NO," she said loudly. "It's happening again."

"THAT'S IT! You're going to the hospital. Pronto. Jack, I'm sorry, but you'll have to stay with Rosie until we get back."

Bob lifted Jean up and quickly led her to the door. Max followed.

"Oh, all right, Max, you came come, but you're going to have to wait in the car. Bob reached into his pocket, pulled out a dog leash and bent down and attached it to Max's collar. He turned back and looked at me seeming concerned. "We'll give you a call as soon as we know something." Then they were out the door.

Jack looked over at me, "I can't have you stay here alone." He looked at Kevin. "I'm sorry, as you can see, we can't go today. Can we reschedule for tomorrow?"

Kevin didn't look happy about this but replied, "Sure, same time?"

"No, we'll head out in the morning and get an early start. I'll talk to you tonight."

I was thinking to myself that Jack had forgotten about helping out here tomorrow. No matter, if all went as planned, there would be no trip tomorrow with Kevin because by then, all of us, including Jack, would know the truth.

Kevin left and Jack commented, "Now what do we do?"

"We run the shop together." I gave him a quick hug. "I'll take the yarn area and you cover the book section."

At that moment, a couple of customers came through the door.

About an hour later, the shop phone rang. I hurried to answer it.

"Hello, Simple Pleasures," I announced.

"Hey, Rosie, it's me, Jean. Is Jack nearby?"

I scanned the shop to see what he was up to. He was talking to a customer about a book. Great, he's occupied. Still, I tried to sound concerned.

"Are you all right? What's happening?"

"We're fine. We're on our way back from Mrs. Rodgers house. It wasn't hard to find. Bob had already done some checking before we went. He found out exactly where she lived."

"And?" I replied. I wanted to say more, but didn't, in case Jack could hear me.

"And she was home. At first, she seemed reluctant to talk to us, but Bob did a good job of convincing her. And you want to know what? She doesn't know a kid named Kevin. Her daughter does live in Pennsylvania, but she doesn't have any children."

That's strange, I thought. Who the heck is Kevin then? Why is he claiming to be Jack's son?

"What are you going to do next? When are you coming back?" I replied.

By this time, I could see Jack had become aware of who I was talking to on the phone. I had to add in a little extra something so she'd know also.

"Well, hurry back as soon as you can. I'm glad to see you are all right and it was only a panic attack. Caused by stress, the doctor said?"

"Okay, I get the message, Rosie. We'll talk more when I get there, which should be soon. Just so you know, I've called Scott and he's looking into this Kevin kid. It's a bit difficult since he doesn't know if this is his real name or not. But, he's also trying to get some info on Karen and how she may be connected to Justin. Maybe we'll know more by the end of the day."

Chapter 19

Bob, Jean and Max, now happy and wagging his tail, were back. Jack seemed relieved as Jean apologized for ruining his plans for the afternoon.

"That's all right," he grumbled. "I'm glad I stayed around so Rosie wasn't alone here. It got kind of busy for a while."

It didn't take long for Jack to leave, though. He put on his coat and gave me a quick kiss.

"I'll see you in a few hours," he called out as he left.

"Phew," I exclaimed as soon as I was sure he wasn't coming back. "So far, so good. Now what did you find out?" I was eager to hear all about their conversation with Mrs. Rodgers.

Bob was the first to start talking. "She's a nice old lady. Her name is Maria. She seemed startled when we came to the door, being strangers and all, but once I explained what our concerns were, she was more than willing to help out."

"Yeah," Jean added. "We asked her about Kevin and if he's her grandson. She'd never seen or heard of him before. Then we asked about Karen, her daughter. She's in Pennsylvania, but travels to Boston once a month on business. Sometimes, she'll come up and visit with her mother when she does. We showed her a picture of Justin, but she's never seen him before either."

"Okay, now we know Kevin isn't her grandson and Karen isn't dead. Is that enough? Too bad we couldn't find out exactly who Kevin really is or even get the connection between Justin and Karen." I sighed. There were still so many more things to find out about this and it had already been a long day.

"Well, that's why, even though you told me to wait, I did put in a call to Scott. He's more than willing to help. It's almost three now. Maybe we'll hear from him soon.

"Almost three?" I said. "Well, I guess it's time for tea. Besides, I've been on my feet for the past few hours. Jack's a lot of help, but, well, he's still Jack. He's not one for showing older women where the best yarns are. I kept him in the book section and, even then, he got tired of talking after a while. I'll get the water boiling."

As I was walking over to fill the electric kettle, Mary walked into the shop. She looked very concerned about something. I wondered why she had come back today after being here all morning.

"Jean. Rosie," she called out frantically as she walked over to meet us. Then, she looked over at Bob.

"Who are you?" she said in a suspicious tone. She shot us a glance like she was wondering if she could trust him.

"This is Bob," Jean replied. "My husband. We're separated, but ah, we still see each other. Long story."

Then I added, "What's the matter? You look bothered by something."

"I am. I've been waiting around outside until your husband left, Rosie. I have to tell you something. I think it's important."

"Go ahead," I said. "It's okay to talk in front of Bob and Jean. That is, if it's okay with you. What's this about?"

"It's about THAT GUY, that guy with your husband earlier! His name isn't Kevin by the way, it's David. And, and, he's not to be trusted."

"How do you know this? How do you know him?" Jack probed.

"Well, ah, Rosie, do you mind if we talk alone? You can tell them later, but it's kind of personal. I'd rather tell you first." She shifted a bit, seeming uncomfortable.

I shooed both Jean and Bob away. "Jean, the water is ready. Go and make the tea. There's a customer already looking like she would like a cup. I'd join you, but right now

I need to talk to Mary. Would you mind if the two of us went upstairs to your apartment for a few minutes?"

"Okay, okay, go." Jean seemed annoyed she couldn't listen in. "But you'd better tell me what this has to do with that Kevin, or should I say this David guy as soon as you can. I'll have to let Scott know. Maybe the information will help him out."

Mary and I walked up the stairs. When we entered the apartment, I motioned for her to go into the kitchen area straight ahead. She glanced around at the surroundings.

"Nice place here," she commented. Great hardwood floors, like in the shop."

We both sat at Jean's 1950's style kitchen table. Gray porcelain top, chrome edging. Mary moved her hand across the top of it. "Cool," she said.

I could tell she was stalling. I looked across at her and she could see my demeanor was serious. I didn't want to talk home décor right now. I wanted to find out what was so important to her, so I figured I would give her a little history to get her started.

"Mary, this guy you call David. Well, he unexpectedly showed up on our doorstep last Saturday claiming to be my husband's son from a former girlfriend—someone Jack knew before he met me. Since then, Jack has gotten kind of close to him and they've been spending a lot of time together."

"That's not good," Mary piped in. She shook her head back and forth. "He's not to be trusted."

"I know, you've said that already, and it's getting me concerned. I'm worried about Jack and I don't trust this David guy either. I've had bad feelings since he arrived, but nothing to base them on. He said his mother just passed away and he's staying with his grandmother. There seemed no reason for me not to believe him."

I paused for a moment and took a deep breath before I went on.

"Jean got some bad vibes also when she met him, so we started doing some research in case our instincts were right. That's when I found Karen, Jack's old girlfriend, on

Facebook and she posted something the other day, so Kevin, or rather David has told at least one lie—she isn't dead. Then Jean and Bob went to visit with the supposed grandmother this afternoon to ask some questions. But she has no idea who this guy is. Karen is not his mother because she's never had any children. The grandmother confirmed Karen's also alive and well in Pennsylvania."

"Wow," Mary's eyes grew wide. "You've found out a lot, but there's still a very important part. That's what I have to tell you."

Okay, now she was ready to talk. I leaned back in my chair ready to listen. "Go ahead. How can you help with this?" I wasn't sure yet if she could, but I wanted to hear what she had to say.

"I've met David before, when I was a patient in a mental hospital being treated for depression."

This wasn't what I expected to hear.

"Oh, I'm sorry, Mary. I didn't know." Although I sympathized with her, it was good to have her finally open up to me. Still, what did this have to do with the guy, whatever his name, claiming to be Jack's son?

"Of course not. I want to put it all behind me now, but that's not the point."

"And the point is?"

"About David. We were in the same ward at McLean Hospital. He was there for another reason—I don't know what the clinical term was for it. All I know is there were times when he would claim to be the devil and it was scary. I mean he really believed he was evil and it would give me the creeps. Then, he'd all of a sudden turn all sweet and kind. He'd go back and forth like that. One moment he acted one way, the next moment the exact opposite. Like I said, creepy!"

"So, you're telling me he's got a mental disease of some kind. And is he dangerous?"

"I would think so—when he's the devil, at least."

"All right. This is important. Thank you, Mary, for coming to me. I know it wasn't easy to talk about, but it might help Jean's friend who's trying to do some background checks right now."

We sat there quietly for a few minutes. Mary continued to glance around at the apartment. She was impressed by Jean's decorating skills.

I was trying to think of how there could be more Mary knew that might also be of help. I tapped my fingers on the table. Thinking. Thinking. Then it hit me. Of course!

"Mary, what did you say the name of the hospital was again?" She could tell I had suddenly become excited.

"McLean. It's a well-known psychiatric hospital. A big place in Belmont, Massachusetts. Why?"

"And when were you and David there?"

"Oh, let me see. A few months ago. Maybe late May, early June even."

Bingo. The timing's right.

"Hold on a minute. I have something I want you to look at. I'll be right back."

I ran down the stairs to the shop and went for my pocketbook. After I grabbed it and headed for the apartment again, I passed by Bob reading by the staircase far away from the several ladies now drinking tea and chatting away with Jean. I leaned down and whispered to him, "Hang around for a few minutes. I think what Mary is telling me will solve another part of this puzzle. A big part."

He arched his eyebrows up. "Oh? Can't wait to hear it."

When I returned to the kitchen table, I fumbled in my purse. There it was. I pulled out a photo I had found late last night. I was surprised I still had it.

"Look at this picture. Tell me if you recognize this person." I held it in front of her. My hand was shaking.

She was silent for a few minutes as she studied the face. Then, after what seemed like an eternity, she finally spoke.

"Ah, yeah, he's a lot older now, but I know him. Hey, that's weird. He was in the same ward as David and me. In fact, he and David became kind of friends. David idolized him, thought of him as some kind of god or something."

"Anything specific you can remember?"

"He was only there for a few days and he wasn't really mental or anything. I think he was just saying that to keep from going to jail. He was given court orders to be checked out by a psychiatrist. From what I recall, he had been involved in some sort of hold up. Pulled a gun on a few ladies somewhere in New Hampshire." Mary sighed. "That's all I can recall."

"He was involved in a holdup, all right. And Jean and I and another woman were the victims. It happened at an inspection of a property we were selling. Or that's what it was supposed to be anyway. That was earlier this year when we both were selling real estate. He pulled a gun on us."

"Really?" Mary seemed surprised.

"Yes, really. And there's more. The guy's name is Justin and he was formerly engaged to me. Long, long ago."

"WOW, I can't believe it. Yeah, that's his name. I remember now. It really is strange, isn't it? How we're all connected somehow."

It sure is, I thought. God's plans never cease to amaze me.

"Mary, you have no idea how you helped me. I have to go and tell Bob and Jean so they can share this with a cop who is helping us. Thanks to you, I think we can wrap all of this up tonight and get that David guy locked up."

"Good, that's all I was concerned about. I didn't want you or your family getting hurt. Now, ah, you think Jean has something good to eat around here?" She glanced toward the refrigerator. "I'm starving."

I looked at her and couldn't help but reach out and give her a big hug. "No problem. Fantastic dinner for you coming up—you deserve it!" She seemed a little set back by the sudden contact. Maybe she wasn't used to it, but I didn't care and I couldn't help it—it was spontaneous. Besides, everyone needs a hug every once in a while.

Taking a fast break to run back down and give Bob the synopsis on what Mary told me, I ran back up again, this time a bit slower from going up and down the stairs so much, and searched through Jean's refrigerator. There was

113

some lettuce, a tomato, feta cheese and an apple—leftovers still from our salad making the other night. I also spotted a carry out container from what looked like L'Italiano's. Peeking into it, I saw some spaghetti with one big meatball. I smelled it. It was still fresh. That must have been from the other night also when Jean went out with Jacob.

I made a salad, even finding a few glazed walnuts on the counter, and heated up the leftovers in the microwave. Mary was as famished as she usually is. It had me wondering when, and if, this girl even ate at all when she wasn't here. And I was happy I could repay her, in some small way, for all of her help.

Chapter 20

It was a few minutes after five and we had just closed up after the last customer had paid for her purchases and departed. Jean was counting the cash drawer. Bob and Mary were in some comfortable chairs reading books. Max was curled up at Mary's feet taking a nap. Scott hadn't called in yet, but he had been excited by the new information Mary had provided and he assured us he would have enough on David tonight to contact the local police station and take the kid into custody by tomorrow.

Then someone started rapping at the front door. A customer who wanted to come in, upset we were already closed? I looked up from the register to find out.

"Jack?" I said.

"What's he doing here?" Jean said.

"I haven't a clue, but he looks kind of upset. Maybe something's wrong."

I sprinted to the door, opened it quickly and looked up at him. "What's wrong? Has something happened? Is Tommy all right?"

"Tommy's fine." He passed by me like it wasn't me he came to see, and headed directly over to Jean who was still counting the money.

Max woke up, stretched, and still in a stupor, slowly walked over to where Jean and Jack were. Bob and Mary joined him.

Looking straight at Jean, Jack said, "Do you think I'm stupid or something?"

"What? What're you talking about?" Jean replied.

"Maria Rodgers, that's what, er who, I'm talking about. I went to see her after I left here to find out more about Kevin." He turned and looked back at me.

115

"Rosie, what do you think? That I don't have any idea what's going on around here? Hey, I was concerned also. What Kevin was telling me wasn't adding up. I had to check it out for myself." He let out a big breath and crossed his arms.

I shifted a bit. I should've talked to him from the get-go but I didn't think he'd take it well.

"Well, you really were hoping he was your son. And we were concerned. Please forgive us. I should've come to you first. I'm sorry, Jack." I gave him a weak smile.

He seemed to calm down a bit. "Yeah, yeah, I'm sorry too. I just got so heated up when I found out what Jean and Bob had done. That means they faked the whole scene this afternoon to get me to stay with you. I wish you would've told me earlier."

"So, now you know Kevin is not connected with your former girlfriend," Bob said.

"And he's not your son," added Jean.

Jack turned around towards them again.

That's when Mary piped in, "And Kevin is David and he's crazy. And he is friends with Rosie's old boyfriend, Justin."

"WHAT?" Jack shouted. He started getting agitated again. However, I knew how he could be. It didn't take much to set him off and likewise, once he got things off of his chest, it wouldn't take long for him to calm down again.

"Uh-oh, maybe I should've kept my mouth shut," replied Mary. She gave me the guilty eye look.

"No, no it's okay. It's time we get this all out into the open and then figure out how Karen and Justin are connected. We still haven't put that piece of the puzzle together," I said. "Maybe Scott will have more answers. He should be calling anytime now."

Jack had just opened his mouth again, but right at that moment, Jean's cell phone began to ring. She looked at the display to see who it was.

"That's him now," she said excitedly, pushing the button and putting the phone up to her ear. "Hey, what did you find out? Any news? Uh-huh, Uh-huh. Really? You're kidding me. Are you sure? Well, maybe he'll say something. When? Yeah, he's right here now. Tonight? Okay. Bye." She flipped the phone closed and looked up at us.

We all stared at Jean, waiting for her to tell us what Scott said. She stood there speechless, shaking her head.

"WELL?" I finally asked.

"You're not going to believe this. Scott's been able to find out more about this David guy, thanks to Mary's information. It seems he likes to pull these types of pranks—long, lost child thing. He gets in good with someone, becomes part of the family, and then rips them off. He's been caught a few times already, but because of his psychological issues Mary has already mentioned, he usually ends up in a mental hospital instead of a jail. He takes his meds, seems to get better, the doctor releases him, and he's back on the streets again pulling the same schemes. He probably makes a living from this stuff and hurts a lot of people along the way."

"But what about Justin and Karen?" Bob asked. "How are they connected?"

"He doesn't know yet. He's headed over here right now to talk to Jack. I told him we'd wait for him. He's already on his way from Dracut, so he should be here within the next hour."

"Oh great!" moaned Jack. "I really wasn't planning on this. There's a Red Sox game starting soon and I didn't want to miss it. Tommy and I were going to watch it at the house. He's expecting us both back for dinner."

"Red Sox?" asked Bob. "Hey, that's right! They're playing the Yankees again. It should be a great game. How about we get some beer, go upstairs to Jean's apartment and watch it while we're waiting. Jean and Rosie can cook up a good dinner for all of us and we can call Tommy to come join us. What do you think?"

Mary's eyes lit up. I think the mention of food perked her interest. Could she be hungry again? Honestly, this girl ate a salad, a big bowl of spaghetti, and very large meatball only a couple of hours ago.

"I like the Red Sox," she said. "Can I stay for a while?"

"Of course you can," Bob said. He put his arm around her and patted her on the back. "Let's go turn on the set and get comfortable. Then, I'll run out quickly to the store to get the beer."

"Hold on a minute," Jean announced. "Sure, you can all watch the game, but if you think Rosie and I are cooking . . . after the day all of us have had . . . and it's not even over yet . . . then you're CRAZY! Rosie, call Tommy and invite him over. I'll put in a call for take-out and will also pick up the beer. Bob, it's your idea, so it's also your treat. Hand over some money to pay for this."

"What're we having for dinner?" Bob asked.

At the same time, Jack and I shouted out "NO PIZZA!"

"Okay, okay, I'll get Mexican—tacos, burritos, nachos. How does that sound?"

"Yumm, GREAT!" Mary was the first to respond.

"Sounds good to me," said Bob.

Jack grimaced. I knew he didn't like spicy foods, and he didn't like to try anything new.

"Don't worry, Jack. We can get you something else," I said.

"Hey, I have some leftovers from L'Italiano's in the refrigerator. Just enough for one. Do you like spaghetti and meatballs?" Jean added.

"Sorry," Mary said from the sidelines. "I already ate that earlier. It was good." She gave Jean a sheepish grin.

I looked at her and cracked a smile. "That's okay. Spaghetti and meatballs it is, Jack. I'll have Tommy order it from the restaurant and pick it up on his way. He can also get the Mexican food for us. Someone will just have to get the beer since he's not of age yet."

"Sounds great. I'll also call in our food order now and charge it," Jean said. "Credit card, please?" She reached out her hand to Bob.

Two hours later, Scott had arrived, ate his share of the Mexican food, and was guzzling down his second beer. He was also sitting in front of the TV set with Bob, Jack, Tommy and Mary and was cursing in unison with them. The game must not be going so well.

Jean had had just about enough of it. Nothing yet had been mentioned as to how and when David was going to be taken in and what Scott needed to talk to Jack about. I have to admit it was annoying to me also that it wasn't the most important thing on these guys' minds right now.

Bob let out a big belch. That did it. Jean stomped over to the television set, stood right in front of it and shut it off. She turned to look at Scott.

"That's it! No more game until you talk, and if you want to see it sooner rather than later, then talk fast, but you came here to share some information and to speak with Jack. We all want to know what's going on. So to hell with the game—business comes first!"

"Okay, okay." Scott held up both of his hands over his head. "I surrender."

"Good, now speak." She crossed her arms and tapped her foot showing her patience was limited.

Scott looked over at Jack. "I'm sorry about what's happened to you the past few days. Jean, Rosie and Bob were all concerned, so Jean contacted me to help in some way. Mary provided Rosie with a great deal of information. She gave us great leads."

Mary was sitting next to Scott. Scott patted her on the shoulder and smiled at her. I think she was already ogling over him—he's definitely a looker even though he's probably twice her age. His comment and attention to her made her blush.

Scott turned back to Jack. "One thing we haven't figured out yet is how Karen is connected. I'm not sure if she has a part in this or if she is also just a victim somehow. As for Justin, we already know he met David at McLean Hospital a few months ago, but there's no evidence he even has any part in this either. Still, Justin is one of Karen's friends on Facebook. There's also a picture of the two of them together. We need to check out how they came to know each other and how David found out about Karen being an old girlfriend of yours."

"Okay," Jack replied. "What are you asking of me? Do you want me to contact Karen? After all of these years?" He shook his head and then added, "I don't know. I mean, is this fair to Rosie?"

It was nice of him to think about my feelings in all of this. "Don't worry about me," I said trying to reassure him I didn't mind. I could feel a pang of jealousy starting up again, but I knew Scott needed to find out if either Karen or Justin were involved in David's scheme. It was important. Not just for Jack's safety, but also for my own and even Tommy's. If Justin was trying to get at my family, I needed to know. "Just do what Scott tells you. It'll be all right."

Jack looked at me and frowned. "Okay, I guess I've got to. When do I call? What do I say?"

"Let's go in the other room. I have her number. You can call right now. The sooner, the better. Ask her if she knows David and also ask her how she knows Justin. You can explain why. I'll be right beside you listening."

"No, I'll do it, but let me talk to her on my own," Jack replied. He took the phone and the number Scott gave him and headed toward the stairway. He would call from downstairs in the shop.

As he was leaving, he turned back to Jean. "Is it all right if they watch the game while I'm doing this?"

Chapter 21

The next morning, after just waking up, with eyes still closed, I recollected the events of the night before. Jack did call Karen and they talked for quite a while. I didn't drill him for all the details, but he did find out Karen had no connection to David. And she had no idea about his scheme. Yes, she knew Justin, but claimed it to be a brief encounter. She met him while on a trip to Chicago when he was there on business. They socialized while enjoying a few drinks together and did whatever else she didn't choose to mention to Jack. I immediately remembered Justin's challenge with Lars, Luanne's former husband. They were business partners and while away on business trips, would tally how many women they could get into the sack in one weekend. The one who slept with the most women won. How disgusting. Anyway, whether Karen slept with him or not, she did keep in contact with Justin afterwards through Facebook. But, according to Jack, she hasn't heard from him for several months and didn't realize he was in jail.

Justin must have viewed photos of Jack and Karen on her Facebook page and he recognized Jack as my husband. Somehow, he must have also shared this with David and I was thinking he put the kid up to this scheme of claiming to be Jack's son. We weren't sure about that at this point. Jack called David last night and asked to see him about something. He met him at the diner, and the police followed undercover. They arrested David and put him in jail. Questioning would take place this morning. Hopefully, we would find out more later.

I glanced up at the clock. 7 a.m. In the meantime, I had to get up, get showered and get into work. The shop would be opening up as usual at nine and this was going to be a busy day. Also, it was Jean's last day before heading off to California with Bob to visit their two sons for a week.

Jack still was sound asleep, so I nudged him awake. "Jack? It's 7 a.m. Time to wake up."

Usually, I would let him sleep longer, but he still wanted to take a drive up north through the mountains. I was thrilled when he asked Tommy to join him.

Turning towards me, Jack was sleepy-eyed, but he had this wide grin on his face. This seemed strange because he wasn't one to wake up in a pleasant manner. Usually, before even getting out of bed, he would list all of the negative things floating around in his mind. He's the kind of guy who sees the glass half-empty first, just like Jean tends to do, whereas I'm the one who views everything at least half-full. Together, we made the perfectly balanced couple.

My eyes widened. "What, may I ask, is on your mind this morning?" I was kind of hoping he might finally want to fool around—a little quickie before facing the day. But I soon found out that wasn't what was making him smile; I should've known. Still, what he shared next with me was a big surprise and just as nice.

"Guess what?" he teased. The smile remained as big as ever.

I sighed. "I can't even imagine. What is going round in that mind of yours to make you so cheery this early in the morning? Especially after all we went through last night." I kind of expected him to be depressed now that we knew the true identity of David. This wasn't like him.

Jack grimaced. "Don't remind me," he replied. "I don't want it to ruin this day."

"Oh, Jack, I'm so glad you're taking Tommy with you for the ride. I wish I could join the both of you, but, you know, I have to work."

His smile broadened again at my comment. "That's a secret I know. Rosie, you don't have to work today. Not at all. Jean told me last night before we left. She said Bob and Mary offered to help out for the day. Bob started his vacation on Monday so he's free and Mary, well, she's just thrilled to have something to do. Also, Gertrude will be there this afternoon. Jean wanted you, Tommy and me to have this day together before he leaves for college."

"But Jean's leaving tomorrow. I want to see her before she goes." I couldn't believe she set this up with Jack without my knowing.

"So, you'd rather work?"

"NO, I'm thrilled to have the day with two of my favorite men. That's so nice of Jean. Let me call and thank her."

"Go right ahead, my dear. I'll wake Tommy and get the coffee ready. But remember, I want us to be on the road by eight-thirty, so make it quick.

Jean answered the phone on the third ring, but didn't say a word.

"Hey, it's me." I said. No response. "Jean?"

"Huh?" she replied. What's the matter with that girl? It suddenly occurred to me she was half-asleep.

"It's after seven already. You usually take a run, and you have to open the shop by nine. How come you're not awake yet?"

"Who's that?" I heard in the background. It was a man's voice. No just any man's either, it was Bob's voice. Now I really understood. Jean and Bob had spent the night together.

"Oh, I get it," I said. "You're tired because you didn't get much sleep and spent the night in the sack with Bob. Honestly, I thought you were going to wait until you went to California."

Now Jean was awake and ready to talk. She chuckled. "We thought we'd have a trial run. Besides, we're still married, remember? We can do it anytime we want to without committing any sin or anything."

"First of all, I couldn't care less what you do in your bedroom, but I am concerned about your well-being. Was it worth it? Do you think Bob now has those feelings for you that were missing for all of those years?"

"I don't know yet, Rosie, but I hope so. The week away

to California will hopefully give me a clue. We'll see if we can stand each other after that. But in the meantime," Jean chuckled again, "yeah, it was worth it. In fact, everything was great." I could hear her pull her ear away from the receiver. "Wasn't it, Bob?"

"You bet, baby, Mmmm, Mmmm"

"Hear that?" Jean asked me after getting back on the phone.

"Yeah, I did and it scares me. Do as you wish, but I hope he doesn't break your heart all over again!"

Chapter 22

According to Jack, we left the house right on time. Why we needed to leave so early, I don't know—we had all day—but Jack is always rushing, even when it's unnecessary. Tommy appeared still half-asleep, disheveled and dragging his feet. He'd agreed to go, probably to please Jack, and not because he was a big fan of riding in a car for long stretches. Jack liked taking long car rides, and Tommy knew it all too well.

When both Jonathan and Tommy were younger, we would all pile in the car at the crack of dawn every Sunday morning. Jack would be behind the wheel and would have no idea where we were headed. All he knew was he wanted to drive, and drive far. We'd travel for hours, stopping to take a hike somewhere, to eat something or maybe to just stroll through an unknown town. It would be dark by the time we'd return back home. Arriving earlier would be against Jack's wishes. The boys would have fallen asleep out of boredom. Jack would be happy we had been able to get out and enjoy the day as he put it, but I'd never hear the end of how tortuous it became for the kids and how much they hated those long rides. They would keep saying once they became old enough to take care of themselves, they would be passengers no longer. Until then, they viewed it as child abuse and didn't think too kindly of Jack for it. They didn't enjoy it at all.

Being the mother, I would sympathize, but being the wife, I would support Jack. No, I wasn't always thrilled with the long rides, either. I would've preferred staying home some Sundays to clean the house or relax a bit before the work week started again, but it seemed more important to make Jack happy. He waited for Sundays. He loved the rides. Having Jack at home grumbling all day would've been more tortuous for all of us, so I supported his favorite Sunday hobby and dragged the kids along until they wouldn't stand it anymore. Looking back on it now, though, there are a lot of good memories of the places we went to. I hoped the kids felt the same.

"I figure we'll travel Route 3 up to Lincoln. Then we can see the sights rather than take boring I-93 all the way," Jack commented as we headed away from the house.

"Where are we going anyway?" Tommy yawned and wiped his eyes. He took a sip of coffee from a thermos I had prepared from him. "Why don't we have breakfast first before we get too far? Let's stop at the diner down the street."

"We already had breakfast. You missed it!" Jack replied rather harshly. Tommy looked at me and rolled his eyes. Oh no, I prayed this wasn't a prelude to the kind of day it was going to be. No way did I want them at each other's throat this early in the morning.

Jack looked over at Tommy and could see his face. He realized what he had done. "Sorry about that, Tom. I'm just being the usual me. Cranky, grumpy as you both continuously say. Can't help myself." He reached over and ruffled Tommy's hair a bit. It was enough to get him to take the scowl off of his face put on by Jack's earlier comment.

"Hey, Jack." I leaned forward putting my arms on the back of the front seat and flashed them both a smile. I usually sat up front, but today I let Tommy sit there instead. "Neither of us ate that much—only a piece of toast and some coffee. How about if we stop somewhere along the way, maybe Plymouth, and have a good breakfast. If that's too soon, there's that diner in Lincoln you like right before we enter Franconia Notch."

Glancing over at Tommy again, Jack said, "How does that sound? Can you make it until Lincoln? You remember the diner, don't you? The silver one right before Clarks Trading Post?"

"Yeah, okay," Tommy answered.

"Rosie, remember when we'd bring the boys to see the bears? Seems like yesterday. Where did the years go?"

I remembered all too well. Good memories, yes, but also hectic ones. The boys would be fighting with each other and whining about the trip. Jack would be grumbling and yelling at them to stop. Tears would flow. I'd feel like I was in the middle, splitting in two, wanting to please everyone. In some ways, it wasn't so bad having the boys all grown up and independent. I miss Jonathan terribly and I'll miss having Tommy around too, but I'll never miss the aggravation that occurred when they and their step-father butted heads so many times. At least now they're old enough to duke it out themselves if they have to. And I can remain as uninvolved as possible. No more refereeing from me just to keep the peace. Besides, they get along better now.

"Remember?" Jack said again.

"Sure do," I replied. "And I never thought I'd live through those days, but somehow I did."

After we all ate more than enough food at the diner, we were on the road again heading north. This time Jack was ready to travel I-93 through the notch. When we were in sight of the Basin, a popular tourist attraction, he took a quick turn into the parking lot. We would stop here every time we traveled through the area.

We got out of the car and walked over to the familiar path and followed it, along with several other tourists, and admired the flowing waters and then the deep pool of water swirling around and around smoothing the big rocks that encased it. It was beautiful and mesmerizing. I glanced at Tommy and could see he was enjoying being here as much as Jack and I were.

Back in the car a half-hour later and traveling north again, we were now in the area where we used to park and view the Old Man of the Mountain, an old stone face displayed on the side of a mountain. It was a New Hampshire

Landmark. I would always look up at his profile and say hello to him, talk to him like he was human, but now I covered my eyes and refused to even take a peek as we passed right by where he once was. In May of 2003, his profile collapsed, worn from the many years it had been perched there and from the often-harsh weather it had to bear. When they announced he'd fallen, I cried my eyes out. I can still remember. I sat at my computer and became inspired to share my feelings. I wrote a story about him. To me, he was a living thing. This area just wasn't the same without him.

We continued on our journey until we reached Littleton. That's when we decided to walk along the still functioning large downtown district. It was like going back into time. One of the attractions was a penny candy store with the longest candy counter around. We marveled at the candy dots, fireballs, Boston Baked Beans, 50 varieties of lollipops. Of course, everything cost more than a penny now. Spotting a jar filled with small packages of candy cigarettes, I was amazed they were still available knowing most people didn't want to promote smoking. I can remember Tommy and Jonathan, when they were young, holding them like real cigarettes. Colored red at the tips, they would pretend to puff on them and try to act so cool. It didn't surprise me when Tommy reached his hand into the jar for a box to purchase.

When we left the store, he took one out of the box and started acting like he was smoking it.

"Don't make me cry," I commented.

"Why would this make you cry, Mom? It's not like I'm really smoking. I can't stand real cigarettes. It just brings back so many good memories."

"That's why. You're all grown up now. I was thinking about those candy cigarettes before you bought them. Yes, good memories, but . . ."

I did cry. I just broke down all of a sudden. Luckily we were outside again walking back towards the car.

"Mom, I didn't mean it. I didn't really think it would cause this reaction."

Jack talked for me. "Tommy, she's going to cry sooner or later, so let her cry. That's what mothers do when their children go off to college."

Tommy came up beside me and put his arm around me. He pulled me toward his side and I buried my head into him. Gosh, I'd never realized how tall he had become. I only came up to his chest, but I still managed to look up at him.

"It's hard to let you go, Tommy. But you'll always be my baby boy—don't forget it."

"How can I?" he remarked. "You'll always remind me." He squeezed my shoulder, flashed a grin, and we proceeded to the car. I was still crying, but was so happy to spend this time with him. After the initial comment Jack made early this morning, it turned into a real nice day for all of us. And it wasn't over yet.

Chapter 23

Later that evening, we were all sitting around the living room watching another ballgame. This time I decided to join them. I had made a nice dinner for us earlier—Shepherd's Pie—Tommy's favorite. We both smothered ketchup all over the top of it—we always did—and the sight disgusted Jack. He, in turn, made a comment about us having a little shepherd's pie with our ketchup.

While watching the game, I started knitting a scarf for Tommy. Soon enough, he'd need to wear it. It was only the end of August, there were a few more months to go before cold weather, but still, it seemed like a good idea.

The phone rang at the beginning of the fifth inning. Neither Jack nor Tommy budged an inch. Okay, so no one's going to answer the phone—it has to be me. I got up and went into the kitchen. Checking caller-id first, I was happy to see it was Jean. She was leaving in the morning before the shop opened and I had wanted to talk to her before she went. Getting wrapped up in spending the day with my family, I had forgotten.

"Hey, Jean. I'm glad you called."

"Well, I had to. I've been waiting to hear from you, but it seems like with only one day off from being here, you've forgotten me." Jean laughed at her own comment.

"Thanks so much for letting me spend the time with Tommy and Jack. It was a great day and I enjoyed it so much. Well, until I broke down and cried about Tommy leaving."

"He hasn't left yet. You still have a few days."

"I know."

"On the other hand, I'm leaving in the morning and won't see you for a week. I'm going to miss you."

That was sweet of Jean to say. "I'm going to miss you, too, but maybe by the time you get back, you'll have a better handle on your relationship with Bob. I really hope you both enjoy your time together, and with the boys."

I was skeptical they were going to be able to stand living together for an entire week. The sex might be good, but I had a feeling they'd start reverting back to their old ways in no time and both Bob and Jean would finally realize that, although they've managed to remain friends, being a married couple is another matter. Still, it's good for them to test things out to make sure.

"Are you still with me, Rosie? Damn, you seem to drift off a lot lately."

"Well, I've been through quite a bit the past few days, don't you think?" I huffed. "Hey, I'm missing the game and I'm knitting right now. Is there anything to tell me before we hang up? I mean, do you want me to do anything at the shop for you?"

"No, got it covered. You're all set for Saturday. Mary's coming in to help Gertrude for the day—they'll be fine together. Both Mary and Gertrude were here today and they hit it off. Mary was a lot of help, and during tea time, Gertrude taught her how to knit. You should've seen her. She was so excited. Wait till you look at the scarf she's started and how neat and even her stitches are already."

"That's great. I'm looking forward to getting back there tomorrow and seeing her. Remember, I'll miss you and I love you, Jean."

"I love you, too, Rosie. Hey, wait a minute, I almost forgot. There IS something I want to tell you. Scott called this afternoon to say they questioned David this morning. He wouldn't talk. They asked him if Justin was involved with this in any way and he wouldn't answer. My guess is Justin put David up to this. Who knows? Maybe we never will, but be careful, Rosie. I don't like it when we're too far from each other. When that happens, I can't watch out for you."

"Don't worry, I'll be okay. After all, Justin is in jail. No plans of getting out for years, either. How could he pull another prank from inside his cell? If he did get David to do this, then he must have arranged it before he was arrested. That's my thought anyway." I tried to sound convincing, but I wasn't so sure. Justin was sneaky and it wouldn't surprise me if he had been involved in this. But what could be done? David wouldn't talk and even if he did, what would they do about it?

Before I went back into the living room, I decided to make some popcorn for the guys. I stuck a bag into the microwave and, not long after it started popping, the smell of buttered popcorn filled the room. When it finished, I carefully opened the bag and poured it into a big yellow bowl. That's when Jack got a scent of it and called out, "Hey, you read my mind. The popcorn smells great. Can you bring each of us a drink also?"

What would they do without me?

Mary was there to meet me at the door to Simple Pleasures the next morning. She had on some new clothes, sported a new hairdo, and looked like a different person from just a day ago.

"I didn't even recognize you at first." I said with a look of surprise on my face. "What's all this about?"

"It was Jean's way of thanking me for helping out yesterday. At lunch, she sent me across the street to the hair stylist." She reached up and lightly touched her hair with both of her hands. "I think he did a great job."

"He sure did," I added.

"Then, after work, Jean surprised me with this outfit. I guess she went out and bought it while I was having my hair done."

I opened the door with my key and we entered the shop. Mary kept on talking,

"And did you hear that I learned how to knit?" She reached into a small bag she was carrying and pulled out

132

her needles. About two inches of the scarf had been done already in a beautiful pink color. I reached out and touched it. Alpaca. Jean was right. The stitches were all even. She may be just starting, but it was beautiful and much better than my first attempt at a scarf.

"You're doing a great job. We'll knit some more this afternoon and I'll show you a new project both Jean and I are working on. It's kind of funky and well, it's kind of a secret. I want to surprise Jack with it when it's finished."

I took a glance around the shop. I already missed not seeing Jean here. And it seemed so quiet. That's because Max wasn't here either.

"I knew I'd miss Jean, but I didn't think about Max," I commented. "It's like he's part of this place—our mascot. I'm going to miss him not being around for a while."

"Me, too, but we'll just have to get by with our other mascot, Bluey. She looked over at the fish swimming around in the vase, acting like a hot shot wanting us to notice. "Speaking of Bluey," she continued, "I'll go feed him before we forget to."

While she was doing that, I proceeded to get the cash drawer set up so we could open on time. When we did open, no one was waiting outside—it had me kind of worried—but it didn't take long before customers started coming in. Some went to the yarn section; some went to the book area. By midmorning, we had already had about a dozen purchases and still more people coming through the door. I was used to it being busy, but not this much. Word must have continued to spread there was a new shop in town.

By noontime, when Gertrude arrived, I was tired and anxious to take a lunch break. I would've enjoyed having someone to eat with, but we had to take staggering lunch shifts so there'd still be at least two people in the shop at any given time.

Jean had said it was okay for us to go upstairs, so I walked into her apartment, and kicking my shoes off, I decided to lie down on the couch. What I didn't plan on was to fall asleep. A couple hours later, Mary was gently shaking me awake.

"Rosie, are you okay?" She felt my ear with her fingertips. "You may have a bit of a fever, you're a little warm. And you've been sleeping for quite a while."

I opened my eyes and looked at her. It took a few seconds for me to get her face into focus. She looked concerned.

"What did you say?" I asked somewhat startled. "What time is it?"

"Just after two. When you didn't come back downstairs, I got worried about you. Then we were busy again and the time flew by. I came up here as soon as possible to see if you were all right."

I sat up quickly and my head began to spin. Could I be coming down with something? My stomach began to feel a bit queasy. Oh no! I was going to barf. I sprinted to the bathroom and made it just in time. Mary came soon after, and held my hair back as I barfed some more.

When I thought I might be finished for a while, she told me to return to the couch. She brought me an empty wastebasket in case I needed to vomit again and then went back into the bathroom, soaked a wash towel under cold water, squeezed the water out, and came back to the living room. By then, I was again lying down with my head on the pillow. She pressed the wet towel onto my forehead.

"Rosie, I should call Jack to come and get you. You're too sick to drive home."

"No, let's wait. I don't want him and Tommy to catch this if it's a bug. Maybe I can just rest a little while longer and see how I feel. Then we can call Jack. Maybe I should even stay here tonight if I don't feel better."

I closed my eyes and my head was still spinning. I thought about Mary. She must be tired from standing so long. And she hadn't eaten lunch yet.

"How are things going downstairs? You say it's still busy? Is Gertrude all right by herself?"

"She isn't by herself. Emma came in and offered to help out. The two of them can take care of the shop for a while.

I'll grab a quick bite to eat. Jean said there's still some left-over Mexican food in there from the other night."

The mention of food made me feel like I was going to vomit again. I reached over and grabbed the wastebasket and gagged a bit, but the feeling passed and my stomach settled down.

Mary reached out and felt my cheek with the back of her hand. "Rosie, you're burning up. I've got to see how high your fever is and then get you some Tylenol. A fever could be high this time of day if it's a stomach bug, but we have to get it down. You'll feel better if we do."

It didn't take long for her to find what she needed in Jean's medicine cabinet. She put a plastic shield on the thermometer, pressed the button and then placed it in my mouth. I felt like a little child and it brought back a memory, a faint memory, of my mother taking care of me. She died in a car accident, along with my little brother, when I was only five, but there were still recollections of when she was alive. For some reason, they hadn't faded completely from my mind. Or maybe, maybe I had made them up when I was younger and just wanted to believe in them.

The thermometer beeped. Mary took it from my mouth, looked at the display and frowned. "Yeah, you've got something alright. Temps 101. It may be a 24-hour bug. You'd better get some more rest and take it easy. You sure you don't want Jack to know?"

"No, no need. What's he going to do anyway? Seems to me I'm having the best care right here. Thanks, Mary, I appreciate it. I hope you don't catch this."

"If I do, then so be it. Hey, go back to sleep. I'm going to go do what I have to do and I'll check back on you in another hour or so." She reached for an afghan on a nearby chair and placed it over me. I must have fallen back asleep instantly because I don't even remember her leaving the apartment.

When I woke again, it was dark outside. It had to be well after five. I started to panic and jumped up again, only to take another mad dash to the bathroom. When I returned to the living room, I heard Mary coming up the stairs from the shop. I glanced at my watch. Almost six.

"Hey," Mary said as she entered the apartment. "How's the patient doing?"

"Not so well and Jack is going to kill me. I'm surprised he hasn't called here wondering if I'm okay."

"Oh, Jack has already stopped by. He came to bring a change of clothes for you after he called earlier and I told him you were sick. He was reluctant to have you stay here tonight, but I assured him I could watch over you. That way, he might not catch the bug and neither will Tommy. He mentioned you're both bringing him to college the day after tomorrow. You should be feeling much better by tomorrow night, but I think you should take it easy for the rest of the week. Emma has volunteered her services while you're ill."

I frowned. I didn't like having everyone else pick up the slack for me.

"Do you think Jean would mind if I stayed here with you tonight, Rosie? I want to make sure you're okay. I can sleep in the chair over there."

"Mind? I think she'll be thrilled you're taking care of me. I'm sure Jack was thankful you volunteered. At least he knows I'm not alone here. He wouldn't like that."

"Well, maybe we should call Jean to make sure it's okay."

"NO," I blurted out. She doesn't need to worry about me. Let's not say anything until she gets back home. I'm sure it's all right if you stay."

"Alright then, do you want something to eat? Jack brought a can of chicken noodle soup and he told me to make you a cup of tea. He said you always like hot tea when you're not feeling well. He also brought some ginger ale and Gatorade to help keep you hydrated."

"Ginger ale sounds good for now. Let's see if that stays down. Besides, my mouth tastes like garbage."

That was so nice of Jack. I'll have to give him a call and thank him.

"Mary, could you go get my purse downstairs behind the cash register and bring it up?"

"Sure thing." Mary was down and back in no time. As soon as she handed me my purse, I reached in and grabbed my cell phone. Flipping it open, I hit the home number on speed dial. Jack answered right away. He must have been waiting to hear from me.

"Jack, it's me. I'm sorry I'm not home, honey. I'm sorry I'm sick."

"It's okay, just get well and get back here tomorrow. It's not the same without you."

I could hear the television in the background. Then I heard cheers. He was watching another game and he wasn't alone.

"What're you doing? Having a party without me?" I felt kind of left out.

"Well, no, not really. Tommy's working his last shift tonight and, well, I was a bit lonely so I invited a couple of buddies over to watch the game with me. You know, the guys I meet with some mornings at the diner. A game is always more enjoyable with company. Anyway, we're also playing some cards."

"Party, party!" I commented. Still, I was glad he wasn't alone. "And for dinner?"

"Pizza. Couldn't think of anything else and it was convenient."

"Okay, get back to your fun. I love you, Jack. I just hope you don't catch this and if it takes a night of sleeping without you beside me to keep you well, then it's worth it. But I do miss you and wish I was home."

"Love you, too, hon. I'll call you in the morning to see how you're feeling. Gotta go." He gave me a smooch through the phone and hung up. No, Jack wasn't going to miss me that much.

So, if Jack was having a nice evening, I thought maybe I could do the same, even if I was a bit under the weather. After all, how often did I get to spend an evening without Jack and also in good company? This time of year, he was watching a game almost every night, too. It felt kind of nice to have a break from that. In a strange way, it's almost a good thing I was sick. Otherwise, Mary and I wouldn't be having this time alone to get to know each other better. Maybe she would open up to me and share something about her life tonight. Maybe I'd find out if she was living in a shelter or if she had a home. Also, I wanted to know what her ambitions and hopes were for the future.

Mary put a glass of ginger ale on the coffee table in front of me. I reached for it and took a sip. It tasted cold and good. My stomach didn't gurgle right away, so I took another sip and then a gulp.

"Hey, take it easy. Don't drink too fast. You must be dehydrated a bit, but stick to sips for a while, okay? Just in case? We don't want you running down the hall to the bathroom anymore tonight." She gave me a grin and went to sit in the nearby chair.

"I'll take it easy. I was so thirsty, though."

"Well, it seems to be settling. Are you getting hungry, too?" she asked. She started to rise like she was going to go heat the soup up.

"No, let's wait and take it easy, like you said." I put my hand up to tell her to stop.

She sat back down and we both were silent. We sat there staring out into space like we didn't know what to do next. Then, I remembered I had mentioned I would share my new project with her today.

"Mary, I'm wide-awake and want to knit for a while. Want to join me?" I reached into my bag again and pulled out my yarn, needles and the bikini bottom.

"Woo Hoo, what is that?" she said. "Lingerie? Weirdo panties?"

"Close," I chuckled. I held it up high in the air for her to see the detail. I had to admit it was unique, but attractive. How attractive it would be with me wearing it was another thing.

"See? It's the bottom half to a bikini—a woolen bikini. That's what both Jean and I are making. I found the pattern in a very old magazine and had to try it. I haven't started on the top yet, but it shouldn't be hard. Like it?"

"Ummm, it's cute, and I like the stripes the yarn creates, but you'd never see me wearing it in public."

"Believe me, I don't plan on wearing this in public. It's only going to be a private showing, if you get what I mean."

"Yeah, I get it." Mary replied. She stood up and went for her bag in the kitchen. She pulled out her own project, came back to sit in the chair, and we knitted together for about an hour. We also talked and I learned quite a few things about her, but there were some things she still didn't want to share. There's no doubt Mary carried around her own secret. What it was, I wasn't sure, but it involved a falling out with her parents. That's why she was living in a shelter right now and just getting by the best way she could. She told me working at Simple Pleasures was the best thing that had happened to her in a long time.

As I listened, I couldn't help but think she reminded me a lot of myself when I was around her age. I didn't know where I was going in life, had experimented with drugs and alcohol a bit, and gave my stepmother a very hard time for a while. But I came out okay, especially after I had my spiritual epiphany in my twenties. I suspect Mary will turn out okay, too. In the meantime, I told her I would hold her close to my heart, which as I explained, meant I would pray for her.

Chapter 24

The sun shining through the paned living room windows woke me up. I looked at my watch. Almost nine. Mary was nowhere to be found. She was probably downstairs getting ready to open up the shop. I could barely hear voices—she wasn't alone. Either Gertrude or Emma must be in already helping out.

I lifted myself up and sat on the edge of the couch. My hair was matted, my body sweaty, but otherwise, I felt much better. My stomach seemed to have settled and the soup Mary and I enjoyed last evening after knitting had given me a bit of strength. Maybe I couldn't work downstairs today—I didn't want anyone else to catch this—but I could definitely get my butt up off of this couch and start moving about.

I shuffled down the hall, still a little unsteady on my feet, in search of the clothes Jack left with Mary yesterday. I found them in Jean's bedroom, neatly folded on her bed. Grabbing what was there, I headed for the bathroom, this time not to barf, but to indulge in a nice, hot shower. I took a pee and was about to get myself undressed and start the water running when I realized it would be best to keep the cell phone handy. Maybe Jack would call, so I shuffled back to the living room to get it and conveniently placed it within reach of the shower.

Sure enough, right after I put my head under the water and was completely soaked, the phone rang. I fumbled around for a towel, shut the water off and reached to answer it.

"Hello?" I sounded out of breath.

"What're you doing? Running a marathon? Why are you so out of breath?"

"Hi, Jack. I just stepped into the shower when you called. I'm feeling better. By tonight, I should be okay."

"Must be a twenty-four hour bug." he replied. "I hope so because Tommy came home last night not feeling so well. Then I heard him in the middle of the night upchucking. Not a good thing right before heading to college." Jack sighed. "Hopefully, things will settle down soon. It's been way too crazy around here. I could use a little peace and quiet for a change."

I wanted to say, "Well, then, why did you decide to party last night? You could have had all of the peace and quiet you wanted," but I didn't. I was happy he'd been able to enjoy some time with his friends. Instead I said, "Tell Tommy I'm sorry. We both must have caught something highly contagious. I hope you're not next. Tomorrow we're supposed to be helping him move, too."

"Don't remind me," he huffed.

My body became chilled from standing in the bathroom wet. My teeth started to chatter.

"Get back in the shower, Rosie, before you get sick again. I'll be round in a little while. Remember, I'm helping out in the shop this morning."

After we finished our brief conversation, I turned off the phone and was about to turn the water back on again. But, then came another interruption.

Rap. Rap. Rap. "Hey, Rosie, you okay in there?" It was Mary.

"Yeah, I'm fine. Just trying to get in a nice shower. I'll feel better if I can. How are things in the shop?"

"Pretty good, but UPS showed up with three large boxes. Two are filled with books and one with some funky new yarn. Want me to unload them?"

"No, put them to the side. Jack's coming soon and I'll tell him to price everything and place them on display. It'll give him something to do this morning. Now, why don't you go back down there? I'm freezing in here and really would like to get back under the hot water."

"Gotcha, I'll check on you later." She walked away and I could hear the door to the apartment closing behind her.

Some time to myself and a little peace and quiet—that was what I could use a little of myself right now. Jack was right—it has been kind of hectic around here lately. With Tommy moving out tomorrow, Jean gone with Bob to California, the shop still to run, and also wanting to find out who my birth child is, I think it's going to remain crazy for a little while longer.

By Saturday morning, I felt completely well again, Jack hadn't come down with the bug yet—maybe he dodged it, and Tommy was on the mend, a little weak, but overall feeling healthy enough to move out. We loaded up the cars with Tommy's belongings. As I took each box from the house, it made the surroundings already appear different. I held back the tears, but didn't know how long I could keep them from spilling over. In only a few hours, I'd be balling my eyes out again as I said goodbye to him. Sure, we'd be in touch by phone and computer, but as I promised, I would have to refrain from contacting him more than once a week unless necessary. It wasn't going to be easy to keep from calling him more often. I was used to having Tommy home almost every night to talk to and I knew most of his current friends. From now on, it would be different. He wouldn't be around, except for holidays and school breaks, and as time went on, his coming home may be less and less. He would make new friends. I'm not going to hear his car pulling into the driveway every night, I won't . . .

"Stop that, Rosie," I scolded myself silently in my head as I tried to arrange the boxes in my car to be able to squeeze a few more in. "You are working yourself up into a frenzy. You know you have to let him go. He's a young man with his own ambitions. You can't protect him for the rest of his life." I know all that, but it's just so hard.

"Mom, you okay?" Tommy asked me as he slid into the passenger seat. I was now behind the wheel looking lost. Jack was going to lead in his car and we were going to follow behind. I hadn't turned the key in the ignition yet. Instead, I was staring straight ahead, like in a fog. I wanted the moment to cease and stand still for a while. That way, I wouldn't have to let him go yet.

On the ride to UNH, which is located in Durham in the Southeast portion of New Hampshire, Tommy shared his excitement about school, as well as his apprehensions. He'd gone to a small high school with only 100 kids graduating in his class. UNH, however, was a larger university. There were thousands of students there. He was a bit scared. Plus, he'd be sharing a dorm with a stranger. His roommate, Peter, was from North Carolina and played hockey. That's all Tommy knew about him. They had spoken on the phone a couple of times planning out how to furnish the dorm room, but that was the extent of it. They'd never met.

I never had the opportunity to go away to college, but I could imagine how scary it might be for my son. So many changes were ahead for him. It suddenly bothered me that, up until now, I'd only been concentrating on my own feelings and worries, not his.

"I'm so sorry, Tommy. It's been so selfish of me to think only of myself and how I'm going to handle the empty-nest syndrome with you gone. I'm sure you'll adjust to the changes quickly. It'll only be a bit awkward in the beginning."

"I know, I'll be okay, but I'm still apprehensive about it all. There are a few kids I know from high school who are going to UNH and we've already planned on getting together later this weekend. Then I'm thinking maybe I'll join a fraternity or something so I can have a group to belong to. It would help me fit in better."

WHAT? Did I hear him correctly? Tommy joining a fraternity? I lost all concentration on my driving at the mention of it and nearly went off of the road. Only after I took a deep breath and gained my composure was I able to respond.

"Do you know what they do to initiate someone into a fraternity?" I asked, trying to remain calm.

"Yeah, sure, they have you do some weird stuff to prove you're entitled to join. They break you, kind of. Like, I heard one kid was dropped off in a strange place in the pitch dark. He had no money on him and they took away his cell phone. He had to find his way back home. He didn't like it, but he did what he needed to so he could join. He says it was all worth it."

"And he probably was drunk, too. Do you know there's a lot of partying that goes on with those groups?" I shook my head. "I don't know, Tommy. I really don't think it's a good idea to join one."

"Of course there's partying, Mom. What do you think, that I'm not going to party? All kids at college party—it's part of the curriculum."

Oh, no. Not worry? I was going to worry double-time now I knew about his plans. Triple-time! "Well, just promise you'll think about it before you join."

"Okay, if it makes you happy, I promise. Besides, I'm also going to join for more important reasons. It's good to have on your resume and you get to know people who can help you with your career plans. Don't worry—I'll be fine, Mom. Okay? Now, let's change the subject."

Tommy continued talking about all sorts of things for the remainder of the ride. I tried to listen as much as I could without butting in. When we arrived at the college, we drove through the campus several times before finally finding the building he was staying in. We then moved all of the boxes inside and when I started to unpack them in his rather small dorm room, Tommy told me not to.

"Okay, I get it. No more doing your chores for you either, right?" I said.

"That's right, Mom. I've got to do them on my own now."
I chuckled and looked over at Jack. "Please remind him

of this the first time he brings home his laundry and wants me to take care of it."

"That won't happen," Tommy replied.

"Right," I answered sarcastically. Suddenly, the tears I'd been holding inside all morning broke through. I couldn't hold them back anymore. I dropped my head and started crying uncontrollably.

"Oh, Rosie," Jack said. He gave me a sad look.

Tommy then walked over, wrapped his arms around me and said he loved me and would miss me, too.

It made me cry more. I couldn't stop.

Finally, Jack put an end to it by telling me I'd better stop NOW, or my eyes would be too swollen to sit in any restaurant. I didn't know it, but Jack planned on taking both Tommy and I out to lunch before we headed back home. That was a good thing. It meant I'd still have more time with Tommy before going back to an empty house. I did my best to smile, sniffled, wiped my eyes and said, "Okay, that's over and done with. Now, let's eat!" Food always did have a way to get me in a good mood and Jack knew it. He chuckled at me as we all walked out of the dorm.

Chapter 25

Sunday morning again. No alarm necessary and no reason to get up early. I planned on sleeping in for as long as I could before having to face the first full day of Tommy not living here. I glanced up at the clock—already 8 am. I looked over at Jack and didn't have to guess if he was still sleeping because he was snoring loudly.

Ring, Ring.

The telephone? That's what it was, but not our land phone. The ringing was coming from my cell phone. Who the heck could be calling on a Sunday morning? Let me guess.

I didn't even have to. Tommy would have called the home number knowing we'd be here. It had to be Jean.

"Okay, what's going on?" I said. "Why are you calling me so early in the morning on the second Sunday in a row?"

No answer. Only sobbing. Something was wrong.

"Jean? Are you okay? What's wrong?" I asked. Now I know Jean tends to get over-dramatic about a lot of things, so I tried not to become concerned, but she was calling from California and it was three hours earlier there. Why was she up? Hmmm, maybe she just had a spat with Bob.

"He's definitely going to move here. He's staying with Matt until he finds a place of his own." Jean replied. "That's not damn fair, leaving me like that."

"I thought you were testing it out to see if you could still make it as a married couple?" I was confused.

"Nah, ain't gonna happen. We found that out the first two days we were here. Sure, the sex was great, it always is with Bob, but damn, he gets on my nerves. And there's no doubt I get on his. He couldn't wait to get out of my sight.

He's been playing golf with the boys in the afternoons and I'm not invited. Now how would that make you feel?"

Not good, I had to admit. "Oh, it sounds like you're having a horrible time. I was hoping it would be a good vacation for you, and you'd be able to spend some quality time with your kids."

"Oh, I've had some quality time with them already. Bob went to a job interview on Friday and was gone for a few hours. Matt, Rob and I took in the sights. Then, the four of us went out on the town last night and had a great evening. It hasn't been all bad." Jean stopped crying. She seemed in a better mood already.

"Well, get to sleep—it's too early to be up—and enjoy your last few days there. Then, come on home. We miss you here."

"I know, I will. I miss you, too." She changed the subject. "How'd it go with Tommy yesterday? How are you doing now?"

"It went all right. We had lunch together in Durham. There was a nice little diner in town a short walk from the college. Then, we met his roommate. He looks like a decent kid. I'm sure they'll get along okay."

"As for you?"

"Well, it's kind of quiet here already. I'm dreading spending the entire day without seeing him. And I promised only to call him once a week. That means I can't talk to him again until next weekend." I groaned.

"You'll get used to it. Just think, you and Jack can have sex in just about any room of the house at any time. You can walk around naked all the time. How great is that?"

I didn't answer right away. Instead, I walked downstairs to get as far away from Jack in case he woke up.

"It would be great if Jack wanted to have sex, but he doesn't," I whispered. "I'm hoping I can finally entice him with my new knitting project, remember?"

My computer was in sight, so I pushed the on button to boot it up. It had suddenly occurred to me with everything happening around here lately, I hadn't checked my email for days.

"I've finished the bottom half of it and I'm already halfway through the top part," I continued whispering. "It's almost done."

"I haven't done any more of mine. I've been too busy." Jean replied.

"OH NO," I said suddenly, not whispering anymore. "I forgot to do my column this week. The editor's not too happy with me. Gotta go, Jean. See you on Wednesday when you get back. Have to run."

I flipped the phone off and sat right down in front of my monitor. What a way to begin a writing career. The editor was a friend, too. How could I let him down like that? To make matters worse, he sent this email to me Friday—two days ago! I read it again.

```
TO: Rosie
FROM: Chad
```

```
Why no column this week, Rosie? I had a hole in
my newspaper with nothing but junk to put in it.
Not happy.
```

What was I going to say? Figuring the truth was the best thing, I typed a quick reply.

```
TO: Chad
FROM: Rosie
```

```
I'm sooo sorry! It won't happen again. It's been
a tough week with unexpected situations. Totally
forgot. Promise to have two columns to you pron-
to. Please forgive me? Rosie.
```

After sending it off, I started working right away on my next story. With any luck, I could at least get one of these done by the end of today.

I must have been at it for close to an hour. Losing all track of time and of my surroundings, I was a bit startled when Jack came up behind me and tapped me on the shoulder.

Looking up at him bleary eyed, I said, "Huh? Oh Jack, I'm sorry. I've been writing."

I can see that. He rubbed my back a bit. My muscles were sore. It felt good.

"Are you okay?" he asked.

"Yeah, I guess so. Jean called earlier—minor catastrophe on her end. Nothing out of the ordinary, but she wanted to talk. Then, I booted up the computer realizing I hadn't checked messages for a few days. That's when I saw a message from the editor at the newspaper. He wrote it two days ago and wasn't happy—I forgot to submit a column last week." I looked up at Jack and frowned. "Honestly, with all that's been going on, I feel like I'm falling apart. That's not like me, Jack, and you know it."

"I know, hon, but you're right, there's been a lot happening around here, a lot of unexpected things, too. That's why I thought we'd both go to prayer group today. It's still early enough to get dressed and arrive on time. I think it'll do us both some good to see everyone for a change."

"Well, the fellowship is always uplifting, and . . ."

Jack cut in, "And don't forget the food! The food is awesome."

"Okay, let's do it. Besides, it will get us out of the house for a while and it's already too quiet around here without Tommy. Just let me do a spell check on this, okay? Then I'll shut the computer down. It'll only take a couple of minutes, and it won't take long for me to get ready."

"Great," Jack said. "I've got some coffee already brewing upstairs and I'll fix us a quick bite to hold us over."

It was about an hour's drive to Jim and Joy's house. They were the hosts of the home church. Driving up their long dirt driveway, which is located in the sticks of southern NH, we passed by their barn and then their beautiful home—a turn-of-the-century farmhouse—came into view.

There were already several cars parked in their drive-way so it looked like it might be a good gathering today. Every Sunday was different. Sometimes only a half dozen would show up, other times it would be a full house, meaning anywhere from 12 to 20. It wasn't one of those churches where you were expected to come every week. Jack and I hadn't even been here for several months. Still, as Jack parked the car, Jim was already on his way over to us with open arms.

"Welcome," he said cheerfully to Jack. "Welcome, Brother."

They embraced. "God Bless," Jim added. "It's nice to see you alive and kicking. Have you recovered completely from the heart surgery?"

"Just about," Jack grinned. "Bless you, too." I could see how happy Jack looked to be here, and was already glad we came.

Then, Jim came over and gave me a hug and a kiss on the cheek. "Hi, beautiful. God Bless you, Sister."

"Amen," I said. This was a certain jargon some Christians used. Brother, Sister, Amen, God Bless. When I first started coming here about two years ago, I felt kind of strange saying those words so freely, but it didn't take long to get used to them.

The wonderful aroma of all of the fixings of a traditional turkey dinner filled the entire house. Joy was busy at the stove stirring something in a pot.

"Mmmm, Mmmm," I commented as I walked over to her and gave her a big embrace. "How are you doing, Sister? Need help with anything?"

She grinned. "So glad you're here, Rosie. It's been so long. Too long!"

Then she handed me the spoon. "And of course I need help. I've been slaving in this kitchen for hours already." Joy left me and proceeded over to the kitchen counter. There, in front of her, was a very large cooked turkey browned to perfection. She covered it with aluminum foil and with another woman's assistance holding it, headed back towards the stove. Knowing what she planned on doing, I opened the oven door and they carefully placed the turkey back in to stay warm. It would be another hour or so before we all sat down to eat at her big farmers table. Worship and fellowship came first.

Several other women were scurrying around the kitchen preparing things. Most I recognized, but some I didn't. The guys were already in the "church" room.

"Okay, ladies," Joy announced. "Let's get everything covered and let's get in there. I'm ready for some singing."

"Oh, no," I groaned under my breath. Not my favorite part, but others enjoyed it. And once the singing ended, we could get into the best part—fellowship. Then, there'd be plenty of food and more fellowship while we continued enjoying each other's company. Those were the reasons why, besides the good friendships we had made, that both Jack and I continued to come back here. Those were the things that made the difference from the other churches we had visited in the past.

SIMPLE PLEASURES

A weekly column by Rosie Blume

My stepmother, Eloise, was always knitting. I can remember when I was young listening to her needles click away as we watched television together every evening (only one television per household back then).

One summer when I was around 12 and bored out of my mind, Eloise handed me a pair of knitting needles and a big ball of bright orange yarn. "Here," she said. "I'll teach you. It'll be fun."

She showed me how to hold the needles correctly, intertwine the yarn between my fingers, and how to cast stitches by looping the yarn a certain way. Then, she taught me how to knit and purl.

It was harder than it looked and, in the beginning, it was also far from fun. I kept getting frustrated. Many times, I wanted to quit.

But, Eloise convinced me to keep at it and, after a few days of practicing, I began to get the hang of it. Before long, I was hooked.

My first knitting project, with that same ball of bright orange yarn, was a scarf for my Dad. It took the entire summer to make and I would constantly measure it to see how long it was getting. When it was finally long enough, Eloise showed me how to finish it by casting off. I couldn't wait to give it to him.

The scarf wasn't very good looking—it was knotted, uneven, and even had a few holes in it—but my Dad didn't mind.

Since then, over the years, I've completed many other knitting projects—mostly hats, scarves, sweaters and blankets. Right now, I'm knitting a hat for a cancer patient and, would you believe, a woolen bikini?

I'll always be grateful that Eloise taught me this craft because it has provided me with many hours of enjoyment and relaxation. Yes, knitting is fun once you know how to do it.

All it takes is two needles, a skein of yarn, and sometimes a little patience. How much more simple can this pleasure get? And how entertaining and relaxing it can be!

Chapter 26

Monday and Tuesday passed quickly, but the house seemed too quiet during the evenings without Tommy there. Jack wasn't one for long conversations, either, so I kept busy with my column stories.

Now it was Wednesday and Jean was coming home. We all were looking forward to seeing her. Both Gertrude and Mary were helping out as they'd been every day since Jean left for California. Gertrude appeared tired from all of the time she spent at the shop lately, but she didn't complain. Mary seemed thrilled to be around as much as possible. She still looked great—not disheveled anymore—and I noticed she'd been wearing some nicer clothes I hadn't seen her in before. Since we didn't pay her yet for helping out, I wondered how she came upon them.

"That's a great looking blouse, Mary," I commented. "Is it new?"

She glanced down at it and smiled. "It's not new. This lady at the shelter saw me with my new hairstyle and wearing the clothes Jean bought me the other day. She thought it was a big improvement and told me she had some clothes at home she wasn't wearing anymore. We were about the same size so she asked if I wanted to try them on. She planned on giving them to Good Will if I wasn't interested."

"That's great," I replied. "I'm sure you've made some friends there at the shelter."

"I guess so, but I don't get too close to most of them—it's not a good thing to do. This lady, she was only trying to be helpful. Plus, I'm sure she thought if I were better dressed and felt better about myself, then maybe I'd go out and find some employment. Maybe even find a place to live. That way they'd have a bed open for another poor soul. There are so many who still live on the streets at night and it's going to start getting cold now that it's September. There are just not enough shelters and beds around here."

It's sad to think of people having to live on the streets in the cold, but I knew we had our share of homelessness around here. That's why I've wanted to help in some way, but as Jean commented earlier, there's a lot on my plate these days to start thinking of some new project like that. Still, once everything else settled down, I wanted to do my part. Maybe I could already, in some small way, by helping Mary out.

"Hey, you like coming here, don't you?" I asked.

"I sure do," Mary beamed.

"Then how about you start putting in a few more hours and getting paid for them? The shop has continued to be busy and the holidays are coming up. I have to discuss it with Jean first, but I think she'd agree that we could add you to our staff."

"Really?" Mary's mouth dropped wide open like she couldn't believe what I had said. "You mean you really would want to hire me? Like a real employee?" She started jumping up and down in place like a little kid. A couple of customers glanced over at her. I put my hands on her shoulders to calm her down.

"I really mean it, but as I said, I have to check with Jean first. I'll let you know for sure by the end of this week. Until then, it's between you and me. Okay?"

"Okay," Mary replied. She immediately went back to work, probably to prove her worth. She set her sights on a customer who seemed to be searching for something special. I watched the customer's expression and I could tell she was grateful for the assistance.

I really shouldn't have said anything to Mary about this before I knew for sure. But she's been doing so much around here lately, and already she's so devoted. Plus, she's starting to take good care of herself and her appearance has improved greatly with the new hairstyle and clothes. I didn't want anyone else to offer her a job before I did. And I really like her. It's a pleasure to see her around here so often lately. Oh, I hope Jean agrees with me on this. I don't want to let Mary down. I don't want to lose her company and trust.

Just before noon, the shop door swung open and there, standing in the doorway, looking so tanned and rested, was Jean. Beside her, tugging at his leash and wagging his tail furiously was a beautifully groomed Max.

"Max!" I called out. "Oh, you look so dapper. I missed you, boy." I squatted down and clapped my hands beckoning him to come to me. Jean let go of the leash and Max was in my arms wiggling about in no time. I patted his head and put my nose up to him. He looked and smelt like a new dog.

"AHEM," Jean said. She was still standing in the doorway, appearing annoyed.

"Isn't anyone happy to see ME?" she asked. She dropped the suitcase she'd been holding onto and crossed her arms. Uh oh, I'd already done it. Jean was mad at me.

I stood up again and walked quickly over to her while Max proceeded to visit everyone else in the shop.

"Of course we're happy to see you. I'm sorry, Jean. I've done it again."

"You sure have and I won't let you forget it. Now get over here and give me a hug." She unfolded her arms and reached out to me.

"You know that I can't stay mad at you for long, Rosie," she said softly. "But, you really annoy me sometimes. Honestly, greeting Max before even saying hello to me! That's an insult."

She's right. I should've said hello to her first. I had missed her terribly and was glad she was back.

After we embraced, I looked right at her. On closer observance, despite the tan, I could tell something was still bothering her.

"Bob?" I asked.

"It's over. We're done for. Like I said Sunday, he's moving to California. In fact, he hasn't left there. I flew back alone."

I frowned. "Why? I mean he has to get everything in order here. He has a job still. He can't not just come back, can he?"

"Sure he can," she replied. "The interview he went to, well, they called to tell him the position was his on Monday. He called work right away and gave his two weeks' notice, but they told him not to bother. It's not like they're mad at him or anything—he's been working there for years—but the work has slowed down. They would've had to lay him off soon anyway."

"You mean I won't get to say goodbye to him?" So sad. I really had grown fond of Bob, no matter what's happened between him and Jean.

"Oh, you'll see him again. We have the divorce to finalize, remember? He told me to meet with an attorney as soon as I could to reschedule it. He's already called his."

It was too sudden. I knew they weren't meant to stay married, but still, I couldn't help feel bad for Jean. Her heart must be broken.

"Ahh, don't look so sad, Rosie. The trip was a good thing— we had to stop deceiving ourselves. It seemed too easy to delay the inevitable. And I'm happy he's going to stay close to the boys—they both love him. He's a good man, I know it, and," she spoke a little quieter now, "we did have great sex." Jean smiled. "No regrets. It's just time for us both to get on with our lives, as so many, including you, have been trying to tell us. Bob told me about your little talk."

"Ohhh," I was thinking she was going to reprimand me for butting my nose into something that was none of my business, but she surprised me by her next comment.

"And I'm glad you had it," she said. "Now, enough about Bob. How's everything here? How's the shop?"

She pointed to her suitcase, knowing I would deliver it upstairs, and went to say hello to Gertrude, Mary and all of the customers.

157

Chapter 27

While enjoying tea that afternoon, everyone marveled at Jean's tan and expressed how glad they all were to have her back. Everything was back to normal, or so it seemed.

Jack stopped into the shop earlier to ask if it was okay if he went to a friend's to see a game that night. Since I wanted to talk more with Jean, I urged him to go. Also, I wondered if tonight would be a good time to open the envelope. That's why I found an excuse to run an errand later in the day and headed to the bank to take the envelope out of my safety deposit box. I also called Jack to make sure he wouldn't be upset if I shared the photos with Jean first. Initially he seemed hesitant, having recently gone through the ordeal with David.

"Are you sure you're ready for this?" he asked. "I mean, after what we just went through?"

"I know, but I figure why not get it over and done with. Then we can get it all behind us. I have to know a little more about the child I gave up. I'm not too sure if I'm ready to meet them yet—we may wait a little while for that, but I need to be prepared if the parents decide to call me."

"And you're curious," Jack added.

"Yes."

"Okay, but then I can see them later, right?"

"Of course," I replied quickly. In no way did I want him to feel left out. "Are you sure you're okay with this?"

"Yeah, I'm fine with it, but still worried about you. I'll be home early enough, by ten, so we'll have some time to talk more then."

"Sounds good. I'll make sure to be home by that time also. Thanks, Jack."

After an afternoon of celebrating Jean's return, Simple Pleasures was closed for the evening. Everyone had gone home and Jean and I were sitting in her living room. She opened a bottle of wine and poured a glass for both of us. Take-out Chinese was ordered and we were waiting for the delivery.

"Thanks, Jean, for letting me stay for a while this evening. I know you must be tired, but I have a few things to discuss."

"I would have been offended if you didn't stay. What's up?" Jean took a sip of her wine and leaned back. She did seem tired, so I'd better get this over with.

"First of all, I thought maybe we could hire Mary and pay her. Not full-time yet, maybe about 20 hours a week. She's good with the customers and the holidays are coming up. We should be busy enough to afford the extra help."

She didn't even hesitate in answering. "No problem. I was even going to suggest it," she replied. "I like the girl. She reminds me of you, Rosie, in a lot of ways."

"Really?" I considered it a compliment. I couldn't wait to tell Mary she had the job.

"Is that it?" Jean replied. "I really thought you had something more important to share with me."

I smiled at her as I reached into my bag and pulled out the large envelope.

"I figured it was long overdue. It's time to find out," I said hesitantly. I was still nervous. In some ways, maybe it would be better off not to know, but no, it had been long enough. I needed to go through with it.

Jean rubbed her hands together. Her eyes lit up. She didn't appear the least bit tired anymore.

"Finally!" she exclaimed. "Ever since the pajama party, it's been on my mind. I really didn't believe you'd ever be ready."

"Well, I don't know if I am, but let's open this before I change my mind." My hands started shaking. I turned the envelope over and undid the clasp that held it shut for all of these years. I emptied the contents into my lap. There were a few letters and several photos. I lifted one up to check it out—a little baby. I could tell its gender by the clothing.

"It's a girl," I said excitedly. "I can't believe it."

I stared at the photo for a few more seconds and then handed it over to Jean who scrutinized it.

"Doesn't look like Justin," she commented. "That's a bonus."

Wanting to view a more recent photo, I took one from the bottom of the pile. I looked at it closely, and gasped. Then, I jumped up and all of the photos and letters fell to the floor. Never did I think—it just couldn't be! The room started spinning and for a moment, I thought I'd be the one to pass out this time.

Jean jumped up as well and looked at me scared. "What's the matter? What's wrong?"

"I . . . I . . . I. The . . .the . . .the . . ." I couldn't talk. I was in shock.

Jean sat down on the floor and started looking through the photos. She picked one up, not the same one, but one when the child was maybe around 15 years old.

She glanced at it and then her mouth dropped. She looked up at me just as shocked.

"Rosie!" she exclaimed. "I mean, it couldn't be! Could it?"

All I could do was shake my head up and down. Yes, I couldn't believe it. The girl in the photo was not a stranger.

The girl in the photo was Mary.

After calming down a bit and after we each had another glass of wine, Jean and I went through and viewed the rest of the photos. One by one, we retrieved them from the floor. Mary was a beautiful child. And so precious. My heart ached thinking I'd missed all of those years with her. We looked at the letters, too. One letter was from the adoption agency specifying the details of what transpired way back then.

21 year old unwed mother has given child up for adoption to an older couple related to mother's stepmother. Couple has means to take care of child, including a nice home. The new parents—Joseph and Olivia Snow—reside in Massachusetts.

That's about all that was written, other than specifying the child's height and weight at birth—information I never knew before.

The other letter was written to Eloise from Olivia, granting her permission to give me possession of the photos when the child turned of age. It also specified that if the child wished to meet its birth mother, once old enough, it could be arranged.

I wondered if Mary already knew I was her birth mother—if she actually didn't just walk into the shop one day without any knowledge. Maybe she arranged our accidental meeting after she somehow found out who I was. If so, then why didn't she tell me earlier? Why did it seem like she didn't know, either? And if not, how am I now going to tell her I'm her mother and explain the reason I gave her up for adoption so long ago? Will she still like me after I do tell her?

The doorbell rang. We were still both in shock. Neither one of us heard it at first.

BUZZ, BUZZ, BUZZZZZZZ. The person on the other side of the door downstairs was getting annoyed. The noise jolted me back to the moment.

"Oh, it must be the food," I said. Jean came around also.

"Sit, you're in no position to move right now. I'd be afraid you'd tumble down the stairs after what we just found out. I'll get it."

She grabbed the wallet from her purse and scurried down to catch the delivery person before he gave up and took the food back with him.

You would think I wouldn't be in the mood to eat after this shock either, but you'd be wrong. I was famished. We didn't even bother with chopsticks. Jean got some forks and both of us dug into the boxes and ate while we continued to discuss the situation. Of course, Jean also poured us another drink. I wasn't quite sure how I'd drive home after three glasses of wine, but I couldn't think about that now. Maybe I'd have to call Jack to pick me up after the game.

"Do you think Mary already knows?" Jean asked.

"I don't know. The other day, I was really sick and Mary stayed with me here until the next morning. We talked for hours. No, I don't think she knows anything."

"You were sick? Why didn't you mention it to me? Are you all right now?"

"I'm fine. I'm fine. Just a 24-hour bug or something. It happened on Thursday and I didn't want to bother you with the details. Mary stayed overnight with me here. I knew you wouldn't mind."

"No, I'm glad she was here with you, since I couldn't be," Jean replied.

"Anyway, we both enjoyed knitting together for quite a while. She told me about herself and how she temporarily lives in a shelter. She explained there'd been some kind of misunderstanding and falling out with her parents. I reflected back for a moment, thinking about her conversation with me. "But, no, I don't think she has a clue."

Chapter 28

"**I**s something wrong?" Mary asked the next morning. "I mean, you're looking at me funny."

Was I? I couldn't help it, I guess. But, I didn't want to tell her she was my child right away. After Jack picked me up last night and we went home to discuss everything, it was decided I should take my time about this. Maybe a few days or so, or even a week or two, before I found the right time and location to share the news with her. As Jack said, it might be quite a shock to her and she's still dealing with other issues; she's unstable as it is. Maybe it's better to take more time and plan out the details first. He's right. Still, how am I going to keep up the appearance everything's the same between the two of us? In the meantime, I decided to share the news she was waiting to hear.

"Good news, Mary. I talked to Jean last night and she agreed you should be working here as an employee starting next week. It would only be for about twenty hours at first, and pays $10 an hour. That isn't much, but it's a start. What do you say?"

Mary started jumping up and down. Customers began turning our way and what Mary did next couldn't help but capture everyone's attention.

"Yippeee!" She screamed out. Then she squealed. "Thank you. Thank you both!" She looked over at Jean who already had a big smile on her face. "I'm soooo thrilled I'll be working here, not only volunteering."

The customers started to clap. The excitement Mary exuded was contagious. A few came over to offer their congratulations.

Mary stayed on for the entire day, even though she wasn't getting paid yet. We honored her with a celebratory

163

lunch, which consisted of ham and cheese sandwiches and leftover Chinese food from last night. All through lunch, she couldn't stop talking about how excited she was. It was a breakthrough for her—a new beginning.

Oh, how I hope she feels just as excited when I share the rest of the news. But it'll still be a while before I can, so I'm going to do my best to put it in the back of my mind right now. It won't be easy.

It seemed like it took forever for Saturday to come around again, although the week went by quickly enough and more than enough had happened since Tommy left. But, I still thought of him every night and missed him. I couldn't wait to talk to him. Finally, on Saturday morning, as soon as I woke up, I hit the programmed speed dial for him on my cell phone. It rang once, twice, six times! Then his voice mail came on . . . "Sorry I'm not available." I hung up knowing he never listened to messages. Darn. Maybe he was still sleeping. He'd call me back as soon as he saw the number on his caller id, though. I got ready for work and said goodbye to Jack.

Six hours later, I arrived back home and he still hadn't called. Maybe he'd sent me an email instead. I went right on to my computer to check, before even saying hello to Jack. There was nothing from Tommy in my Inbox, only an email from the editor of the newspaper. I opened it up.

```
TO: Rosie
FROM: Chad
```

```
Thank U for the articles. Good response to the
first two weeks columns. Attached are some com-
ments we've received.
```

It occurred to me that I didn't even bother to pick up the paper this week. What's going on? It wasn't like me to forget these things, especially since I've wanted to be a columnist for as long as I can remember.

I didn't bother to read the attached comments yet, either. My mind remained on Tommy. Why hadn't he called me? Was something wrong? Was he sick again?

"JACK?" I yelled upstairs to him. No response. I walked up the stairs looking for him and found him in the bathroom. He was leaning over the toilet bowl, puking his guts out. It was an all-too-familiar sight.

"Oh, no," I said. "You've got the bug Tommy and I had."

"Delayed reaction, I guess." He moaned.

I grabbed the wastebasket nearby and then reached for his hand.

"Here, hold onto me. Let's get you to bed."

Once I had him settled down, I took his temperature—101.5. He had the bug all right. Then, I gave him some Tylenol and he took it down with a few sips of water.

"Ohhh, this isn't fun." He moaned.

"No kidding. I've gone through it, remember? I thought you dodged it. Guess you weren't going to be that lucky."

That's when Jack shared the good news with me. "Oh, I almost forgot, Tommy called earlier. Everything is fine. He didn't want to bother you at work, so he told me to have you call him when you got back home."

I let out a big sigh. "Are you going to be okay for a few minutes?"

"Yeah, I guess."

"Good, because I'm calling Tommy. I can't wait to talk to him."

Heading into Sunday, Jack still wasn't feeling well, but, at least he wasn't running to the bathroom every few minutes anymore. It had been a long night. He couldn't keep anything down and his fever remained high. Not to mention, he wasn't very patient and continuously needed my help.

Men! They always moan and groan when they're sick, wanting us to take care of them like their mother's did when they were children. But when we're sick, well, that's a different story. It disrupts the whole household and they more or less just want us to snap out of it. That's another reason that when I was sick, the best idea was to stay at Jean's and away from him. Remember that, ladies. If you get sick, get as far away from your husband or significant other if possible. It makes it easier all around.

I could hear Jack snoring. What a relief. He was finally getting some sleep. I quietly got out of bed and went into the kitchen to make myself some coffee. Honestly, I couldn't have been gone two minutes when he started calling for me.

"Rosieeee," he whined out in a pathetic "I'm weak and need your help" tone. Oh no, so much for rest and relaxation. I sighed and then put on a nice smile and went to see what he wanted.

"Hi, honey. How are you feeling? Can I get you anything?" I sat down beside him and stroked his forehead. He didn't seem to be running a fever anymore. If he was, it must be a low grade one.

"I think I'm feeling better, although I'm still weak. Weak and sweaty." He reached for his blankets, trying to pull them off of him, but I was sitting on them so he couldn't. I got up and pulled them down just a bit. I could see his pajamas drenched in sweat. He must've broken his fever some time during the night.

"Jack, you're sopping wet, you must be uncomfortable. Here, take my arm. I'll bring you to the couch and get you settled there. Then, I'll get you a change of clothes and will put new sheets on the bed. How does that sound?"

"That sounds good, hon. And can you make me something to eat? Maybe a little toast and ginger ale? I think I can keep something down."

Yeah, yeah, I thought. I could see how the day was going to go. I'd be wiped out by the end of it, with Jack having me run around waiting on him hand and foot. Not that I really minded much—it was nice to be wanted—and I did understand how sick he must still be. Not to mention, I'm probably the one who gave it to him.

I felt exhausted already. It had been a long night, and a long week with all that went on. My emotions were frazzled and I needed some rest and relaxation. Hey, maybe there's a game on this afternoon that I could get Jack interested in. There's always at least one game on Sundays. He'll want me to watch it with him, of course, to keep him company. But that's okay—just being able to sit and have his thoughts occupied for a few hours will help. And maybe I can even knit for a while.

Still, it'll be a chore taking care of him. Hopefully by tonight, he'll almost be back to normal again.

Chapter 29

By Monday morning, Jack was well and rested, but I was a wreck. I started to look like Mary did when we first met her—disheveled, pale, out-of-sorts, with a lot on her mind. Jean noticed my demeanor right away when I came through the door. Max was just happy, as he always is, to see me. He came bouncing over to me, sniffing my pockets for a treat. Luckily, I always carried some treats around with me now.

"Here you go, boy," I said in a less-than-upbeat tone and I patted him on the head. When I looked up again at Jean, she was in a rigid stance, her arms crossed in front of her. She was also scowling.

"Look at you!" she commented. "You look awful. This is not the Rosie I know. I really think you need a vacation."

"Yeah, right," I scoffed. I proceeded across the shop to start preparing for the day. With the way I was feeling, I already knew it would to be another long and tiring one.

Jean didn't let up. "No, I mean it. You need to get away. When's the last time you and Jack took a vacation, just the two of you?"

"Ahhh." Jean was right—it had been a long time. Too long! "Let me see," I said, placing my right index finger up to my chin, "Two years ago, maybe three?"

"Then, that does it. Pack your bags. Call Jack. You're getting away. Not today or tomorrow, I need you, but Wednesday. Plan on it. I've got enough help here with Gertrude and Mary. I may even ask Mary to put in a full-time schedule this week. I'm sure she'd be thrilled to get in the extra hours and make the extra money. And then I'm sure Emma would be more than happy to be a backup."

"That's short notice," I commented. "Where would we go?

"I've got that all figured out for you, too. You'll go to the ocean—York Beach. That's where my cottage is. With the summer season now over with, it's not rented and it's yours for the rest of the week. You'll be only a few steps from the beach and there's a great view of the ocean right from the bay window. The cottage has a nice front porch to sit out on, too. Plus, there's television and cable for Jack's games and some of the restaurants and stores are still open. Come on, say yes already."

"Okay, yes, YES!" I exclaimed. The life in me was starting to come back just thinking about getting away. It would be great for both Jack and I, and we could talk about how we're going to proceed with Mary, and also about our future without children at home. I could . . . . Oh, I thought, it would be perfect.

"Jean," I said excitedly, "my bikini's done. I could bring it along, put it on for Jack. Maybe?"

"Now you're talking," she replied. "Okay, enough, it's settled. Tell Jack at lunchtime. Right now, it's time to get this shop opened and I have a hunch it's going to be busy."

My pace had picked up again and my energy was renewed. In no time, customers started streaming in. The morning, as well as the next couple of days before we headed out, went by in a whirl.

York Beach. I marveled at it as we drove north along a coastal road toward the cottage. The tide was in and the waves were high, crashing against the rocks. I could see the Nubble Lighthouse in the distance, a familiar sight.

When I was younger, I would go here often. My aunt owned a cottage around here she'd rent out for the season, and she would keep a few weeks open for Dad, Eloise and I. We'd have such fun spending days on the beach and I can recall getting more than my share of sunburns. Back then, lathering yourself with tanning oil to promote the sun's rays was the ritual, not putting on sunscreen to keep it away. We didn't think about skin cancer then, and since I'm half Irish, I'm susceptible to getting it. So is Jack.

I remembered back to many times waking up at the crack of dawn, heading to the beach with Eloise, and walking along it as I watched the sun rise over the ocean alongside the Nubble. It was breathtaking and also good for the soul. It made me realize every day was a new beginning.

"There it is," Jack pointed at a gray weathered cottage right across the street from the beach. It was situated at the corner of another road, the very road that my aunt's former cottage was on. What a coincidence.

Jean's place was perched up on a knoll, so I could see how there must be spectacular views from the windows and it did have a front porch with ocean views, like she said, yet much larger than she described it.

Jack turned onto the side street and into the driveway at the back of the cottage. I noticed a picnic table and covered grill on the lawn. Awesome! We could even barbecue here.

I told Tommy about the vacation before we left and he seemed happy we were taking some time off and getting away. Since York was less than an hour from Durham, where he went to school, he decided to join us at the end of the week, after his classes had finished. He said he'd be able to get a ride up Friday, and would stay with us until Sunday. It will be nice to spend some time with him so soon, while still giving Jack and me a few days also to be alone together. After all, I had plans of an intimate vacation. My bikini was packed in my suitcase, in a side compartment, hidden from sight so Jack wouldn't see it before I put it on and modeled it for him. I figured I wouldn't do that right away, maybe I'd wait until tomorrow night. That way, he'd be settled in, relaxed and, hopefully, ready for some fun between the sheets.

Although the cottage was weathered, looking a bit aged from the outside, inside everything appeared brand new. There were all modern appliances, including a dishwasher, although with just the two of us, I refused to use one.

The floor plan of the cottage was open concept and the décor and furnishings were ideal. The place was beautiful. Jean had really decorated it nicely. And I even noticed a nice gas fireplace in the far corner of the living room. What a perfect way to heat up the place. I went over and flipped the switch to turn it on. In no time, the cottage was nice and warm.

Jack found his way directly to the couch, I knew he would, and turned on the very large flat screen television set suspended on the wall.

"Wow," he exclaimed. "I think I'm going to like it here."

I stood right in front of him blocking his view. "Hey, wait a minute. Don't get too comfortable yet. There will be plenty of time to cozy up in front of the fireplace and watch television later. This is our vacation and that means going out and seeing the sights, and absolutely NO cooking, unless we decide to boil up a few lobsters and grill up some steaks when Tommy comes this weekend."

"It's only noon now, Rosie. We could sit here and enjoy the news, then maybe get the update on sports. After that, well, whatever you want to do will be fine."

That sounded fair. "Okay, I'll compromise, but as soon as the news and sports are done, which means about 12:30, you and I have to bring in the rest of the gear from the car. Then, we'll go to the restaurant down the road. I used to go there and I think it's still open. They'll have fried clams and scallops and that's what I want for lunch."

"Uckk!" Jack faked a gag. "It's going to smell fishy. You know I can't stand fish."

Jack used to eat fish when he was a kid. It's the tradition for Catholics to have fish on Fridays and his parents forced it on him. When he left his childhood home, he decided never to eat fish again. Now he's decided I can't even cook it in the house.

"Well, I'll tell you what, Jack. We'll get the food and bring it back here to eat then. But don't think I'm not going to have seafood and lobsters while I'm here. Maine lobster is the best and their seafood is to-die-for. I plan on having it morning, noon and night every day we're in Maine. In other words, get used to it."

"All right, All right," he groaned. "We'll eat there, though. I'd rather smell it for an hour instead of smell it for the entire night if it comes back with us."

I took my knitting out while we watched television. I was working on the scarf for Tommy and, since I also knit for most of the ride to the cottage, a good portion of it was done. Already I felt more relaxed than I'd been in a long time. When it was 12:30, I promptly reached for the remote, shut the TV off, and said, "Okay Jack, let's go. I'm hungry."

The clams and scallops were scrumptious. I ate way more than I should've and used more tartar sauce than the average diner. What a great combination. I also ate all of my French fries with loads of ketchup. Jack enjoyed a nice steak, baked potato and corn on the cob. The corn couldn't compare to the farm fresh butter and sugar corn we enjoy in the late summer months in the Lakes Region, but he seemed happy with his meal and didn't even comment about any fish smells. Honestly, I think it's all in his mind. If he would just sample some of the seafood I eat this week, he might be surprised at how much he might like it. Not worth even bothering trying to get him to taste it, though. I learned that long ago.

By the time we left the restaurant, I was so full I could hardly move, but knew the ideal thing would be to take a long stroll along the beach. It was a bit chilly and breezy, but we had brought along sweaters. We walked hand in hand right along the shoreline marveling at the sights. I noticed a couple of young boys building a sand castle and couldn't help but reminisce about when my boys were small. We used to come to this beach from time to time, even though the cottage had been sold off by then. Eloise would join us most times and Jack would always opt out. We'd sit in the sun, while they played nearby. They loved building the castles and then tearing them down before the water came inland. They also enjoyed jumping the waves and would stay in the water so long their legs would go numb. Then, they'd collapse in the back seat on the ride back home. Their faces and shoulders would be red from the sun, even though I made sure they both stayed saturated in sunscreen.

Back at the cottage, Jack turned on the television set again, but we both fell asleep on the couch. Several hours later, we woke up to a dark room, except for the glow from the fireplace. The place was toasty and Jack seemed in a good mood. My temptation was to go and put the bikini on, sooner than planned, but I refrained. No, I should wait.

That evening, we ventured out again to take a drive along the Nubble Road. We stopped to enjoy some homemade ice cream from a landmark ice cream shop always packed during the summer months, and then we went downtown, but because it was after Labor Day, most places were closed because the summer season was over. Luckily, though, we found an arcade still open for business so we went in, played a few games of Skeeball, and then grabbed some pizza. It wasn't very good—in fact it was quite bad, the kind of pizza you'd find in a convenience store that's been sitting under the heat lamps all day. But it was also cheap and available and we were still hungry.

Returning to the cottage around nine, Jack watched a game on TV while I explored the place more. I discovered some board games and a few puzzles. Choosing one of the puzzles, I spread the pieces out on the kitchen table and began to put it together. I can't remember the last time I had done one of these. Truth be told, I wasn't very good at putting puzzles together, but Jack was, and I hoped maybe he'd perk up an interest to help me with it during our week here.

It was the next morning and I knew the shop hadn't opened yet, so I gave Jean a quick call on my cell. I wanted to thank her again. Besides, I knew she'd want to hear from me.

"Hey, Jean, it's me. I just wanted to say thanks for convincing us to take a vacation. We're having a wonderful time already."

"Glad to hear it. How's Jack doing?"

"So far, so good. The 55 inch flat screen television on the wall is a big help. No, seriously, we had a great first day yesterday. I enjoyed some seafood, Jack ate a nice steak, we walked along the beach and we even played Skeeball last night at the arcade. How about that?"

"When in York, Maine, that's exactly what you do. Now remember, all of the stores should be open starting Friday for the weekend. Be sure to visit the place where they pull and sell the taffy—it's called Goldenrods—and make sure you bring me back some. A box of peanut butter taffy would be ideal."

"You've got it. It's the least I can do for all you've done for us. This place is fabulous. Honestly, how come you don't come here more often?"

"Well, I rent it out during the summer as you know," Jean replied. "But it holds some memories I'd rather forget. Bob and I used to have some hot and wild times there. I'm hoping you have some of the same."

"Me, too. I'm following through on my plan later this evening. Wish me luck!" I giggled at the thought of even discussing this with anyone else. Only my best friend could know my intimate secrets.

"Well, be sure to give me the results. No specific details, thank you very much, but let me know if it all works out. I'm thinking positive for you. Good luck."

"Thanks, Jean. See you soon. I hope all is going well at the shop and everyone misses me a little bit."

"More than a little bit. And Max has been searching for you high and low. Every time someone enters the shop, he hopes it's you."

Chapter 30

It was time to show off my new knitting project, and I was more than a little nervous about it. If Jack took this bikini thing in the wrong way, if it irritated him rather than aroused him, then it could ruin the rest of the vacation for both of us. I didn't want that to happen, but I had to go through with this.

Jack was perched in front of the television set watching *Law and Order*.

"Hey, I've got a surprise for you, hon," I announced. I came over to him and gave him a kiss. He was responsive. Then, I gave him a more intimate kiss.

"Love your kisses, babe." He said. He reached around and slightly squeezed my butt. My mind said the timing was right. It was now or never.

"I made something just for you. It's in the other room. Wait, I'll be right back." I touched his face with my fingertips and let them trail down the front of his chest. He had to have an idea of what I was thinking now. Still, he didn't seem turned off by it.

The bikini was more than revealing, and I was hoping it would help. I took a quick look in the full-length mirror in the bedroom before parading out in it. "Oh no!" I could see I'd gained a little weight the past few weeks—probably from eating all of that pizza and take-out since the shop opened. And then there'd been all of the seafood and ice cream indulgences the past two days. I'd been packing the weight on lately and not taking the time to exercise enough to get the pounds back off again. Oh well, this was how I was, pleasantly plump. Since Jack never complained about my weight and how I looked, I hoped it wouldn't matter to him.

It didn't. I sauntered out expecting to have to put on a little strip show or something to arouse him, but he was already aroused and waiting for me to return. He had stripped down to his boxer shorts and was lying on the couch. He motioned me over.

So much for the striped woolen bikini! I didn't need it after all, but he still took the opportunity to admire it.

"Mmmm, nice," He said as I stood there next to him. "Seems like it could be a little itchy, though."

"Just itching to be with you," I replied with a chuckle.

He undid the tie and the top of the bikini feel down to the floor. Then, slowly and lingering along the way, he pulled down the bottom half.

This is the moment, I thought. We're finally going to be together.

The lovemaking brought smiles to our faces that remained for the rest of the evening. Mission accomplished—the vacation was a success. Jack didn't have a heart attack, not even a slight pain, and now we could start making love on a regular basis again. At least I hoped so. And, as Jean commented earlier, since both of the kids were gone, we could do it in every room of the house if we wanted to. There are some things about the empty nest syndrome that aren't so bad.

We settled into bed that night totally exhausted and soon we both were fast asleep, but it was only a few hours later when I woke up in a panic. I also woke up Jack.

"JONATHAN!" I cried out. Jack immediately fumbled around looking for the light switch on the bedside table and turned it on. Then, he looked at me strangely and said, "What the HELL is going on, Rosie? What about Jonathan?"

"I forgot to call him," I replied much calmer now. "His apartment isn't far from here, right?"

Jonathan lives in Wells. We have only visited there once since he moved to Maine after graduating from college. That's when he got his new teaching job at the local elementary school. We've seen him several times this past year, but except for that one instance when we wanted to check out his new living quarters and where he worked, he was always the one to come home and visit us.

"I think it's the town just north of here. It's not that far. Why?"

Now I was looking at Jack strangely, wondering why he couldn't figure this all out. I wondered myself why I didn't think of this earlier—to invite Jonathan to come visit us while we were here. With Tommy coming this weekend, they'd want to see each other. And, of course, I wanted to see them both.

"We have to call him!" I started getting excited again. "We have to find out if he'll join us tomorrow for the cookout, if he can visit us here this weekend. It would be great, all of us together again and not even a holiday. Like a family reunion of sorts. Wouldn't it be wonderful, Jack?" I had already pulled the covers off of me and was about to get up. I wanted to get to my cell phone fast to call him before Jonathan made other plans.

Jack reached over and held me down, though. "HOLD IT RIGHT THERE! Are you crazy, Rosie? See the clock?" he griped. We both glanced at the illuminating digital alarm clock on the bedside table. The time was only 3:15 am.

"So?" I said. "I'll only wake him for a minute."

Jack rolled his eyes and gave me a glance that said, "Now I know you're crazy!"

"NO!" he replied. "Not on your life."

"But what if he has plans already? I've got to call him as soon as possible," I pleaded. Jack was still holding me down.

He didn't respond. He rolled his eyes again, took his arm away from me and reached over to the nightstand and turned the light off. The room was pitch dark. I couldn't see anything if I attempted to get up now. Just what Jack intended.

"If he's busy, he's busy," he grumbled. "I'm not going to have you phoning him in the middle of the night. He'll think something's wrong. No, that's that. You can call him later when the sun rises, at least wait until then. Now, go back to sleep!" Jack turned onto his side facing away from me and soon I heard him snoring.

"I tried to sleep also, I really tried, but my mind kept spinning and spinning with thoughts of this upcoming weekend. I couldn't stop thinking and it kept me awake. If Jonathan's free this weekend and could come by for at least the day, then the family would all be here and I could finally tell them both about their half-sister Mary. Of course, I wouldn't mention her name or reveal she worked at the shop. No, not yet. I'd have to wait until I let her know as well, but I could at least prepare them for the time when they would meet her, which I hoped wouldn't be too long from now. In the meantime, I could unload this secret I've carried for way too long. It would be a relief.

Really wanting to wake Jack up again to share my thoughts with him about telling the boys finally, I was just about to nudge him, but then decided against it. He needed his sleep and it'd be better if only one of us had to deal with insomnia. So instead, I just stayed as motionless as I could, not wanting to stir him, and waited for what seemed like forever. At some point, I must've dozed off.

When I woke again, the sun was peeking through the Venetian blinds of the bedroom window. The room was getting lighter. The nighttime had passed. I glanced up at the clock again. Ten past six. Good enough, I thought. I quietly got myself out of bed, went out into the other room and grabbed my phone. Jack was still snoring. Great. I called Jonathan.

"Please answer. Please answer," I whispered to myself hoping he'd still be at home. Being a teacher, he left early for work, but maybe if I was lucky enough, he'd still be there.

After four rings when I'd almost given up hope, a strange voice answered the phone.

"Hello?" It was a woman's voice.

Did I put in the wrong number? Couldn't have—I had it programmed into my phone.

"Hello." I replied hesitantly, not knowing whom this strange voice belonged to. Jonathan, as far as I knew, lived alone and I'd called his land line. He was one of those people that didn't believe in using cell phones except for an emergency, and then only if he made the call, not the other way around, so he usually kept his cell phone shut off. His land line was the only way we knew how to reach him.

"Uhmmm. My name's Rosie Bloom. I'm calling for my son, Jonathan."

"Oh, Mrs. Blume," the woman replied in an excited tone. "I'm Laura. Wait a minute. I'll get him for you."

"Jonathan." I could hear her calling for him. He was probably getting ready for work. I remembered the name Laura—she's the girl he told us about, the girl of his dreams he recently met. She was also a new teacher at the same school he worked at. I wondered if they were already living together. That would explain why she was there so early and had answered his phone.

"Hello?" Just hearing his strong deep voice made me anxious about seeing him soon. Oh, I hoped he was free.

"Hey, Jon Jon," I said cheerfully, forgetting he didn't like to be called by his childhood nickname anymore. When he graduated from college, he informed us he was giving up the name, retiring it. Too bad, I still liked it, and to me he will always be my Jon Jon, but I could understand why he preferred the name Jonathan or even Jon now.

"Sorry, no one by that name here," he replied slightly annoyed.

"I'm sorry—Jonathan. It just slipped out naturally. I wasn't thinking."

"I know. What's up, Mom? Something wrong?" He seemed concerned. It wasn't like me to call him on a weekday. Good thing I listened to Jack after all and didn't call him in the middle of the night.

"Oh, no, nothing's wrong. Quite the opposite. We're spending a few days at York Beach. My business partner, Jean, owns a cottage here and kindly offered it to us free of charge."

"Nice," he commented. "It's a great place to go to once the summer tourists have left. Otherwise, it's a bit crowded."

"It's not that far away from you, is it?" I asked.

"No, we're only about 20 minutes away."

I caught the word we—that's it! They must already be living together. Instead of commenting, I let it slide. As long as he was happy about this new girlfriend, so was I. Besides, she sounded sweet.

"Do you want to meet for lunch or something?" he asked. "I mean, you could come by here, but I'd have to clean the apartment first because Laura and I have been busy with the start of school and all. Oh no, speaking of school, make it quick, Ma. I've got to get to work."

"Okay, I'm sorry again." Why was I always apologizing to everyone? This was something I had to work on. "Yes, we'd like to meet for lunch, but we'd like you to come here. Tommy's arriving this evening and we're planning a big surf and turf lunch for Saturday. We'll cook up some steaks, boil some Maine lobsters . . ."

Jonathan cut in. "You're making me hungry! If you add in steamers, we'll definitely be there."

"Of course, I forgot. You love steamers." Jack wouldn't be thrilled, not liking fish of any kind, but he'd have to deal with it. After all, we were in Maine and Maine's seafood is the best.

"Just kidding," Jonathan added. "Well, not really, I'd love to have steamers, but we'll be there anyway, no matter what. I'll even bring some beer and stay to watch the game with Jack and Tommy. How's that? But in the meantime, I've really gotta run, Mom. Laura doesn't have to be in to work until later, so I'll hand the phone back over to her for the details. See you soon."

"I love you," I said. But it was too late—Jonathan had already passed the phone over to Laura.

"I'll be sure to tell him," she said. "I love him, too. Now, what time should we arrive and how do we get there? I can't wait to finally meet the family."

I gave Laura the directions to the cottage and told her we'd be starting up the grill around noon. We'd have the barbecue first. Then, we all could enjoy a walk on the beach together.

The game started late afternoon according to Jack, and I was hoping Laura would like to go shopping with me at the outlet malls in Kittery while the guys had their own time together. That would give us some time alone to get to know each other. I could also pick up some early Christmas gifts, a thank you present for Jean (reminds me I've got to get her peanut butter taffy, too), and maybe even something special for Mary. Then, when the game ended, I'd gather up the nerve to sit the boys down and tell them they have a half-sister. If all went well and they reacted positively to it, we could enjoy some sandwiches and leftovers from lunch after, before Jonathan and Laura headed back home again. Or, better yet, they could stay the night. There's plenty of room here for all of us.

After getting off the phone with Laura, I snuck back into bed. Jack stirred, reached over to me, and we made love again. It was blissful. We then showered together, dressed and went for another long stroll along the shoreline, stopping at another restaurant for breakfast. Life was good. As soon as we returned back to the cottage and I became out of earshot of Jack, I called Jean again on the cell phone.

"BINGO!" I announced when she answered and then hung up the phone. I'm sure she knew exactly what I meant. As for details, I'm one who believes lovemaking is a personal thing, so she wasn't going to get the details later, no matter how many questions she asked.

My arms wrapped tightly around Tommy when he arrived at the cottage Friday evening. I reached up onto my tiptoes to plant a kiss on his check. It had only been two weeks since we'd last seen him, but I could've sworn he'd grown another inch. He was already over six feet tall.

Tommy glanced quickly around the inside of the cottage.

"Wow, look at this place. It's so awesome! You said Jean owns this?" He continued checking it out, but his eyes kept going back to the television, the one Jack had been in front of for the past few hours. I was becoming annoyed he hadn't even gotten up to say hello to Tommy yet. This was an addiction already.

"Good thing we don't have one of those," Tommy chuckled. "Jack would be sitting in front of the TV more than he already does at home."

He took the words right out of my mouth.

"No kidding," I said sarcastically. "Jack, aren't you going to come and say hello to Tommy?"

No answer. I noticed I couldn't see the back of his head. Maybe he was in the bathroom or went to lie down in the bedroom when I wasn't looking.

"Jack?" I called again.

Tommy and I walked over to the couch. He was still there. His head had dropped down and he was leaning against a pillow. No wonder he hadn't answered when I called for him. No wonder he hadn't greeted Tommy when he arrived. Jack was out like a light, fast asleep.

I gently lifted both of his legs onto the couch so he'd be more comfortable. I grabbed a nearby afghan from a chair and placed it over him. He grunted and moved a bit, even opened his eyes for a second, but then he fell asleep again.

"It's my fault," I whispered to Tommy as I tiptoed away from the couch. "I woke him up in the middle of the night thinking about Jonathan. I called Jonathan first thing this morning to invite him here tomorrow for a barbecue. He's coming with Laura, his new girlfriend, and as I presume, his now new roommate."

"Great," replied Tommy, almost a little too loud. I was hoping Jack wouldn't wake up. I wanted Tommy for myself for a while so we could talk—just the two of us—like we used to almost every night at home.

"It'll be good to see him," he continued talking as we walked toward the kitchen area. He pulled out a chair at the table and sat down. "It's been a few months since he's been home, right?"

"Yes, it was the Fourth of July, remember?"

"Yep, that's right." He started glancing around again—along the counter, at the refrigerator.

I sat down next to him, hoping we could keep chatting for a while, but it became apparent Tommy had something more pressing on his mind.

"Ah, you got anything to eat around here?" he asked. "I'm starving."

Luckily, we'd done a bit of grocery shopping earlier in the day knowing Tommy would be hungry when he arrived. In fact, Tommy is always hungry. Who knew what he was eating now that he's in college and I'm not making his dinners for him anymore.

I prepared a couple of ham and cheese sandwiches and placed them in front of him, along with a tall glass of cold milk. It only took a few minutes for him to wolf them down. After he finished eating, he sat back, legs outstretched, and looking rather satisfied that he now had a full belly, he said, "Okay, Mom, whaddaya want to talk about?"

He knew me well. We were able to engage in a great conversation about his school, his new friends, the shop, and unfortunately, he didn't leave out the fact he still planned on joining a fraternity. He told me initiation started in a couple of weeks.

My stomach flip-flopped thinking about what he might have to do to become a member, but he added, "Don't worry, Mom. I can't tell you anything that goes on so you won't have to know."

Good grief! Like he thought a comment like that would ease my mind about it?

Chapter 31

I f I could've captured one day into a bottle to preserve it forever, it would've been Saturday. Jonathan and Laura arrived right at noon. Jack was just starting up the grill and I was attempting to get my nerve up to take the live lobsters out of their boxes and drop them into the hot boiling water on the stove. For some reason, it occurred to me I had never cooked them on my own and may not be able to do this—send live lobsters to their immediate death. The fish market where we went to pick them up earlier that morning had asked me if I desired them cooked already, but wanting to save the extra few dollars they would charge us for it, Jack had quickly said no thank you, we'd cook them ourselves. Of course, Jack wasn't about to touch the things. He not only didn't like to eat fish of any kind, he didn't even like to see it, especially alive. The clams weren't a problem for me, though. They were in shells and I didn't have to look at their tiny faces (that is, if they even have faces). I could steam them without any guilt. They were already cooked and sitting in a big bowl on the table next to some melted butter waiting to be eaten.

My eyes lit up as soon as I saw Jonathan and Laura getting out of their car. I was so happy to see him and so glad to meet her. As he reached out for her hand, I could tell already they both seemed happy and very much in love.

I turned off the stove. I would start the lobsters later. Right now, I wanted to say hello to my oldest son and his guest, so I hurried outside, joining Jack and Tommy, to greet them.

"Hi, Mom," Jonathan reached out and gave me a big hug. Then he shook Jack's hand and high-fived his brother. "I'd like you all to meet Laura." He leaned toward her, giving her a kiss on the cheek and making her blush.

I smiled at her to relieve any tension she might be feeling. She smiled back, it was a warm smile, and I knew my initial observations about her were correct—she was a sweetheart. I immediately liked her and I could tell both Jack and Tommy were also taken by her.

"Welcome," I said. "Welcome to the family. I motioned them all over to the table. Now, before we do anything else, let's start eating those steamers Jonathan demanded. They just came off of the stove and they're nice and hot."

"Yummm," said Tommy

"Awesome," commented Jonathan.

"No thank you," Jack added. "Count me out. I'm going back to the grill."

"Uhm, may I help you?" Laura said quietly to Jack as she turned away, not even wanting to have a glance. "I don't want to offend anyone, but I'm not into fish, so I don't like steamers. Can I hang out with you while they're eating them?" She looked up at him.

"A girl after my own heart," Jack chuckled. He put his arm around her and they walked over to the grill, far away from the picnic table and steamers. I could see they were already engaged in conversation and it was nice to see Jack already enjoying her company.

I didn't mind and wasn't offended she didn't want to join us. As much as I wanted to get to know Laura, there would be time for that later when the guys became engrossed in the game. And right now, I had my two wonderful boys all to myself for a while. Now, how long has it been since that happened? What a blessing!

"These are soooo good," Jonathan commented. He had already eaten a plate full and was still showing no signs of slowing down.

"We have plenty. I didn't know Laura didn't like them and I knew what you and Tommy could eat alone, but please remember to save some room for the rest of the meal. We have steaks, potato salad, fresh corn on the cob and lobsters. Oh my, the lobsters," I remembered. "Jonathan, have you ever cooked lobsters before?"

"Plenty of times," he answered. "It's easy. You simply drop them into boiling water and when they stop moving and turn red, they're done."

I shook all over at the thought of it. "Good. Then you and Tommy can prepare them. As for me, I can't do it. I don't want to be a lobster killer."

Both Tommy and Jonathan laughed.

"Come on, Tommy, let's make Mom's day and cook those critters up. You are going to eat them, though, aren't you, Mom?"

"Are you kidding? Of course I am. It's my favorite meal."

After enjoying all of the food, none of us could even consider moving, never mind walking a couple of miles along the beach.

"Let's wait until sunset to take a walk," Jack suggested. "Besides, there's an early game on as well. We can watch it before the other one comes on."

Laura and I glanced at each other. I rolled my eyes and, at the same time, she rolled hers.

"Don't worry, Laura. We don't have to spoil our day sitting in front of that set all afternoon. I was wondering if you wanted to do some shopping while these guys had their fun. Maybe go to the outlet malls in Kittery?"

"I'd love to," she said. "I've got Christmas shopping to do and maybe I can take care of Jonathan's gifts. You know him better than I do, so you can help me."

"Great idea," Jack replied, cracking a beer open.

"I'm glad you agree," I said. "Now, remember not to groan when you see the credit card bill."

Chapter 32

Laura talked nonstop on our way to Kittery. She's 23, the same age as Jonathan, and she grew up in Maine. She graduated from college this past year and was thrilled about landing a teaching job right after graduation. When she met Jonathan in July, being first introduced as a new addition to the teaching team, she fell in love with him at first sight. According to Jonathan, she said, he felt the same way. They started dating only days after meeting and she moved in with him two weeks ago. So far, it's been a whirlwind romance and she confided in me that she hopes it will last forever. In my heart, I do, too.

As we parked the car at a large outlet mall, I began to think of Justin again and how much I became infatuated with him when I was a few years younger than Laura. We, too, started dating almost immediately after meeting. He worked at a bank where one of my best friends also worked. She introduced us to each other. Later, she also slept with him right before we were planning to get married. That wasn't what called off the wedding, though, because I didn't even know about the incident when Justin disappeared into thin air before we were to tie the knot. Not a word from him. Not a sign of where he went. He just vanished. Only days later did I find out about him shacking up with her and also that he'd embezzled funds from the bank. The authorities were onto him and that's why he split. From what I know now, they tracked him down soon after and he spent two years in jail for the crime. If all of that hadn't of happened, I would've married him. Good thing. Sometimes what seems terrible at the time ends up being the best thing.

Laura and I enjoyed shopping together. She bought several clothing items for Jonathan, and seemed thankful I was able to assist her by letting her know the right sizes to choose. She also bought him a new best-selling mystery novel to read. I was thrilled to find out she also enjoyed reading as much as I did and didn't think Christmas was complete without receiving a new book.

"That way, when the excitement wears down, you can curl up and become lost in it," she said.

"I just love to get into my pajamas, drink a glass of wine and get absorbed in a book. I'll read for the entire day after Christmas," she continued. "Mysteries are okay, but I prefer a woman's novel. You know, one that includes some romance, a great looking guy or two, and a little tension or sadness leading up to a good ending. That's my favorite type. Oh, and I also like Christmas stories—all kinds. But I usually read those before Christmas. It gets me into the spirit of the season. Not a year goes by without picking up a new one and enjoying it right after Thanksgiving."

Laura and I seemed to have a lot in common when it came to reading books. I'd have to find her a special Christmas novel from the shop and send it her way.

When we returned to the cottage, the guys were still glued to the game.

I groaned as I approached them. "It's going on seven o'clock. The sun will be setting soon."

Jack turned off the television. "We were waiting for you to come back. The game is all over anyway. It's the top of the ninth with two outs. There's no way the Red Sox will catch up. They're three runs behind and no one's on base."

"Are you sure about that?" Tommy questioned. "You know they have a habit of catching up right at the end."

"Maybe, but we're taking a walk anyway. If they win while we're gone, I'll be ecstatic, but your mother's right and I promised her that walk."

The sun setting was a majestic sight. It looked like the sun dropped right into the ocean, turning it, as well as the sky, beautiful shades of orange and red.

I wanted to continue walking to the end of the shoreline and back again, but after the sun set, it began to get dark fast. I knew we needed to go back to the cottage, and I needed to tell Tommy and Jonathan about having a child out of wedlock. My stomach was doing somersaults in anticipation of what I was going to say. I hoped it wouldn't ruin the evening. After, I'd fix them dinner. It was almost 8 now, but too early to eat again. I had eaten too much at lunch and still felt full. I'm sure they all felt the same. Maybe later on they'd be hungry, provided the boys still wanted to stick around after what I had to do.

As we approached the cottage, I gently grabbed onto to both of the boys arms, pulling them back from Jack and Laura who were already heading to the cottage door.

"I have to share something with you guys. Something very personal," I said softly. "Do you mind if we stay outside for a couple more minutes, just the three of us?"

They both looked at me perplexed.

"Ahh, sure Mom, okay," Jonathan said and Tommy nodded in agreement.

I called out to Jack. "Go ahead inside with Laura. We'll be right in, okay?"

Jack already knew my plans so he wasn't surprised.

"Okay, Rosie. Come on, Laura, let's see if there's another game on TV," he said as he opened the cottage door.

Once they were inside, we all sat down at the picnic table. I was worried how I was going to begin. "This might come as a shock," I blurted out.

Neither of them spoke. Both of their eyes were glued on me.

I took a deep breath. "Maybe I shouldn't have started that way. Okay, I'll begin again."

"Before I met and married your father, I was engaged to someone else. Someone I met in my early twenties."

"So?" Jonathan asked. "What's so strange about that? Why do we even care?"

I shot him a glance.

"Well, hear me out. You'll come to understand. Anyway, the guy left me at the altar so to speak. He took off before we said our vows. A few months later, I found out . . ." I hesitated. My mouth was dry and my insides were shaking.

I took a few more deep breathes, gathering up enough nerve to continue.

"Okay, I'm just going to come out and say it. Well, a few months later, I found out I was pregnant. I almost chose to have an abortion, but then Eloise knew of a distant relative who desperately wanted a baby. So, instead I went to a special place for unwed mothers, gave birth, and then gave the baby up for adoption. Until recently, I never knew if it was a boy or a girl or if I'd ever meet them."

"I can't believe this," said Tommy. "First, Jack has some kid claiming to be his son which turned out to be a farce. Now you're claiming you've had another child? Why didn't you tell us sooner, Ma?" Tommy looked hurt. My heart was breaking knowing he was right. I should have.

"I was afraid to, Tommy. Can you understand that?"

He put his head in his hands and shook his head no.

"C'mon, Tommy," Jonathan piped in. "Let's give her some slack. It couldn't have been easy keeping it from us for so long."

"It wasn't," I added as I let out a deep breath. "I was embarrassed and ashamed and wanted to keep the past behind me, but Eloise saved pictures in case I wanted to find out someday. Then the adopted mother called her a few weeks ago, asking to get in touch with me. I knew it was time to face it all. And it wasn't fair for both of you to not know you have a half brother or sister."

"And did you find out?" asked Tommy, looking directly at me again. "Is it a brother or is it a sister?"

"It's a sister. You have a half-sister. She's 25 years old. I know you will like her."

"And when will we meet her?" This question came from Jonathan.

"Soon, real soon. I know who she is, but she doesn't know about me yet. I have to tell her first, and then I promise you'll all be introduced."

Suddenly, there was nothing but silence. They were trying to take it in. I rose from the table and walked inside, leaving them alone to discuss what I had said.

SIMPLE PLEASURES

A weekly column by Rosie Blume

Sometimes a simple pleasure isn't what you seek out or plan to do. Instead, it comes from somebody else's efforts and often when you least expect it.

It could be a letter in the mail from a person you love

A Facebook friend request from someone you care about, but haven't seen or heard from for so many years

A hug, a gesture, a kind word, a sincere thank you

Or a bunch of beautiful flowers arriving to lift you up when you're feeling down

And there are also times, plenty of times, when a simple pleasure doesn't come from anyone's efforts at all, but rather from an act of nature itself.

The sun peeking through the clouds on a dreary day

> The sound of falling rain

> Birds chirping

> A gentle, soothing breeze

> The smell of fresh green grass

No matter where simple pleasures come from, they are blessings, and many times go unnoticed, especially when life gets
tough.

But that's exactly when you need them most.

So, do me a favor—stop what you're doing, right now, wherever you are. Just take in a deep breath, relax, clear your mind
from all its worries, and spend the next few moments to ...

Count your blessings.

It's another simple pleasure that will make such a difference.

(And then maybe consider being a blessing, in some simple
way, for somebody else.)

Chapter 33

Well rested from the vacation, I was thrilled to be back to work. Max scurried over to greet me. I bent down, gave him a hug and a pat, and reached into my coat pocket.

"Okay, Max, today you get two. Now, give me your paw."

Reaching out my hand, he lifted his right front leg up to me. He was shaking all over with excitement.

"There you go, boy." He gobbled the biscuit down in two bites and kept lifting his paw to me to show he wanted more.

"New trick. Lie down, boy."

He immediately dropped to the floor.

"Now roll over," I motioned with my hand to show him what I wanted him to do. He rolled quickly and then sat down and lifted his paw.

"Okay, okay, buddy. Good job!" I gave him the second biscuit, ruffled the top of his head, and stood back up. Expecting Jean would give me grief for paying so much attention to him before I'd even said hello to her, I was surprised she hadn't said anything yet. I glanced around. She was nowhere in sight, so I started up the stairs.

"Jean? Where are you? Are you coming downstairs?" I called out. Still no answer. I let myself into the apartment, and as I walked around in search of her, I heard a moan. Then, Jean finally called out, "I'm in here. In the bathroom."

That's when I heard the heaving. Oh no, Jean had caught the same stomach flu.

I peeked in at her. She was squatting on the floor, her auburn hair pulled back and her face almost into the toilet.

"I've been puking since early this morning. There's no way I'm going to be able to work in the shop today. It looks like you came back just in time." She moaned again.

"Oh, Jean, I'm so sorry. Maybe if I hadn't stayed in this apartment when I was sick, you wouldn't have gotten it." I rubbed her back in a gentle motion knowing it would help her feel a little better. "Let me get you back to bed. Then, I'll bring you a cool washcloth and something to keep by the bed in case you get sick again. Also, I'll pour you some ginger ale. There should be some left in the refrigerator."

After getting her settled under the covers, I quickly went and got the wastebasket from the bathroom, minus the partially filled trash bag in it that I tied up and put aside. I ran a washcloth under the water before I headed back to her room.

"Rosie, please sit for a minute. I want to talk to you and ask you how your vacation went. You can get me some ginger ale before you go back downstairs in a couple of minutes. I know you have to get the shop ready to open, but I want to see you first. I've missed you."

Pressing the cool towel on her forehead, I replied, "I've missed you too, Jean. We had a wonderful time, thank you so much. It was the best vacation ever. Jack and I spent a lot of quality time together and our kids were with us all weekend."

"And you finally did it!" Even though Jean wasn't feeling well, she still was able to chuckle at the thought of me seducing my husband with that handmade woolen bikini.

"Yes, we did. Several times. Jack's not afraid anymore and that bikini is going to be framed and hung on our bedroom wall reminding us to never be afraid of something that's so damn good!"

"Rosie, you swore!" Jean looked shocked.

"Of course I did. Everyone swears sometimes, what's wrong with that? You think because I'm a born-again Christian means I don't swear?"

"Well, some would say . . ."

I didn't give her a chance to finish. "Yeah, some would, but no one wins their way to heaven. It's a gift, plain and simple. And after you receive it, it gets planted in your heart. That's another thing for you to remember."

Jean closed her eyes and drew in a deep breath. "It feels so good to be back in bed. I've been in the bathroom for hours. Oh, I almost forgot to tell you, Mary was sick also."

"Oh?"

"Yeah, she got the bug, too. She came down with it right after you left for vacation. That's how I finally must've caught it. I guess it's highly contagious."

"Oh, that's terrible. It must have been awful being sick and living in a shelter. I wonder if she had anyone there able to watch over her."

"She didn't need to. Of course, I wouldn't let her be alone and sick there. I let her stay here with me until she felt better. It was the least I could do with all she's done, and also knowing she's your daughter."

I put my finger up to my lips. "Shhh, remember you can't breathe a word to anyone, at least not until I've told her."

"Whoops! Rosie, I think I blew it. I mentioned it to Gertrude, but I told her to keep quiet about it. Don't worry, she won't say anything."

Don't worry? "Jean, how could you? Can't you keep a secret?" I became so mad at her all of a sudden. What was I going to do? I hadn't planned on telling Mary right away about this, but now I had to. I couldn't chance her hearing it first from someone else. She'd never forgive me for it.

"Is Mary coming in today?" I asked, trying to calm myself down. I knew Jean hadn't meant any harm, but it irked me she had such a big mouth.

"She'll be in this afternoon, right after lunch. This morning, it'll be just you and Jack."

I glanced at my watch. Quarter till nine. "Okay, we'll manage, and after work tonight, I'll have to use your living quarters to break the news to her. Thanks to you, I need to tell her as soon as possible."

"Do the kids know already? Did you tell them this weekend?"

"Yes, and they took it well, after the initial shock. Still, I have to get in touch with Eloise to see if she's heard anything else from the adoptive parents, and I need to tell her I know now and am planning to tell Mary. I'll have to do that before Mary arrives."

I went into the kitchen, poured the ginger ale for Jean, and brought it back to her. I asked her if she'd taken any Tylenol—she had—so she was all set for a while. I hurried back downstairs to prepare to open the shop. No one was at the front door waiting to get in. What a relief. My mind was racing thinking about the day ahead and a few more minutes without customers would be helpful. Jack was due to arrive at ten. I could manage alone until then.

It was still quiet when Jack arrived. I asked if he could handle the shop himself for a few minutes and explained what I had to do. He was okay with it, so I ran upstairs and, after checking to see if Jean was okay, I called Eloise.

"Eloise? It's me, Rosie."

"Oh hello, Rosie. So nice to hear your voice. Is everything okay?"

"Yes, everything's fine. I called to tell you I finally opened the envelope. I now know my birth child is a daughter and she's very pretty. Thank you for collecting all of those pictures for me over the years."

"Oh, I'm so glad you finally opened it. The mother has called again and has plans to contact you soon. She said their daughter, Mary, had been upset at them. There was a falling out of some kind after they found out about her dating this guy they didn't like. He'd been a bad influence on her and she got involved in some drinking and drugs. Then she became depressed. She was going for psychiatric help and that's why they wanted to contact you before—to see if depression ran in the family. I told them of course it did, your dad was depressed and so was your grandmother, but it was because of the accident that killed your mother when you were young. Anyway, she and her parents had a big fight and Mary took off. They haven't seen her since and it has now been several weeks. So, naturally, they're very concerned."

I didn't want to speak with them right away. First, I wanted to talk to Mary and get her side of the story—it could be quite different. I did want to tell Eloise to inform the parents not to worry, though, imagining how distraught they must be unaware of where she is and if she's okay.

"Eloise, please do me another favor. Call them back and tell them I will be in touch soon. Tell them I know where Mary is and she's okay, but I can't say anymore right now."

"You know where she is? How could you? You just found out about her."

"I know, I know, but believe it or not, she was already in my life when I found out. You see, Mary came into the shop when it first opened. Now she's working for us part-time. Long story. I'll explain more later on and please keep this confidential for now. I don't think she knows about the adoption and she definitely doesn't know I'm her natural mother. I've got to tell her. Today. Tonight. Say a little prayer for me that it will all turn out fine."

This was playing out like a novel or maybe even a soap opera. How can things happen like this? A child I gave up for adoption 25 years ago comes back into my life by coincidence? I didn't believe in coincidences. Everything happens as it is destined to be, that's what I believe. Knowing this is the only thing that's kept me from getting overwhelmed by all that's been happening this past month. Otherwise, it's all, well, unbelievable.

The day continued to be slow, so Jack excused himself soon after Mary arrived. A lot of restocking had to be done since several boxes of books arrived in the past week and Mary didn't want to shelf them until I gave the okay. We spent most of the afternoon unloading them, cataloging them on the computer and placing them on the shelves and display tables. We took a break at three to drink tea and chat with a couple of new ladies who'd discovered the shop and were visiting for the first time. By five, when the store closed, we were both ready to sit down again and relax.

"Whatcha doing for dinner?" I asked Mary.

"Nothing planned. Why?"

"Jack isn't expecting me until later. How about we go check on Jean and then have something to eat? I can make us an evening breakfast, how does that sound?"

"Bacon and eggs?" she asked. "That sounds delicious."

"Better yet, since I don't know if Jean has any food up there, I'll order two full breakfast platters from the diner next door—they serve breakfast all day—and I'll even get some soup for Jean. She should be feeling better by now."

"No clean up—sounds great. Here, let me give you some money." Mary reached into her pocket, pulling out a couple of bucks, probably all she had.

"Not on your life," I said. "I'm paying for this. Go on upstairs and tell Jean I'll be right back. I headed to the front door with Max at my heels whining to go with me. Mary had taken him out earlier to do his duty, but he probably wanted a walk. I could walk him around the block after I placed the order. It would only take about ten minutes or so, and the food would be ready by then. It would also give me a chance to clear my head and gather my thoughts about what I was going to say to Mary. How would I be able to explain to her why I had to give her up for adoption? Would she understand and still like me after I told her?

"Remember, Rosie, all things work out as they are meant to," the little voice in my head reminded me as Max and I were walking out of the diner. We strolled leisurely down along Main Street, up Pleasant Street and then circled back. Returning to the diner to pick up the food, I felt much more relaxed and relieved the time had finally come to tell her. Even if Jean was a loud mouth and couldn't keep a secret, I had been delaying what needed to be done and was glad I wasn't going to delay it any longer.

When I entered the apartment, Jean was feeling better. She was sitting on the couch looking less pale than before, although still dressed in her pajamas. I could tell by the smile she greeted me with, the worst of the stomach flu was over for her.

"Hungry?" I asked both of them.

"Famished," Jean was the first to reply. "What did you get me?"

"Well, since I didn't know how you were feeling, I got you some homemade chicken noodle soup."

She frowned. "I thought we were having breakfast. Mary said you were getting bacon and eggs."

"I did get that for Mary and me, but I didn't think you'd be up for it. It's a little much after just being sick, don't you think?"

"No." She looked like she was going to cry. Honestly, what a pain in the butt she can be.

"Don't cry," I replied. "We can share. They always give more than enough anyway. I'll give you a little of each of ours and will put the soup in the refrigerator for later on. How does that sound?"

"Sounds good," Jean said. "Now, let's stop figuring this all out and eat before it gets cold. I can't eat eggs when they're cold."

"She's definitely feeling better," added Mary, "but I agree, let's eat."

After dinner, Jean left me with the dishes to wash and went back and sat down in the living room. I was about ready to kill her. Sure, she wasn't feeling well earlier and I probably was the one who started everyone getting the stomach flu, but she seemed to be feeling okay eating our meals. Since we had ordered out, there were only a few plates to wash, so it didn't bother me much. What did bother me was that Jean was fully aware I needed time alone to talk with Mary. So why was she still hanging around? I decided instead of sending her back to her room, I would find an excuse to bring Mary down to the shop and we could talk there. As Mary finished wiping the last dish dry, I suggested it.

"Now that we're done, come downstairs with me. I need to show you something."

Jean stood up from the couch like she wanted to go with us. I gave her the evil eye, sending her the message she'd better smarten up and smarten up fast. There was no way she was going to be with me when I told Mary the news.

She got the message and sat back down. "I'm too tired to join you," she said. "I think I'll stay up here and rest."

"Good idea," I replied.

Mary looked suspiciously at both of us. She knew something was going on.

"What're you going to do, give me the boot? You don't like how I stock the shelves or talk with the customers?"

"No, nothing like that. Just come downstairs. Like I said, I want to show you something."

We both sat on the antique couch in the sitting area. My hands were shaking and I think Mary could see I was nervous. She was nervous too, not having any idea what was going on. I rose to get my bag in its usual spot under the cash register. Bringing it back with me, I sat down again next to her, opened it, and pulled out the manila envelope. I undid the clasp of the envelope carefully, hesitated, looked up at her, and then pulled out the photos.

"Here, look at these." I handed them to her.

She took them and started glancing at the one on top. It was a photo of her when she was only about a year old.

"This one seems familiar," she said. "It almost looks like . . ."

She carefully looked at the next photo and the next one. Her mouth opened wide in disbelief. She then glared at me, suddenly angry.

"Are you a friend of my parents? Did they hire you to spy on me?"

Never did I guess I would be accused of something like that. I'd thought the pictures would do most of the explaining.

"No, please don't be mad. I don't know your mother or father. I've never even talked to them."

"Then why do you have pictures of me? What's this about?" Mary appeared puzzled.

I took the photos from her and placed them on the table in front of us. I reached back over to her and took her hands.

"You were adopted when you were a baby."

"NO WAY," she yelled. Tears started flowing from her eyes.

"Yes," I replied gently. "You were adopted. Twenty-five years ago. I know because I'm your birth mother."

"Screw you!" she said. She got up from the couch and headed to the door. "I need to get the HELL out of here NOW. You're crazy!"

"No, no I'm not," I pleaded with her as I followed behind. "Please don't go. Please! I didn't know you were my daughter. I didn't even know I had a daughter until right before I went on vacation. I just saw those photos myself the other day and found out about you. I'm so sorry, Mary."

She turned on her heels and faced me, her eyes still pouring out tears, her face red with rage. "I always suspected I was adopted. I didn't look like my parents and somehow felt different. But they never told me. And now this! This! If you are my real mother, then why'd you give me up? Huh? WHY?"

"BECAUSE I HAD TO," I screamed back. I started becoming angry now, not at Mary, but at the memories of losing her the first time. I didn't want to lose her again.

Tears were now streaming from my own eyes. It was hard to talk. I was choking up, remembering how I felt back then giving up my child. How awful it all was. How I had my baby safe inside of me, moving around, and then my precious child was gone. There'd been a hole in my heart since then. I had given my baby away to strangers. Still, I was

202

telling the truth. I had to do what I did back then.

I tried to calm down, but the sobbing wouldn't stop. All of my energy was drained. I collapsed down to the floor. Closing my eyes, I cried and cried. Mary was going to walk out that door and I may never see her again. I wanted to continue pleading for her to stay, but I was wrapped up in my own grief and couldn't even talk. I couldn't hear anything. Maybe she'd already left.

A hand reached down to me. It was Mary's. "Please get up, Rosie. I'm sorry. Let's go back to the couch and talk. I want to know what happened. I want to know why you had to give me away."

She was offering me the chance to explain. I managed a smile, but she didn't smile back.

"I'm still angry, but if I don't hear you out, then I'll never know the truth," she added. "I still may walk away."

I understood. But, she seemed willing to listen first. I got up from the floor, wiped my eyes with my sleeve and we proceeded to the couch. We sat there in silence for a few minutes, not looking at each other, until both of us calmed down a bit. Then I started to talk.

"I was only 21 years old and my fiancée had just deserted me. I didn't know until after he left that I was pregnant. I thought about having an abortion. He wasn't coming back and I felt desperate. There was no way I could handle being a mother. Luckily, though, I confided in my stepmother, Eloise, about my plans. She offered to help."

My eyes began to tear again, so I wiped the tears away with my hands before proceeding.

"She was distant relatives with a woman who'd tried to conceive for years, but was unable to. She and her husband were older and getting beyond the age where it would be safe for her to carry a child. Eloise thought it would be a blessing to them if I carried the child full term and let them adopt the baby. As part of the arrangement, the new parents were willing to pay for my expenses of staying in a home for unwed mothers until the birth. This included all medical expenses being paid by them, something I couldn't afford. They also agreed to send photos of the child every year to Eloise who would give them to me when the child turned eighteen. Then, I could find out who they were and decide if I wanted to contact them."

"But I turned 18 seven years ago. You told me you just found out."

"I never opened the envelope until last week. I was afraid to. I didn't even know if I'd given birth to a boy or girl. I never even got to find out. They were afraid I would change my mind if I saw my baby and they were right! We were already bonded—I regretted ever giving my baby up for adoption."

Mary put her head in her hands. She was sobbing again. I wanted to reach over to her, but it was best to just keep talking. To get it all out of me, no matter what the outcome was.

"That was me!" she replied. "That was me you gave up!"

"Yes," I said softly. "I'm sorry. I didn't want to give you up. I loved you with all of my heart. For the past twenty-five years, there's been an empty feeling inside of me. It was selfish of me, I should have let you be, but I couldn't get you out of my mind. Then, your mother called Eloise. She was concerned about you and wanted to talk to me. She said there were problems and she wanted medical history."

Mary looked up again. "You said you didn't talk to her."

"No, not yet, I haven't. She called Eloise a second time to say something had come up, and she'd call again in a few weeks. I had to find out who my child was before she contacted me directly. It was time to know. Imagine my surprise when I saw those photos."

"The same way I felt," Mary said somberly.

"Yes." That's when I reached over to her and took her hand again. "It wasn't an accident that you found your way into this shop. It's all meant to be. Neither one of us knew. Neither one of us could've imagined."

Mary leaned toward me placing her head on my shoulder. I hugged her tight. "Forgive me, Mary. I'm sorry. I'll leave you alone if you want me to, but I love you and I'm so glad I've finally found you."

She didn't pull away. We just stayed there for a long time hugging each other and crying together. When the tears stopped and both of us were ready to talk again, Mary said, "So, I'm not an only child after all."

"No, you're not," I smiled. "You have two brothers. Tommy, who you've already met, and Jonathan—he's 23 and lives in Maine."

"Not the same father?" she asked.

"No, I never saw your father again until. . .well, until earlier this year."

"Oh no, my father is that Justin guy—the guy I met at McLean Hospital. You mentioned you were engaged to him."

I lowered my head. "Yes, Mary, Justin is your father."

"Does he know about me? Does he know he fathered a child?"

"Not yet. That's a long story. We'll figure that out together as to when, and if, we should tell him. And not even Jack knows about this yet, so let's keep this to ourselves for now. I'll tell him soon enough."

Mary nodded in agreement.

"Hey, it's getting late," I said. "And Jack would probably appreciate me getting home at a reasonable hour. How about if you stayed over? We have plenty of room at our house. You don't have to sleep in the shelter anymore. You can stay with us until you figure things out with your parents."

"You know about that?"

"Not much more than you've already told me. Eloise said there was a fight between you and your parents and you took off. That's how you got here, I guess. Weird, huh, how things work out even without us being aware of what's going on?"

"Yeah, REAL WEIRD!"

"But beautiful, too. Like I said, I'm so glad I found you. And everything will work out, just wait and see. I'm sure your mom and dad are scared to death about where you are right now and if you're okay."

What a relief to know Eloise would tell them Mary was okay. That would have to do until Mary decided to talk with them again. I couldn't push her on that. It was her decision.

I was thrilled when she decided to take me up on my offer to come back and stay at the house. We said goodbye to Jean, stopped by the shelter to pick up her belongings, and Jack welcomed her when she got there, already knowing what my plans had been. He glanced over at me to get the assurance everything was going to be okay, and then after I gave him the thumbs up, proceeded to entice her to sit down in front of the television and enjoy the rest of the game with him. It was a bonus Mary also was such a sports fan.

"How about making some popcorn for us, Rosie?" he called out to me.

"And something to drink?" added Mary.

"Yeah, sure," I replied.

Everything's going to be okay after all. Everything's going to be fine.

Chapter 34

It was already the middle of September. Tonight was going to be our first knit and read event. Mary was still staying with us, and hadn't called her parents yet, but was at least thinking about doing so in the near future. She wanted to eventually tell them her plans for staying in the Lakes Region, hopefully getting a small apartment she could afford, and also about her new job. They still didn't know she was working in the shop. Jean and I decided that within the next month, if sales kept up as well as they have been, we would hire her on full-time. She was wonderful with the customers, knew a lot about books and even was becoming quite the knitter. Already she had finished the scarf, a hat to go with it, and was currently working on a sweater—a challenge I hadn't even seen Jean try to tackle yet. She also planned on making one of those bikinis.

I gathered a few books to suggest for our first reading assignment, and Jean made copies of a hat pattern she wanted the group to knit.

"How many are we expecting?" I asked.

"At least nine," Jean replied. "I talked with Emma earlier and she's still hoping her son George will join in also, even though he hasn't committed to it yet. How about Jack?"

"Well, I thought he would enjoy it, but he's opting out for tonight. He's really not into the group things, although I know he'd like it. Maybe I can convince him to come next week, but quite honestly, I didn't have the energy to try too hard to get him here tonight."

Jean looked at my stack of books. "That's a good assortment. Which one do you think they'll choose?" she asked.

"Beats me. I already have plenty of copies of *The Cheerleader* and it would be nice if they chose that one with the author being from New Hampshire and all, but I could order more of the others and get them here within a couple of days."

"What about this Anne Tyler one? Sounds interesting. Isn't she your favorite author?"

"She's one of my very favorites. I love all of her quirky characters. Just like all of us."

When Emma arrived with George, I thought Jean was going to pass out again. There's no doubt about it, he was as handsome as they come—wavy dark hair, deep brown eyes, muscular, a nice smile. It seemed he had it all. Except that he was shy and appeared nervous. That's when I remembered he was agoraphobic, like Jacob was.

Still, she was gawking at him and doing everything but drooling. It didn't take a rocket scientist to see she was mesmerized right from the start.

"Hey," I whispered to her, "try to close that mouth of yours. It's so wide-open, a bird could fly in it."

"What?" she looked at me like she was in a daze.

"And remember," I continued, "this is a knitting and reading class. It's not let's just stare at Emma's son and fantasize time."

"Huh?" she replied, still apparently lost in another world.

"Snap out of it!" I said a little louder, but out of earshot of the others. "Pull yourself together and get over it for now. We can talk about how good-looking he is later. And maybe if he'd talk a bit tonight, you could even get a glimpse of his intelligence and personality."

"Okay, I know. It's just he's soooo . . . "

"Yeah, I know that. Now, let's start up. Everyone is here and waiting for us to begin."

She continued to be paralyzed with her gaze on George, so I could see she needed help. I took her arm and walked her over to a chair. Then I sat down beside her. The rest of the group was already seated in a circle facing us.

"We're a bit nervous about tonight, so please forgive Jean for seeming lost for words." I glanced over at her. It looked like she was beginning to come around. "Not that Jean's ever lost for words," I added, "but I'll begin tonight. First, let's discuss the book we might want to read and discuss these next few weeks and then Jean will get you started on the knitting. How does that sound?"

Everyone nodded in approval.

"Great! I have a few here to consider, but I encourage all of you to also make suggestions. We'll then take a vote and the book that gets the most votes will be the one we read first."

I reached down and picked up four books from the table. "Let's see, this one is *The Cheerleader* by Ruth Doan MacDougall." I lifted it up so everyone could see the cover. "She's a New Hampshire writer and she wrote this best-seller, the beginning of a series, back in the 70's. It contains many landmarks of the area, so I thought it would be a good choice." I passed the book to Emma who was sitting on the other side of me. I wanted everyone to also be able to read the description so they would get a better idea of what it was about.

"Okay, the second one I suggest is *The Help* by Kathryn Stockett."

"Oh, I've been wanting to read that," commented Morgan, one of the young mothers in the group.

"Me, too," said her friend, Heather. It was nice to see both of them here.

"Yes, it's very popular. It's a debut novel and very well-written. You won't be able to put it down. Is there anyone here who has already read it?" A couple of hands went up. I passed the book to Jean to circle around the other way.

Both of these seemed to generate interest, but there were still two more to consider before anyone else offered suggestions. I'd already taken up about 15 minutes and the gathering was only scheduled for an hour-and-a-half, so I decided to move things along.

"I'll just pass these other two books around for consideration as well. *Water for Elephants* by Sarah Gruen is a great read. Everyone I know who has read it already puts it on the top of their list of favorites. And the last one is by my favorite author, Anne Tyler. It's called *Digging to America*. Now, while you're looking these over, Jean can go over our first knitting project. Then, we can have other books suggestions and make a final decision. Sound okay to you?"

Everyone nodded again in approval.

Jean finally joined in. "As everyone knows, we're going to start with a basic hat—a chemo cap. It's fast and simple and, although you knitting pros will make one in no time, you'll be able to also help those just beginning to knit."

"I'm going to need all of the help I can get," said Heather. "I've never knit anything in my life."

"Oh, don't worry, we'll help you," replied Emma. "It'll be fun and you'll get the hang of it fast, I promise. Right, Mary?"

"Oh, yeah, I just started knitting as well and now I'm making a sweater, see?" She lifted up what she'd been working on since the beginning of the gathering.

"That's good to know," added Heather. "I really came here for the book discussion, but now I'm also anxious to learn how to knit. I'm a bit uncoordinated, though. I'll warn you ahead of time."

Jean passed out the pattern and told everyone what supplies they would need to purchase to start their first project. The classes were free, but she also had done her best to keep the costs down on the necessary supplies so everyone could afford to participate. The hat would only require one set of size 10 needles and a skein of cotton yarn.

After a few other book suggestions, we voted, and the book *The Cheerleader* won for two specific reasons. One was that no one in the group had ever read it, and the other was because of the local landmarks. It was the perfect choice and there already were enough copies here for everyone to either purchase or borrow—they could start reading the first few chapters right away.

I went to get the copies I'd put aside already and brought them to the counter while everyone was browsing through the shop and picking out their yarn and needles. Only Mary needed to borrow a book. The others decided to purchase theirs outright.

"Helps support the shop," Emma said as she paid for two of them—one for herself and one for her son.

George still seemed withdrawn. He didn't leave his seat to look for yarn. He didn't talk to anyone. When we all sat back down again in a circle, I looked at him more closely. He appeared white as a ghost and scared. Jean, who kept gawking at him all evening, also noticed his demeanor. She went over to him, whispered something in his ear and, holding onto his arm, walked with him to the other side of the shop. Then, she sat him down, proceeded to run upstairs and came back with a small paper bag.

"Here," I heard her say. "Breathe into this slowly. It will help."

Okay, so he was hyperventilating. It was nice to see Jean helping him. The others, except for Emma, were so thrilled looking over their new books and yarn that they failed to notice George and Jean had gone missing. Since it would probably be a few minutes before they both came back to join us, I figured I would get everyone started on their knitting.

"Now when you're ready, cast on 40 stitches. If you don't know how to do that, maybe someone who does can show you how."

Mary paired up with Morgan and Emma with Heather.

"Once you get that done, follow the instructions. It's a simple knit pattern for the next six inches of the hat. Again, for those who already know how to knit, please help the others just starting out."

I went over to our sound system behind the counter and

turned on some soft music hoping the newbie knitters, once they'd gotten over the initial frustration of learning, would be able to relax. It worked. They were all engrossed in knitting their hats, some slowly, some quite fast, and enjoying each other's company in the process. Since I didn't have to speak anymore, I rose again from my chair and started the coffee. I set out pastries Jean had purchased at a bakery earlier, along with plates and utensils. We'd end our first gathering with some refreshments.

There were many comments of gratitude as everyone left the shop. I told them all to read at least a couple of chapters before next week so we'd be able to discuss the book. Phew, I was glad it was over. Jean didn't appear to be, though. She spent most of the evening nursing George in the corner and keeping him from getting a full-blown panic attack. It seemed she enjoyed being with him way too much.

"Don't think that I'm going to let you leave me alone to give this class one more night. Next week, I'm the one who's going to sit back as you do most of the talking. Fair is fair," I said.

"But, he needed my help," she replied defensively.

"And you loved every minute of it!" I said back to her. I knew Jean all too well and she was crazy about any good-looking man who happened to come along. Tonight, it just so happened to be George.

Chapter 35

"**R**osie!" It was two weeks later, on another Sunday morning. I didn't know why Jean was calling me and why she seemed in such a panic. Maybe it was because her date with George hadn't gone so well. Since he still had a hard time going out in public, Jean went over to visit him at Emma's house. I wonder if Emma stayed around to chaperone. I would have to ask her.

"What's wrong, Jean?" Didn't go so well last night? Did Emma stay around and mess up your plans to seduce him?" I chuckled.

"Don't even talk about my date last night! Yes, it was a disaster, but that's not why I'm calling. There's even a bigger problem—something that would ruin my life forever."

Okay, this was Jean being dramatic again. I should be used to this by now. It could be she just ruined a few of her nails, or that Jacob didn't Skype her, or he'd gotten mad at her for dating his new friend. Nevertheless, I had to listen to her apparent problem—that's what best friends do for each other.

I tried to sound serious. "All right, Jean. What's going on? Maybe I can help you figure things out."

"Well, I don't know if you can, but I have to share this. It's awful, absolutely awful."

My patience began getting thin. It was so early, the sun had just come up, and this was the only day of the week I could sleep late. This better be good, I thought.

I waited for her to continue talking, trying not to doze back off.

"Rosie, you didn't fall back asleep, did you? ROSIE?"

"I'm here, now tell me or I will fall asleep." I took a glance at the alarm clock—six o'clock! "Gosh, Jean, this is a record for you. Please, why'd you have to call this early?"

"I had to, that's why. I'm worried, Rosie. I don't want to say this, don't want to even admit it, but I didn't use any contraceptives when I slept with Bob—didn't even think about it—and now I'm two weeks late for my period!" Jean let out a breath, like it was a relief blurting it out to me. "Please help me, Rosie. You're the rational one. Tell me what to do."

"Have you considered buying a pregnancy test and finding out the results? I mean, that's the easiest way and you may very well be worried for nothing. You're fifty-one years old, you know, and probably going through menopause. It's not unnatural to skip a period."

"Well, I've never skipped one before and I'm not having any hot flashes or anything. You're making me feel old, real old. And as for the pregnancy test, I can't get myself to do it, I'm too scared. Instead I'm thinking of setting up an appointment to see a gynecologist. I haven't gone to one in five years, so maybe I should."

"Maybe?" I was shocked. "How about a mammogram? Have you had one of those yet?"

"No, why would I? I've heard it feels like two 2x4's smashing your breasts and flattening them like pancakes. The pain must be unbearable. Besides, no one in my family has had breast cancer. There's no need."

Now I wasn't just shocked, instead I was madder than hell. Jean's an idiot. She hasn't been having her annual check-ups or mammograms. These were important, especially at our age.

I took a deep, long breath. After taking a second to calm down, I thought up a plan. Jean was willing to see her gynecologist, so maybe if I promised to go with her, she would also agree to be thoroughly checked out.

"Tell you what, Jean. Go ahead and call for an appointment. Get it as soon as possible. But if you want my support, you'd better have the full exam. And if it turns out you're

not pregnant after all, I want you to also have a mammogram—it's for your own good. I'll go with you, too. That way,
if the pregnancy result comes back positive, which I doubt
it will, then you'll have someone to cry on."

Jean hesitated. "I don't know. I think your tricking me
into something I don't want to do. Isn't the pregnancy test
enough? I mean, what if I am pregnant? What am I going
to do about it? I can't have a baby at 51. It can't even be
healthy to have one at my age. And what would Bob say?
Damn, I must be the most fertile woman around. I became
pregnant the first time I ever had sex with Bob and now,
after abstaining from it for so very long, the first time I
sleep with him again, I get . . ."

"Don't even say it. You're working yourself up over nothing. Like I said before, I don't think you're pregnant. I think
it's only the changes. Face it, Jean, these are the menopausal years."

Jean scheduled an appointment for Tuesday morning.
We had Mary and Gertrude covering the shop and, since my
own gynecologist was in the same building, I decided to stop
at the reception desk while Jean was in with her doctor to
schedule my own appointments. There was a last minute
cancellation that came in—they were able to take me right
away for the mammogram. What a convenience. I decided
I'd be done and over with it before Jean was finished with
hers.

The procedure took no more than 20 minutes, but when
I returned to the waiting room, Jean was there waiting
rather impatiently. I observed her closely—there were tears
in her eyes. Oh no, I thought, can she really be pregnant
after all?

"Sorry, Jean, I was able to get my mammogram done
also—last minute cancellation. I hope you haven't been
waiting too long."

She flipped her hair back showing her annoyance with
me and started walking out the door. I followed behind.

"Jean, I said I'm sorry."

"You said you'd be here for me for support. You weren't. And now what am I going to do?" Jean face crumbled and she started crying even before we got to her car. She unlocked the doors, slid into her seat, and dropped head forward onto the steering wheel.

I slid in next to her and placed my hand on her shoulder. "Like I said, I'm sorry. I really thought I'd be done in time, and I never believed the results would be positive."

She didn't look up, but she did stop crying. "What? Who said the results were positive? I'm not pregnant, Rosie. It was like you said, I skipped my period. I'm menopausal, I'm, I'm . . . ," she stammered. "I'M AN OLD BAG!"

The dramatics had returned. I threw my head back and started laughing. I couldn't stop. This made Jean all the madder.

"What the hell are you laughing about? I'm old, I said. Old. Lady. Old! The gynecologist told me I was indeed menopausal and should expect my periods to cease completely soon. She told me there's no way I would ever be pregnant again."

"Well?" I continued chuckling. "That's good news, right? You won't have to worry anymore if you decide to sleep with Bob, or George, or anyone else."

"Just stop talking," she said. "Damn, you really make me mad sometimes. You really don't understand. After all, you're still a few years younger. You haven't even hit the big 5-0 yet. Life goes downhill after that!"

"Does it?" I stopped laughing. "Well, maybe you've had your traumas, but life's not so bad now. You have the new shop and you've met a new man. You've recently gotten back from spending a week with both of your boys. What's missing?"

As soon as the words were out of my mouth, she yelled back "BUT I DON'T HAVE A MOTHER." Then, she cried even harder.

Okay, I understand now. I lost my mother when I was only five and, still to this day, I wish I could talk to her.

Everyone wants a mother to talk to, and even though Jean held a grudge against her mother marrying Walter and they didn't talk for two years, they reunited earlier this year and Jean was able to spend some quality time with her. The bad part, though, was not long after they reconciled, her mother was diagnosed with inoperable cancer and died soon after. Their time together was short and Jean still feels cheated.

"I understand, Jean. Go ahead and cry. It will be good for you. I'll give the shop a call and tell them we'll be a little late. We can go through the drive-through at Mr. Burgers, grab some food and something to drink, and then we'll head over to the park and talk for a little while longer. That way, you can get your feelings out and I'll listen. Then, we'll go back. Your red eyes should be clear by then. No one will notice anything's wrong."

That's exactly what we did do and it was just what both of us needed. Jean shared her grief in losing her mother and in also letting her husband go. She also talked about Jacob and how she still wished she felt differently about him. She really believes he's her soul mate and misses him terribly, even though it's only been about a month since he went back to Cleveland and they still talk and see each other almost every day on Skype.

When she finished talking, I also shared my feelings—about not having Tommy home anymore, about Mary being my birth child, about finally making love with Jack. I didn't share the details—they were private—but I did thank her again and mentioned how important the vacation had been for both of us.

By the time we returned to the shop, it was close to tea time and there were several women and even a couple of men sitting around chatting with each other. Emma was knitting away and George was beside her. He looked up eagerly at Jean when she came near. I could tell he'd become infatuated with her, but I couldn't yet tell what she thought about him. I had the feeling, though, he was just a replacement for Jacob and I hoped she wouldn't break his heart as well. Later, I'd have to discuss this with her and stress how important it was to share her true feelings with him right from the start.

"So there you two are," commented Emma. "We've been here close to an hour waiting for you to get back. George has something important to tell you. I'm sure you'll want to hear it. Go ahead, tell them George."

"Uh," George shifted his eyes toward the floor and seemed to be stammering. I didn't realize how shy he really was, but I wasn't surprised. It had been years since he even dared walk out of the house and this is as far as he's gone. I do know he's in therapy now, though, thanks to Jacob's urgings.

"Go ahead, George. Tell them."

"Okay," he replied. "I did something good today—I went for a job interview."

"He did. He really did. Can you believe it? I am so proud of him," Emma cut in.

Jean blew up over Emma's intrusion. She crossed her arms and glared at her in defiance.

"Stop talking to him like he's a child. He's a grown man. He has agoraphobia, that's all." She then turned and looked at George. "That's great. When will you know if you get the job?"

"Next week," he said. He was still looking down. I don't think he knew how to deal with his controlling mother. We all liked Emma, and I hoped how Jean addressed her now didn't upset her to the point she wouldn't want to come around anymore. However, it wasn't looking good. Emma seemed clearly upset and was about to speak her own mind.

"Now, see here young lady." She put her knitting needles back in her bag, stood up and gave Jean the evil eye. As she pointed at her repeatedly with her right index finger, she said, "Don't EVER try to talk to me like that again. You don't know George that well—I do. And he doesn't mind the way I speak to him. Do you, George?" She glanced his way briefly before glancing around at all of us. "I'm being a good supportive mother and I'm proud of him, that's all."

George didn't respond. I could tell right away he was

afraid of her. Still, I didn't want Emma to leave angry. Jean shouldn't have come on so strongly. She should've known better. Too late now—what's said is said. But I needed to say something myself to help calm everyone's feelings.

"Emma, Jean does realize you care for George. Don't you, Jean?"

I looked at her intently, so she would get the cue. You'd better agree, I thought.

She nodded her head in agreement. So far, so good.

"I'm pretty sure Jean just wanted George to have the chance to speak himself. It's been a hectic day for both of us. We're both tired and on edge. Don't take it personally." Again, I looked at Jean.

"Isn't that right?" I asked her.

She nodded yes again and then she opened her mouth to say something. Oh no, I hoped she would be helping instead of hindering. We couldn't afford to tick off our customers, especially when they were so supportive of our business and we'd become so close to them.

"Yes, Rosie's right," Jean said. "I'm sorry, Emma, I am frazzled and it all came out wrong. We're all proud of what George accomplished today. I'm sure it wasn't easy for him and I know you feel the same."

That was what Emma needed to hear to calm down. I wanted to commend Jean for saying she was sorry, but I couldn't right now. I'd have to say something to her later when the shop was closed. It was hard for her to apologize, especially since I was aware she meant every word she said defending George. She'd already told me Emma was always butting in, and when she was at Emma's house with George, she never left them alone for a minute. She was always nearby chaperoning to make sure they didn't get that friendly. George must be in his mid-fifties, so even I agree behavior like that is a little extreme. What he needs to do is get a job, as he is trying to do, start making enough money to afford his own apartment, and get some space between him and his mother. Otherwise, she will hinder his ability to become independent again, no matter what she says. It's just the way Emma is—a nurturing sort who can get a little too carried away. She has already tried to mother both Jean and I before and offer us advice. I have the ability to brush it off, but if she keeps on doing it to Jean, there will be a major blowout between the two of them before too long. At least we were able to keep it from happening today. In the meantime, George hadn't been able to tell us any more about his job interview so I asked him again. Maybe this time he wouldn't be so nervous to answer and his mother would stay quiet long enough so he's able to speak on his own.

Emma was sitting down again engrossed in her knitting, not looking directly at Jean, but not seeming angry anymore. The others sitting around were chatting amongst themselves while sipping their cups of tea.

"George, please tell us how the interview went and if you think you'll get the job. We all want to know," I said. Everyone around the table stopped talking to listen. They all were interested.

"Well, it went as well as expected. At least I didn't have a panic attack, but I was nervous," he replied. "And I don't know who else applied for the job, so I don't know my chances. It's in a printing shop. I'd work in the back room with a few other guys. They said they'd call me by the end of the week."

"Well, I'll be hoping and praying for you, George. It would be a good start." I shot a glance over to Emma. She seemed happy he was sharing the details with us. The others added their support saying they'd be rooting for him. Jean was quiet in the corner, probably thinking about something else. For all of the comments she'd made earlier about George after she met him—how handsome he was and all—I didn't sense she really had become very interested in a relationship with him. She'd better not lead this guy on. He was a nice person and I didn't want to see him get hurt. He'd already been through a lot with his wife dying of cancer and losing his employment and his home.

Chapter 36

In only two weeks after announcing she wanted a place of her own, Mary had rented a small apartment in the downtown area within walking distance from work. She dragged me from the shop one afternoon to show it to me.

"It's so exciting," she squealed. "My very own place. I can't wait until you see it."

It made me smile seeing her so happy. Still, I would miss having her stay with me and Jack. With Tommy gone, the house had seemed so empty. Since Mary had joined us, it came back to life again. I know I'd work with her daily in the shop, and we'd go out occasionally, and continue to get to know each other better, but I was especially going to miss our nightly chats after dinner while Jack had his eyes and ears glued to the television set. Of course, if there was a game on, Mary would watch it with him. It made me realize how much Jack was going to miss her, too.

We walked up three sets of stairs before reaching Mary's door. I'd become so out of breath by the time we got there. Geez, I really was out of shape.

She nervously placed the key in the lock and demanded I close my eyes first.

"Taa Daa!" she exclaimed as she nudged me forward into the apartment. "Now you can look."

I slowly opened my eyes, kind of scared of what I might see. What if it turned out to be a dump? How could I react without hurting her feelings, especially since she's so excited about this place?

It was a pleasant surprise, though—much better than I expected. The apartment seemed spacious, and so nicely decorated. I was instantly impressed. However, it didn't take long for it all to register in my mind that she couldn't have possibly done this on her own.

"The place is beautiful, Mary. But, ahhh, how did you afford all of the furnishings and decorations? I mean, you were living in a shelter before coming to stay with us, and you only work part-time."

Mary gave me a big grin. "That's what's so wonderful, Rosie. It was all Jean's doing. She found the place, decorated it without anyone knowing, and then surprised me with the key. Jean also paid my deposit and first month's rent. Can you believe it?"

Sure I could, I should have known. A pang of jealousy instantly shot through me. How could she do this without telling me? After all, I'm Mary's birth mother. If anyone should've helped Mary find and decorate this place, it should've been me.

"Oh no," Mary said suddenly. "I blew it, I promised not to tell."

"Promised who?" I asked, like I didn't know already.

"Promised Jean—she thought you'd be mad at her."

Oh, she was so right. Wait until I get back to the shop. Now it's my turn to tell Jean to stop butting into MY business!

I continued to seem happy for Mary, but inside I was fuming.

Mary hadn't come back with me after showing off her new apartment, and the shop closed soon after, so I was able to talk freely and tell Jean exactly what I thought about her getting involved.

"How could you, Jean? The place is beautiful, but I should've been the one to help Mary find it. I'm her birth mother, remember, not you."

Jean had just finished replenishing some yarn that had sold earlier "Oh, for heaven's sake, Rosie, get over it. I didn't want Mary to tell you because I knew you'd be upset. The opportunity arose, and I took advantage of it. If I hadn't of acted on it fast, someone else would've instead, and it's so close by, she can walk to work. You should be happy she has a nice place to live now. I was going to tell you, but I wanted you to see it first. I didn't want to ruin Mary's excitement in showing it to you herself, that's all."

"But...." I stammered. "Mary's going to be living right next door almost. You'll get to see her all the time." The jealousy I was feeling was now full blown and I was surprised by my own comments to Jean. My anger annoyed me. What was all this really about?

I had become close to tears. Mary had a nice place already—she was living with me and Jack. Now we won't be able to talk every evening. The house will be empty again. I won't have anyone to hang out with while Jack is glued to the television. I then realized being upset had nothing to do with Jean finding and decorating the place. Instead, it had everything to do with Mary leaving our home. I really didn't want her to go, at least not yet.

It was as if Jean had been reading my mind. She came right up to me, placed her hands firmly on my shoulders and looked directly at me.

"She's not going anywhere, Rosie. She'll still be at the shop," she said sternly. "She'll have her own place, that's what she's wanted, and you and Jack will also have some privacy again. It's all good news and I only helped her out a bit to get her started."

"Okay, okay, I'm sorry. Forgive me?" I frowned.

"Of course I do," she said. She lifted her eyebrows and made a funny face to try to cheer me up.

I did manage a weak smile. "Thank you, Jean, but I'm still concerned about Mary. She's only working twenty hours a week now. How can she afford a place so nice, even if you did pay her deposit and first month's rent?"

"Well, that's something I wanted to discuss with you. The customers love her and she really does help us. Also, it's continuing to stay busy at the shop and the holidays are approaching. How about if we begin to schedule her full-time? What do you think, Rosie?"

"Oh, Jean, that would be wonderful! Getting a full-time paycheck will definitely help.

I felt much better now—the jealousy had gone away. I reached out to Jean and gave her a big hug of gratitude for all she had done for Mary.

The following day was Saturday, and it was a beautiful crisp October morning. Gertrude offered to help Jean at Simple Pleasures, so Mary and I could spend the time together and take a drive down to Manchester to visit with Eloise. The ride down was enjoyable and both of us marveled at the colors of the autumn leaves along the way—vibrant reds, yellows, and oranges all mixed together creating an awesome display. What a sight! New Hampshire is especially beautiful this time of year and many people from all over come to admire the foliage during these months. There's no other place I'd rather live, especially in October.

Eloise was thrilled to see both of us. She embraced Mary like she'd known her all her life, although this was the first time they'd met. Mary also seemed comfortable with her right from the start, so she wasn't shy like she sometimes tended to be.

Within a first few minutes of meeting, Mary had already told Eloise all about how she had been depressed and how her parent didn't understand what she was going through. She shared how she had taken off without their knowledge, heading north, and not knowing where she'd end up.

"It was scary living in a shelter," she said. "I was almost out of money and about to head back home. But somehow, I found my way into Simple Pleasures. A sudden smile came over her face. "It has made all the difference!"

Eloise turned my way and winked. We both knew there were no coincidences in life.

As we were sitting on the screened porch of the nursing home, continuing to talk while enjoying the foliage and crispness in the air, Mary reached into her rather large pocketbook and pulled out a small gift bag. She handed it to Eloise.

"Here, I made something for you," she said.

Eloise seemed surprised and delighted. "For me? Why, you shouldn't have."

"It's nothing big—just something I knitted recently. I hope you like it." Mary gave her a shy smile.

Gently, Eloise removed the tissue paper to reveal what was hidden underneath.

"Oh my," she exclaimed. "It's beautiful." She pulled it out to admire it.

It was a purple scarf made with alpaca yarn.

Continuing to admire it, Eloise held it between her hands, patting it gently to feel the softness of it.

"You're a great knitter, Mary. The stitches are so even. It's the nicest scarf I've ever seen. I can't believe someone as young as you enjoys knitting. I thought no one knit anymore, except us old folks."

"Hey," I protested. "Watch out who you're calling old! Remember, I knit, too, and I don't consider myself a senior citizen yet."

Both of them chuckled.

"Really, a lot of young people like to," I added. "Mary's one of them now, thanks to Jean and the other customers who frequent the shop and knit during our afternoon tea time."

"And it's such a relaxing hobby," added Mary. "The only hard part is deciding what project to do next."

We spent a few hours with Eloise on the porch, eating some sandwiches I had brought along for lunch. Then we took her for a stroll in her wheelchair. As we were walking and continuing to admire the foliage, Mary came up with an idea.

"Hey, let's collect some leaves. Then we can press and preserve them," she said.

Eloise's eyes lit up. "I haven't done that for ages. Wouldn't that be fun, Rosie?" She turned and looked up at me.

"I think it's a great idea," I replied as I reached down to pick up a beautiful yellow leaf off the ground.

We became engaged in gathering leaves of all different colors and sizes, enough so Eloise could share them with her friends at the nursing home, and enough so we could also bring some to Jean as well as the participants in the knitting and reading group. Mary also thought it would be a great activity for the group while we discussed the book we were reading, especially since it was not only by a New Hampshire author, but also took place in New Hampshire.

When it was time to go, Mary asked Eloise about her parents. "Have you heard from my mom and dad lately? I'm wondering if they're still mad at me."

I could tell that, despite the separation, she cared deeply for them.

"Yes, honey," Eloise replied. "I've heard from your mom and I assured her you were fine. She's anxious to speak with you."

"Did she seem mad at me?"

"No, I don't think so, only concerned. You did say you'd call them soon?"

Mary hesitated and then said, "Yes, I did, and I will in the next few weeks. I really want to patch things up with them, let them know I'm okay and tell them what my plans are now. I'm just afraid to."

"Now, now, Mary," Eloise gave her a pat on the shoulder. "It'll all be okay. I know your mom well and she loves you. If you're doing fine, and I can see you are, then that's all she'll be hoping for as long as the drugs and alcohol are no longer in the picture."

Mary raised her eyebrows in surprise. "Drugs and alcohol? Did my mom also tell you about all that? Why would she do such a thing?"

By the look on Eloise's face, I could tell she immediately regretted what she had said.

"I'm sorry, honey, she was only reaching out for help. She said the doctor needed to find out if it ran in the family."

"And it does," I interjected. "I started abusing drugs and alcohol when I was younger. Eloise can attest to that. It took a revelation to get me over it."

"You? Had an abuse problem?" Mary eyes were wide open in astonishment. "I can't believe it. You're so straight and narrow."

"Yeah, I know, but it happened and I'm not proud of it. Still, I don't regret it because of where it led me to. The same is true for you."

"You're right," Mary replied. "I never thought of it that way. If I hadn't gone through all of that crap, I wouldn't be here right now. I wouldn't be working at the shop and I wouldn't have met you."

It was like the revelation was a sudden relief. I could see her begin to relax.

"All worth it, right?" I asked, hoping she wasn't regretting all this.

"You betcha!" she said. "I love you, Birth Mom!" She reached out and gave me a kiss on the cheek.

When she did, my eyes filled with tears. So did Eloise's. Who would've ever imagined how wonderful it could all turn out after all these years of missing her?

Eloise looked up at me and then over at Mary and said, "Never doubt. All things work out one way or another—in God's time, not ours."

I can remember her saying that very comment to me when I was mourning the loss of giving Mary up for adoption.

And many years later, look where we had come. A wonderful afternoon together, a bonding long overdue, a future filled with hope and promise . . .

And no more secrets.

Chapter 37

Our last knitting and reading class was about to happen, and everyone had already finished reading *The Cheerleader*. Most had knit their hats, too, except for George who decided it wasn't his thing. Still, he had come to most of the classes and seemed much more comfortable in a group setting. He had also gotten the job at the print shop and was doing well. It paid nowhere near as much as he was used to getting, but it was a start. Jean still flirted with him, too, and they dated occasionally—if you could call visiting each other's homes a date. She'd made it clear to him, though, that they were just good friends.

It was almost closing time. Mary was busy preparing for the group to arrive. She had already put out a display of leaves on the table, as well as wax paper, scissors, card stock, glue and a big box of crayons. She also set up Jean's ironing board and iron.

"There, we're all set," she said as she rubbed her hands together in anticipation. "I can't wait to do this. I've already done some research on the Internet and I've added a little something to make it special. Be prepared, ladies, for some arts and crafts tonight."

"Can't wait," exclaimed Jean as she rolled her eyes. "This looks like a project for a six year old."

"And those are the best kinds," I added, not wanting to ruin Mary's excitement. I knew it would be fun. "What's wrong with being a kid for an evening, anyway?"

"I don't know, I guess you're right," said Jean. "Sorry, Mary, I'm sure we'll have a good time."

"Just you wait and see," replied Mary. "In fact, I'm willing to bet you're the one who gets into it the most when you find out what we're going to do with these leaves once we press them."

As soon as everyone arrived, Mary took over the class. She explained how we would discuss the book as planned, but that she had a little project for us to do as well.

"Can you remember the last time you pressed leaves?" she asked everyone.

"Oh, it's been ages," replied Emma. "When the kids were young, we'd do it every autumn. We had so much fun."

The others nodded their heads in agreement.

Morgan's eyes lit up. "This would be the perfect project to do with my five year old. She's been bringing me leaves for the past week, but they're just collecting on my kitchen table. Now I'll know what to do with them."

"My daughter and I have also been collecting leaves, but I've never tried this before," Heather commented.

"That's great," said Mary. "So let's get started. Find a leaf and then cut some wax paper so you can cover it on both sides. I'll stand by the ironing board, so once you're ready, form a line over here and I'll show you how to press the wax onto the leaf to preserve it. Oh, Jean, I forgot, I need a cloth so I won't ruin your ironing board. Can you run up and get one?"

Jean rolled her eyes again. She still wasn't thrilled by this idea.

But a little later on, after everyone had pressed their leaf and Mary explained how we were going to cut them out, glue them to the card stock, and then create a card for someone very special, Jean got right into it, like Mary said she would.

"So who'd you make your card for?" I asked Jean after everyone had left.

"Who do you think?" she replied.

I decided to get her worked up again. "Was it Bob?"

"Are you kidding me?" she huffed. "After he dumped me again? No, it's not for Bob."

"Hmmm, let me think....maybe George?" I did everything I could to keep myself from laughing, but I couldn't help but snicker.

"NO, NOT GEORGE." Jean became irritated which made me snicker some more. "I've told you already, he's only a friend—no one special. Our cards are for someone special, remember? So who're you giving yours to, like I can't guess?"

"All right, I'll answer first. I was going to give it to Jack, like I know you thought I was, but he's not into this stuff and wouldn't appreciate it. So, instead, I'm giving it to you, my very best friend."

"Really?" Jean's eyes opened wide. "Oh, now I feel bad. I'm really sorry. I should've made my card for you. It's just . . ."

"I know, I know, you don't have to tell me. You made yours for Jacob, right? And why? Because you miss him and wish he was still here."

"Yeah, I did, and you know what Rosie? I'm beginning to think I've been comparing him to Bob all this time, like he was supposed to turn me on the same way or something. But it's different with Jacob. I only want to be with him and miss him when I'm not. Maybe that's telling me something. Maybe it could work between us after all."

"You think?" I replied. "Jean, I believe you're beginning to see what love really is all about. Sex is great, but it's not the only thing that matters. Only time will tell if you're meant to be together in that way."

"You're probably right, but I've been such a jerk to him lately, telling him all about George like he's my new boyfriend. I think I was only trying to replace Jacob, but it didn't work because he's not Jacob."

Jean covered her hands with her eyes. Her body started to shake and tears began to seep through her hands.

Then she leaned in towards me for comfort. "Oh Rosie, after how I've treated him, I hope he still wants me."

Chapter 38

The mammogram and other gynecology results for Jean came back normal. Everything was fine, despite her lack of check-ups in earlier years. As for me, I hadn't heard anything back regarding my own mammogram and I was starting to get concerned as to why not. I decided to contact the office one morning when the shop was slow. I went up to her apartment, claiming I had to use the bathroom so I could make the call.

"Hi, this is Rosie Blume. I came in a few weeks ago for a mammogram and I haven't heard anything back yet. I have a yearly exam coming up in a few weeks, maybe the doctor's waiting for that, but I want to make sure everything is fine." The receptionist excused herself and put me on hold for more than a few minutes.

Ordinarily, I would've assumed all was okay, as it always was. A postcard would usually end up arriving in the mail with a big smiley face affixed to it. That's their way of saying results were normal—nothing to worry about. But no card had come and I had been doing my own self-exams lately, every time I took a shower and when I remembered. And it was just the other day I thought I may have felt something on my right breast not far from my armpit. It felt like a small pebble, a little bump. At first, I didn't think much about it, but I became anxious to get the results to confirm it was nothing to be concerned about.

The receptionist came back on the line. "Name again and date of birth." She sounded like a recording, not pleasant at all. I tried to stay cheerful in case she was having one of those days, but I was slightly annoyed she had me wait on hold for so long.

I gave her the information she requested. I could hear her keyboarding through the phone line.

"So you're 47 now. Okay. I don't see that a postcard has been mailed to you. You may be right—the doctor may be waiting to speak to you when you come in again, but also there is a backlog—she's been very busy." The reception-ist paused briefly, and then said, "Wait, what's this? Okay, maybe . . ." She stopped there. I wondered if she was going to tell me something might be wrong. Maybe they found something unusual.

I figured I'd let her know my concerns. "I recently did a self-exam and thought I felt a small, bump. It's really important I talk to the doctor as soon as possible." I still tried to be pleasant, but wanted to also be direct and insist-ing. I wanted to make sure the receptionist didn't take my request too lightly.

"Okay, the doctor's with a patient now, but I'll give her a message to contact you as soon as possible. You should be hearing from her by the end of the day."

"Sounds good. Thank you so much and have a nice day."

She didn't respond, she just hung up. What's happened to quality customer service these days?

"What's wrong, Rosie," Jean asked as I closed my cell phone. I didn't hear her enter the apartment and had no idea how long she'd been listening.

"Oh nothing much," I replied. "I haven't gotten the results of my mammogram back and I was wondering what was taking them so long, that's all. I figured I'd check in with them." I didn't want to mention I had felt something on my right breast the other day. There was no need to get her concerned.

"Are you sure you're telling me everything?" Jean looked at me suspiciously. "If there was something wrong, you would've heard right away. I wouldn't worry about it."

Hmmm, what a good thought. Maybe I'm getting wor-ried over nothing. At least I didn't have to wait much longer. By the end of the day, I should know for sure.

My cell phone rang later that afternoon. I looked at the display—it was the doctor's office. If I ran upstairs again, Jean would really be suspicious, so instead I found a quiet place in a nearby corner of the shop before I answered.

"Ms. Blume?" Dr. Reynolds asked.

I could feel myself starting to shake. From the sound of her voice, I sensed right away something wasn't right.

"Yes," I replied quietly.

"Well, er, ahh, first of all, I'd like to apologize for the delay in getting back to you. I've just reviewed your mammogram x-rays. It seems they should've gotten to me days ago, but it's been very busy and I was on vacation for a few days last week. Still, that's no excuse."

No it wasn't, but what could I do? I wanted her to tell me what was wrong.

"I've had a chance to look them over and I'm a bit concerned," she went on. "There is an abnormality on your right outer breast. It could be only thick tissue matter, or a small cyst, but I really think you need to be set up for an ultrasound to be sure. Are you free Tuesday?"

That was only four days away.

"Well," I glanced up at Jean who was standing by the register with a customer.

"Yes, I think I can arrange that," I said, still a bit quietly so Jean wouldn't hear. "When should I be there?"

Jean looked my way and her eyebrows rose. No luck—she had heard me. That woman hears everything and I could tell as soon as I got off of the phone, she'd drill me for all of the details. I'd better be sure to get some before I hang up.

"Let's say around 10 am. I'll confirm it, but if you don't hear back from me, expect to be there as planned. Also, they may call you for some more medical information beforehand. Oh, and while you're waiting, start thinking of who you'd like to choose as a surgeon. That'll be who reviews the ultrasound and determines what might be wrong."

"Is there anything else you'd like to know?" Dr. Reynolds added.

I didn't know if I could speak anymore. A surgeon? Wasn't that an extreme measure? I cleared my throat and luckily the words came out.

"Yes, please tell me more about what I'm facing. What are the chances it could be something else, like cancer?" I hated to say the word, but I had to. It was the only thing on my mind right now.

"Oh, it's too early to tell. The records here say you haven't felt anything abnormal, is that right?"

"Well...."

"Well?" she replied.

"At the time, that was correct, doctor, but I'm not one for doing self-exams. After having the mammogram, I did check and I felt something. I'm surprised it wasn't noticed during the examination. Right breast like you said. It's not very large, but it's been on my mind since."

"I'm sure. Well, this makes a difference. I think we've already wasted too much time. Under the circumstances, we need to move the ultrasound up to the earliest available slot. Let me make a few phone calls and someone will get back to you. With any luck, we'll have you there tomorrow morning instead of next week."

As soon as I got off the phone, Jean was by my side and had me by the arm. She signaled Mary and Gertrude to take over as she marched me right upstairs.

What am I going to tell her? I don't know anything yet. All I know is I already don't have a good feeling about all of this. But I'm hoping I'm wrong.

I told Jack as soon as I arrived home that night. He seemed concerned, but told me not to worry. Jack said everything would turn out fine and we shouldn't jump to conclusions before I knew anything else. I reached for his hand, putting it under my shirt and bra so he could touch the outer side of my right breast. I was hoping he couldn't feel the small bump, like I had, but he did feel it. He took his hand back quickly—a reaction I'm sure out of fear—but then he wrapped me in his arms and tried to console me.

"It's really small, Rosie. Are you sure it's not just a blemish or an ingrown hair follicle or something? Maybe it's a new mole." He reached towards my breast again. "Take your top off, let me take a look."

I didn't want him to now. I didn't want him to see anything else there. Feeling a bump was scary enough. What if he could also see it?

"Jack, later, you can look later. Right now, let's forget about it and have some dinner. As you said, there's nothing we can do about it—it's just wait and see—so I won't worry and I don't want you to either."

But, as much as I tried to forget, it was the only thing I could think about all night. We sat in front of the television together watching the nightly news while we ate our dinner. Despite what I said, I couldn't concentrate at all, but didn't want Jack to know. I tried to act like everything was okay and I wasn't too concerned. After all, what could I do? And what's any different from this morning? I knew there was something there that shouldn't be; the doctor had confirmed it with the x-ray. But it's still unknown as to what exactly is there. And it would take the ultrasound tomorrow and maybe even a few more tests to find out so I'll know what I'm facing—what Jack and I are facing—if anything. And maybe the doctor was right; maybe it's just a cyst after all. No need to overreact so soon.

Chapter 39

An ultrasound was only the next step. Then, there was the biopsy the following Monday. A couple days later, an appointment with the surgeon, Dr. Chow, quickly turned into a consultation. He broke the news to me the best he could. There wasn't a doubt; I did have cancer—the invasive sort. The ultrasound revealed the tumor was still small, about 2.5 cm, but something had to be done right away. His suggestion was a mastectomy, but he also said I could consider a lumpectomy with some lymph node removal for testing. There'd be radiation or chemotherapy needed afterwards. I had to make up my mind what I was going to do.

"I don't know what options you have, Rosie. Whatever they have to do to assure your safety, let them do it. Go for the mastectomy." Jack had gone with me to the consultation. The doctor had left the room for us to discuss this alone. I didn't have to make up my mind immediately, but Jack didn't want to waste any more time. I could tell he was shaken, as I was, by the news.

"But, Jack, it's so drastic. I'm not going to look the same. You're not going to want to look at me anymore." I started to cry, but stopped myself. I didn't want him to see I was already having a hard time handling all this. He always viewed me as the strong one in the family, and I believed everything was meant for a purpose. I didn't want to let him down.

"God, Rosie. We've been together for all of these years. It's not your body that's important, it's you—what you are on the inside, who you are. You could be missing a leg or an arm, or be totally paralyzed and I'd still love you."

"So why the indecisiveness?" he continued. "I think we have to face this now and move forward. I don't want that cancer hurting you any more than it has to. I want you alive."

Jack was sitting beside me and suddenly put his head in his hands and covered his eyes. Then his body began to shake. He was sobbing. My tough, sometimes hard to get along with, husband was broken.

Still, I couldn't make the decision right away. I needed a little time, only a little, to digest and sort it through. After all, it was my body being attacked. It was my breast they wanted to dissect. I tried to explain this to Jack and promised I would make a decision soon. I just needed to talk to another woman first, someone who would know how I felt. I just needed to talk to Jean.

That very evening, I was in Jean's living room. She took the news hard and was in shock.

"I can't friggin believe it, Rosie! Of all the people it can happen to, it shouldn't happen to you. It should have been me."

"Don't say that," I snapped back. "You don't deserve it any more than I do. Still, it's a fact, I have cancer. And I still believe there's a reason for everything. I just don't understand why yet."

Jean let out a big huff. "Oh stop it, Rosie! Stop it right now! You and your reasons, you and your faith, don't you ever question it? I mean all the shit that's happened this year? All the bad things you've gone through? Haven't you had enough?"

If I hadn't had my own spiritual experience so many years ago, I would've doubted. I would've been mad at what was happening to me now. But life was a balance. And sometimes what appears to be bad at first turns out to be a blessing—maybe not for me, maybe for someone else. And if that's what it takes, then so be it.

"I'm tired, yes, but I still believe. And look at all the good things that have happened this year. Finding Mary, the shop, the column . . . Oh no, the column! I need to write another one. If I'm late again, they're going to fire me!" I jumped up from the couch in a panic.

Jean rose from her chair also and threw up her arms. She now looked angry. "I give up! I will never understand you! You have broken the news to me, have gotten me all upset, and all you can think about it your stupid column?" She threw her arms up again and shook her head.

"I know, I know, but I've got to write it. Besides, I promised. But I'm not going anywhere yet, Jean. Let's sit down again. I need you to help me make a decision."

We both sat next to each other on the couch and within minutes, both of us had calmed down. Then I discussed my dilemma as to whether I should opt for the mastectomy or go for the lumpectomy and hope it gets it all. Jean became upset again having the same reaction as Jack.

"Wait? Are you crazy? Get that cancer out of you. Get rid of that breast, even both breasts if you have to. Jack is right."

Jean let out a sigh of frustration, then reached over and put her arms around me.

"Oh, Rosie, the last week has been tough on you. You must be so confused over all of this." Her eyes suddenly brightened. "Hey, you know what? I think you need another vacation, this time with me! So keep your calendar open this weekend."

"And don't worry about Jack—I'll tell him."

It was late Friday morning and Jack and Mary were busy stocking shelves. We had just had a rush of people, but now it was quiet again. Jean turned my way and winked at me. Oh no! What was she up to?

She went right over to Jack, stood right in front of him, and with her hands on her hips, she gave him a serious stare.

He put a book on the shelf, brushed his hands together, and then looked right back at her.

"Well, all right, let's not stand here and have a stare down. I might as well get right to the point," exclaimed Jean. "I'm kidnapping Rosie this weekend."

Oh no! She didn't even ask him if he'd agree to it, she just came right out and told him. Jack didn't like pushy females. I had no idea how he was going to react.

He glanced over at me and raised his eyebrows. He wasn't smiling. I didn't know what to do, so I simply shrugged my shoulders, trying to act like I didn't know a thing. I could tell he was bothered, but good for him, at least he didn't yell at her. Instead, he continued to look at her with not much expression on his face and said, "Excuse me, what did you say? I couldn't have possibly heard you right."

"You heard me," replied Jean. "I'm kidnapping your wife for the weekend. We need time to talk and deal with a decision she has to make. And, let me add, I'm in full agreement with you—she shouldn't stall anymore on this, so in a way, I'm kind of helping out."

Okay, that softened the blow a bit. I could see his shoulders sink a little, no longer crunched up against his ears in a defense mode. The redness in his face was leaving, also. Still, I didn't know if he was okay with this.

Jean went on. "Don't worry about spending the weekend alone while Rosie's gone, either. I figure Max can keep you company. How about that?"

That did it. Jack was angry. He was just about to yell at Jean when Mary came over beside him and placed her arm on his shoulder. She turned toward Jean.

"Can't you take Max with you? I was hoping since Rosie will be with you, I could steal Jack for myself this weekend. I happen to have two tickets to a Monarchs game, their opening one, in Manchester on Saturday and I want him to join me. It'd be no fun going alone."

The anger left his face again instantly. He looked at Mary. "Really?" he asked her. "A hockey game? Wow, that would be great! Is it okay with you, Rosie?"

I smiled. "Seems like a fair trade. I promise not to get jealous." I hesitated a moment before continuing. "So it's okay if I'm away for a while? I do need time to sort this all out, Jack."

"Sort what out?" Mary asked.

"I might as well tell you now, Mary, but keep it confidential for a while. I still have to break it to the boys."

It was hard to say what I had to say next. It still seemed so unreal to me.

"I've been diagnosed with breast cancer. They want to operate as soon as possible."

Mary gasped. Jack bowed his head in sadness. Jean's eyes started to water up.

"They want me to choose between a mastectomy and a lumpectomy, and I'm...I'm scared." I also started to choke up.

Silence. No one spoke for a few seconds.

"I'm so sorry," Mary finally said. Her voice was barely audible. "Everything's going to be okay, though, right?"

"Oh Mary, I hope so, I really do."

Chapter 40

J ean wouldn't tell me where she was taking me when she picked me up that weekend. Max was in the back of the car, so excited about coming along. His tail couldn't stop wagging.

"It's none of your business," she said when I asked.

Okay, well, one way or another I'd figure it out.

As soon as we passed Portsmouth and headed into Maine, a little over an hour into the trip, I was sure of where we were going—we were headed to York Beach where her cottage was. Although it was early October, it appeared to be Indian summer. Temps were already in the 70's, and Jean had asked me to bring my woolen bikini along, as she was also planning to do. Warm weather or not, I wouldn't be caught dead wearing it in public. I had no idea what she was thinking. Still, I tossed it into my suitcase before leaving.

The weather made it too nice to be inside. As soon as we entered the cottage, Jean announced we had to get to the beach, pronto. She kicked off her shoes and put on flip flops. Then she threw me over a pair.

"Here, I bought you some, also. They were on sale—only $2.99. I got you bright pink ones to pay you back for those ugly polyester pajamas you purchased for us."

I hesitated to put them on. I preferred the Crocs I was already wearing and didn't like flip flops. But I didn't want to disappoint Jean. After all, she did purchase them for me and even knew what size I wore.

I grinned. "Okay, they're not my favorite footwear, I hate

the thong part that goes between the toes, but I'll wear them if it'll make you happy."

Jean gave Max a dish of water, and we both had a bathroom run. Then, she put a leash on him and we were out the door. The beach was only a few steps away.

Max's tail kept wagging furiously as he was leading the way, panting even though he'd just had plenty to drink. He was so excited to be here. As soon as we were down near the water's edge, he began chasing some seagulls. Since there weren't many people nearby, Jean was able to extend his leash to quite a distance so he wouldn't choke himself.

We took a long walk stopping to turn over rocks to see what was hidden underneath—a starfish, some shells, plenty of tiny crabs. Afterwards we decided we were hungry and climbed up some bigger rocks to a drive-in restaurant overlooking the water. We both ordered fisherman platters. When our order was ready, I gasped. The paper plates were overflowing with shrimp, clams, scallops and haddock. Not to mention French fries and coleslaw. Max started licking his chops in anticipation of leftovers.

"If you think you're getting any of this, you're crazy," Jean said to him, but then I saw she had ordered him a separate hamburger minus the bun.

"I know, it's probably not too good for him, but it's better than fried food. Besides, it's a special treat," she said.

"As long as he doesn't start farting later on," I added. We both couldn't help but giggle, remembering our first pajama party and how he stunk up the house after eating leftover Chinese food.

As we sat at a picnic table enjoying our seafood, we marveled at several surfers riding the waves. Max finished off his hamburger in about three bites and scurried under the table to lie down. Every once in a while he would look up at us with sad eyes, hoping to get some of our lunch.

By the time we finished eating, the tide had come in. We put the leftovers into some Styrofoam take-out containers, and went back to the cottage. Placing the food into the empty refrigerator, we changed into other clothes, and then drove into town. It was later in the season, but Jean was hoping the place that sold her favorite taffy was still open on weekends. We were in luck. After admiring their window display showing how the candy was made, Jean went in and bought several boxes—a couple for her, one for Mary, one for Jack, and a couple more boxes for the shop. I stayed outside holding onto Max's leash. NO DOGS ALLOWED was displayed boldly on their entrance.

"I really love this stuff," Jean commented as she came out of the store. I could hardly understand her, her mouth was full of taffy.

"Samples," she said. "Here, have one." She handed me one with pink stripes on it.

Jean put the boxes in the car, and then we walked around. Most of the shops were closed now, but we enjoyed window shopping, and sitting on the sidewalk was a woman with a head wrap. Next to her was a big sign that read: PALM READING $10.

"Hey, let's get our palms read," Jean exclaimed.

"Not on your life," I replied. "I don't believe in it."

"Ah c'mon, Rosie. You're not supposed to believe in it, it's just for fun." Jean nudged me and smiled, but it wasn't going to work this time.

"No, you go ahead if you want to waste your money. I'll stay and wait outside with Max."

"Party pooper!" she exclaimed as she shook her head at the lady, indicating we weren't interested. "It's no fun having it done alone."

When the window shopping was done, and after Jean got over her pity party about not getting our palms read, we stopped at a store on the way back and bought a few groceries. As we passed by the wine aisle, Jean said, "Should we get some?"

"I don't know, maybe just some cocoa tonight. And some toast. How does that sound instead?"

"You know what? It sounds great. Besides, there are no hangovers with cocoa."

"Exactly," I replied.

Chapter 41

After relaxing a while at the cottage, we treated Max to another short walk, and then polished off the rest of the leftovers from lunch. None for Max, though. He had some dog food.

Jean was now lounging in a recliner, skimming through a Cosmopolitan magazine. Some of her twangy ommm music was playing. I was comfortable on the couch, my bare feet propped up on her coffee table. I tried to reach Jack on my cell phone, no answer. Oh well, he must still be out with Mary. How I wish he'd carry a cell phone, but he refuses to have anything to do with modern technology. He has to be home to reach him.

I was just about to start talking about the breast cancer to Jean when there was a rap on the back door.

"Who could that be?" I asked. We weren't expecting any company, at least Jean didn't give mention of anyone else showing up.

But she gave me a broad smile. "I know who it is." She went to the door and opened it wide. "Surprise!" she exclaimed as Mary entered the cottage.

"Wha...but...I thought you were spending the day with Jack," I said.

"I was, I did, but now I'm here. Jean asked me to come." She grinned.

"And how'd you even get here?" I asked. "You don't even own a car."

"Oh, Jack brought me. Jean had it all planned out. She gave us the tickets to the Monarchs. Then she convinced Jack to bring me up here. He's staying with Jonathan tonight. Then . . ." Mary stopped talking and looked over at Jean.

"Can I tell her the biggest surprise?" she asked.

"Go ahead, Mary. Tell her what's happening tomorrow," Jean said.

Mary took a deep breath and exclaimed. "Tomorrow, Jack, Tommy, Jonathan and Laura are coming here. We're going to have a picnic. I'll get to spend time with my half-brothers and we're all going to celebrate your birthday early."

My birthday, oh, I had completely forgotten. It was only a week away. How did they know? Hmmm, Jack must've told them. As if Mary joining us wasn't enough of a surprise already.

Jean then announced, "Okay, Rosie, go and get your bikini on."

My mouth almost dropped to the floor. "Are you kidding me? I'm not wearing any bikini, thank you very much!"

"Why not? I'll wear mine," Mary commented. She reached into that big pocketbook of hers, still slung over her shoulder, and took out a knit bikini. As she sat down in a nearby chair, she held it up, one piece at a time. It was pink. It was skimpy. It was beautiful.

"I like it," I said. "You are such a great knitter, but still, neither one of you are going to convince me to change into the thing."

"Ah, be creative, Rosie." Jean replied. "I'm not asking you to ONLY wear your bikini. Why don't we all just put on whatever we've brought to sleep in? Then, we'll put the bikinis on over our clothes. I want to have some fun, take a few photos modeling them, maybe even dance and sing together. How about it?"

"Kind of a replacement for the polyester pajamas?" I asked.

"Yeah, exactly," Jean said.

And that's exactly what we did. Wearing our bikinis over our clothing (which looked ridiculous, by the way), we took a few photos and then put on some disco dance music. Why Jean had a disco CD, I haven't a clue, but we all had fun trying to move like John Travolta in *Saturday Night Fever*. In fact, it was hilarious. I can't remember when I laughed so hard—probably at the first pajama party Jean and I had earlier in the year.

After a while, we became tired of the dancing, but we still needed to talk. I heated up some milk on the stove for cocoa and Mary toasted some bread. Jean made sure she cut each slice of toast into four squares.

As we all sat at the table with our toast and a mug of cocoa in front of us, Jean lifted up a square and said, "In memory of Mom." Then, she dunked it in her cocoa.

Later on, after the dishes were done, we sat around the living room with the twangy ohmmm music back on. It was softly playing in the background.

"Now it's time to talk," Jean said. "And, Rosie, we want you to make the right decision, but we know it's your decision to make. We're here for you. Tell us how you feel."

I looked over at her and then at Mary. Both of their eyes were on me, waiting for my reply.

"Well, I understand how you all want me to have a mastectomy, but it's not that easy of a decision. What if I go with the lumpectomy and everything is all right? Then I won't have to lose my breast."

"But you'd be risking your life, right? What if that wasn't enough and it was too late when you found out? Doesn't the doctor recommend the mastectomy?" Jean snapped back, now sitting on the edge of her seat.

"Well, yeah, he does," I whispered and put my head down. I really didn't want to discuss it anymore. I had to decide this one on my own. Besides, Jean was already too pushy about it.

But we did discuss it for the next few minutes. Jean wasn't about to stop there. She did her best to stress the importance of opting for the mastectomy and "going all the way" as she said to ensure my well-being.

Mary didn't give an opinion one way or the other, but did comment about the ability to have reconstructive surgery as well, something I hadn't even considered before she mentioned it. I wondered why the doctor hadn't earlier. Maybe he was waiting for my decision.

Still, despite the concerned and helpful comments, we were getting nowhere. I still hadn't made up my mind. Somehow, I think, I was hoping there'd been a terrible mistake and everything would just go away on its own without having to make up my mind.

Finally, I was through with all the talking and started to yawn.

"I know you promised Jack I'd decide what to do, and I promise you I will, but right now I don't want to think about it. I'm really tired and want to relax a bit before bed. How about if we maybe watch something for a while on your big screen TV, Jean? Kind of unwind before bedtime."

"Sounds like a great idea," Mary commented. "Why don't we watch a football game?"

"That's NOT what I was thinking," I scowled. "I have enough of sports with Jack. No, I was thinking of a sitcom or a reality show maybe."

Jean looked at her watch and then reached for the remote on the coffee table. She switched the television on and changed the channel.

"It's nine o'clock now, perfect timing. My favorite show *House Hunters* is on," she said.

"You miss real estate already, don't you, Jean?" Mary asked.

"Yeah, I kind of do, but I still have my Broker's license. And Rosie has her license, too. We can still sell real estate." Jean's eyes widened like she just remembered something.

"And we still have to list and sell your condo, right?" I said, already knowing what she was thinking of.

Jean flashed a big smile at me right before the show started. "That's right, we do. Are you ready for a new real estate adventure, Rosie?"

"Sure, why not," I replied, smiling back at her.

Chapter 42

"**O**kay, sleepyhead, wake up," I said as I shook Jean awake.

She opened one eye and peeked at the alarm clock on the bedside table.

"It's 5:30 in the morning. It's still dark outside. Why're you doing this to me?" she moaned. She closed her eye tight and rolled away from me.

I shook her again. "Wake up!" I said louder. "We have to see the sunrise. If we don't hurry up, we'll miss it."

Mary was standing next to me. We were both dressed and ready to go.

Jean moaned again. "You really are a pain in the ass, Rosie. What the hell do we need to see the sunrise for? I'd rather sleep."

"You'll thank me for it after. Now GET UP," I said loudly. That did it! My loud voice startled Jean and she immediately sat up straight. She gave me an evil eye and grumbled.

"It better be good, because if it isn't spectacular, you're done for, lady."

"Okay, deal," I replied. "Now hurry up and get dressed. We have to leave in five minutes max."

As I walked out of the bedroom door, now trusting that she wouldn't go back to bed again, I added, "And we've prepared a thermos of coffee for you already. No need to thank me yet."

I chuckled to myself, knowing this would cause another sarcastic reaction.

"Don't worry, I won't," she barked. Jean before coffee can be scary.

We made it to the beach right on time. The sun was beginning to peak over the horizon. It was absolutely breathtaking. Max even sat there quietly like he was as much in awe watching it, as we were. He didn't even bother with the few seagulls already flying about.

While we sat on the rocks admiring the new day, we all sipped our coffee. Jean was beginning to come around, her caffeine fix being satisfied. She actually didn't appear mad anymore.

After the sun had risen, we began to walk the length of the beach. A few other people were doing so as well. Some were jogging. They all waved and greeted us as we strolled by them. There's something about a new day that puts everyone in a happy mood. It's like starting over.

Max waded at the edge of the shore. Mary took her sandals off and joined him. Pretty soon, we were all knee deep in water, splashing about, splashing each other, and laughing again.

"Remind me to thank you," Jean said.

"I told you it was worth it," I replied.

"Just don't die on me," she said more seriously. Her laughing had stopped.

"I won't, I promise." Could I promise? The reality I was facing came back full force.

Jack, the boys, and Laura all arrived around noontime. Max was so excited to have more company. His tail wagged furiously as they emerged from their cars.

Jonathan carried a big box of live lobsters in one hand. In the other, he carried a bag of clams. Tommy brought the steaks, and Laura had a big bowl of homemade potato salad, along with some fresh picked corn and a birthday cake. Jack was holding some soda, and what was that?

"Beer?" I asked. "You brought beer?"

"Yeah, why not? There's a game on today. What's a game without beer? Besides, you can drive home. I've done enough driving the past few days." He came up beside me and gave me a quick love pat on my behind, along with a kiss on the cheek.

Okay, sports. Why did I think we wouldn't be watching it? Besides, Mary likes sports also and maybe this would be a way to bond with her stepbrothers.

After introducing Mary to both Jonathan and Laura, and reintroducing her to Tommy as his stepsister, I said, "Now who's going to cook the lobsters and clams this time?" I asked.

"Ewww," Laura commented.

"Double ewww," added Jack. "C'mon, Laura, let's get the grill going and cook up some steaks."

"Tommy and I will take care of the seafood," Jonathan volunteered.

They went inside, found a few big pots, and got busy. Mary went to join them.

"Hey, Jean, let's wrap up the corn to put on the grill," I said. "Then, we can set the table and get the rest of the condiments out."

"Great idea, Rosie. Much better than watching live lobsters boil to death," she said with a grimace on her face.

Two hours later, after all of us had eaten way more than we should've (including Max, who was able to beg himself into a few pieces of steak), and after we'd had a great time talking and laughing together, Jack announced a game was about to begin. This time it was football—the New England Patriots against the New York Jets.

As much as I'm not a big sports fan and neither is Jean, we decided to join the others in front of the big screen. In no time, Jack started yelling at the set, along with the boys and Mary shouting out their own comments. It was exciting and close right up until the end, but the Patriots won by three points and so everyone was happy.

"What a great game," Jack said. "I wonder if another one is on."

"Not on your life, Jack Blume. One game's enough for today. Besides, we have to still clean up from lunch. Is anyone hungry? We still have some yummy birthday cake here."

Everyone groaned. "Guess not," I added.

By the time we finished washing the dishes, the sun had already set and I still needed to talk to the boys alone. I had to tell them what was going on with me.

"Jonathan and Tommy, how about you both come with me to take Max for a walk before we all leave here?"

Jean opened her mouth and was about to speak. I was certain she was going to ask if she could come along. I gave her a look to convey it wasn't a good idea to join us. Luckily, she got the message.

"I'll stay here and pack up the car with Jack and Mary. How long will you be gone?" she said.

"Oh, only about 20 minutes or so—not too long," I replied as I attached a leash to Max's collar.

The tide now was in, so we had to walk along the sidewalk above the beach. There was a full moon out and it cast enough light on the ocean so we could admire the waves crashing against the rocks. No one else was around. The only sound, besides Max's panting from tugging so hard, was the mighty sound of the ocean. Oh, how I loved this place.

Jonathan walked on one side of me, Tommy on the other. They both towered over me.

As soon as the cottage became out of sight, I started talking.

"I have something else to tell you both, but I don't want you to worry."

Not the right way to start a conversation. Immediately Jonathan replied, "What's wrong, Mom? Is Jack all right? Does he need another operation?"

I shook my head. "No, no, Jack is fine. It's not about him, it's about me."

"Don't tell me you're getting divorced," Tommy said. "All of my friends' parents are divorced."

"No, Jack and I are not getting divorced." I couldn't believe Tommy could ever consider that. Sure, Jack could be hard to live with sometimes, but he knew I loved him.

"Okay, then what is it?" he replied. "Just tell us."

I took a deep breath and slowly blew it out. Then I took another one. My insides were suddenly shaking again. This wasn't going to be easy.

"I...I...I've got breast cancer. It was diagnosed last week."

Both of them stop walking. Neither of them said a word. They were in shock. I stopped a few feet in front of them and turned around to look at them. Tears began to well in my eyes, but I had to stay strong. I didn't want them to think I was scared by this.

Max stopped tugging and sat down. Good dog.

Another deep breath went in and out of me before I could proceed.

"It is in one of my breasts, a small lump diagnosed early enough to treat. The doctor is suggesting a mastectomy, but I can also opt for a simpler procedure called a lumpectomy. It may be possible to get the cancer without losing the breast entirely. I don't know. It's a decision I'll have to make soon. Either way, there will be either radiation or chemotherapy treatments needed afterwards. It will make me weak and tired for a while and I might even lose my hair."

"Oh, God, Mom, I can't believe this is happening. Laura is planning on walking with Making Strides in Portland this year and she says one out of eight women get breast cancer. Her Aunt had breast cancer several years ago and died from it." Jonathan closed his eyes like he was about to cry. I can't remember when I saw him cry last. He clenched both of his fists. Tommy noticed and put his arm around Jonathan and drew him close.

"Don't worry," Tommy said, his voice cracking just a bit. "Mom's going to be all right. Maybe Laura's aunt found out too late, but Mom's cancer was found early." He looked up at me for reassurance. "Right, Mom?"

"Yes, it was," I said. "Mine is treatable and, like Tommy said, I'm going to be all right."

Still holding onto Max's leash, I reached out to both of my boys and embraced them for several minutes. None of us spoke. Then, I let go and glanced at them once more, being sure to flash them a smile of reassurance before I turned and started walking again with Max.

"Okay, let's go," I called back to them. "Let's finish this walk and get back to the cottage. It's getting late and some of us still have to work tomorrow."

Chapter 43

J ack slept for most of the ride home. Two beers and plenty of food will do that to him. I didn't mind, it gave me some time to think.

Mary drove back with Jean and Tommy stayed with Jonathan and Laura for the night. Tommy didn't have a class again until later Monday afternoon and Jonathan had taken a personal day, so he was going to drive Tommy back to school in the morning.

When we finally arrived home, it was late. Jack turned on the eleven o'clock news and in no time, was fast asleep again. I grabbed my pajamas and went into the bathroom.

A shower would feel good after being in the sun all weekend. I stripped down and stood naked in front of the mirror. Turning from one side to the other, I examined myself. My breasts were small, always had been, and they were already beginning to sag. Both silver-lined from stretch marks—the results of three pregnancies—one breast was slightly larger than the other and it had always bothered me. Still, they were my breasts and I was used to seeing them. "What if I were to opt for a mastectomy instead of a lumpectomy?" I thought. That's what everyone wants me to do, but how would I feel about myself after it's done? How would Jack feel? I know he keeps saying he doesn't mind, the only thing important is there's no cancer left in me, but how would he really feel when he saw me? Would he even want to look at me again?

Here I stood, completely naked in the bathroom, imagining the changes a mastectomy would make and wondering what it would be like if I never looked this way again.

I had to admit it to myself, despite my belief all things are as they're meant to be, I was still afraid. Brave little Rosie with all of her faith was scared. I knew better, but it still didn't matter. My mind couldn't stop worrying about this disease.

Backing away from the mirror, I sat on the edge of the tub. Crossing my arms, I cupped each breast with the opposite hand. They fit inside each hand nicely. I could feel their warmth and, yes, even though I didn't want to, I could also feel the small tiny lump already seeming a bit larger. Was it just my imagination?

As I bent forward slowly, in a fetal position with my face now almost to the floor, I closed my eyes and began to pray quietly for the peace and strength to make it through whatever I had to face next.

And then I cried, until I couldn't cry anymore, not just for myself, but for all women with breast cancer.

After what seemed like a very long time, I stood up and wiped the remaining tears from my face. Standing nude in front of the mirror again, this time straight, strong and with renewed faith, I said . . .

"Okay, Jack and Jean, I'll do it, I'm ready. I'll have the mastectomy."

For better, for worse, my decision had been made.

Chapter 44

For some reason, we tend to think life will never change beyond the very moment we're in, but it does nonetheless.

There are many great things that have happened to me over the course of this year. Jean and I became best friends and business partners. My dreams of owning a bookstore and writing a column have both come true. Jonathan has found the woman of his dreams, and Tommy is doing well in college. I've met many new friends at Simple Pleasures, and, after 25 years of waiting, I've finally met my birth child, Mary. Life has definitely been grand.

However, life doesn't come just one way—it requires balance—so there have also been challenges. Justin came back into my life and tried to ruin it. Jack had a heart attack—I almost lost him. Later, while he was on the mend, a stranger knocked on the door claiming to be his son. It turned out not to be true. And then there was the diagnosis of my breast cancer a few weeks ago.

Now, I'm sitting at the edge of my hospital bed clothed in an ugly gray hospital gown. The mastectomy is scheduled for tomorrow. Jack and the boys are with me and so are Mary, Jean, Laura, Emma and George. Seeing George makes me remember his wife died of breast cancer. No wonder he is showing so much concern.

Dr. Chow was in to see me earlier and assured me he'd do everything he could to remove the cancer. Still, he couldn't promise me anything. Reconstructive surgery would have to wait until chemotherapy and further testing were done. He told me to be prepared for a very challenging year ahead.

I guess I'm ready for it, what else can I do? I looked over at my loved ones again and managed a smile. None of them were talking. No one knew what to say.

A nurse entered the room and walked towards me. She was holding a bouquet of beautiful roses.

"From you?" I asked Jack.

"No, wish they were, hon," He replied, looking sadly at me.

"Jean?" I asked next.

"No, but I did bring you something." Jean reached into her pocketbook and revealed a fuzzy multi-colored knit chemo cap. "I know you don't need it yet, but if you get scared tonight thinking about the surgery, put it on. It'll comfort you."

"Thanks," I said reaching for it. It felt so soft in my hands.

It was weird being here like this. I felt like I was in a dream. Could this really be happening to me?

"Jonathan and Tommy, these flowers aren't from you, are they? Because if they are, I'm going to be upset you spent so much."

"No, Mom, we couldn't afford a dozen roses," Tommy replied.

"I know, I know, having you all here means the most to me," I responded.

My eyes were back on the flowers, wondering who could've sent them.

"Why don't you open the card and find out who they're from?" said Jack, fully aware of what I was thinking.

The nurse handed me the envelope, so I opened it and started reading the card inside.

Life –
I hold a portion of it in my hands.
I can smell it
and I enjoy its fragrance.

I can touch it
and I like the way it feels.
I can see it
and I recognize myself in its plan.
But I cannot possess it,
or change it,
or perfect it.
It is already perfect.
So I choose to simply accept it
and I let its course include me.
I breathe it in –
and I relax.

Om Mani Padme Hum

Jacob

"They're from Jacob," I announced to everyone. "That Jacob," I looked over at Jean, "is a very special man."

The nurse placed the flowers into my hands, and I held them up close to my nose. Slowly, very slowly, I took a deep breath in . . .

While I counted my blessings.

About the Author

Catherine Dougherty, a native of New Hampshire, lives with her husband in the beautiful Lakes Region area, near Lake Winnipesaukee. She is a member of the New Hampshire Writers Project and currently serves as social media chair for the Greater Lakes Region Making Strides Against Breast Cancer.

Her debut novel *in Polyester Pajamas*, the first book in the Jean and Rosie series, was released in June 2012. She has also published several essays and poems, and is a featured author in the 2012-2013 publication *50 Great Writers You Should Be Reading* presented by TheAuthorsShow.com.

To find out more about Catherine, visit her author site at:

catherinedougherty.com

Made in the USA
Charleston, SC
08 July 2013